THEY LOOKED AT ONE ANOTHER WITH HORROR

It lay on the ground bleeding red and gray blood. Its legs jerked spastically once, twice, then stiffened out in sudden rigor, the tendons showing under the fur. It thrashed again and grew still. Sato couldn't watch anymore and glanced up and away. Another one stood before them, arms spread and a single claw on each hand extended.

"Antonia," he said slowly.

"Pictures." She jabbed him in the ribs.

"Christ—"

"Pictures, I said!"

He held up the camera, feeling sick inside.

The live creature did not move for a few moments, then knelt next to the dead one. It laid the body across its back and backed away cautiously into the trees.

25887

ISAAC ASIMOV PRESENTS

CALIBAN LANDING

STEVEN POPKES

WORLDWIDE®

TORONTO · NEW YORK · LONDON · PARIS
AMSTERDAM · STOCKHOLM · HAMBURG
ATHENS · MILAN · TOKYO · SYDNEY

This book is for my parents, Earl Lesley Popkes, Opal Rogers Popkes, who always knew I could do it.

Supporting Cast:

These people are as important to this book as people get.

Steven Caine	Pat Cauduro
Kathy Marquis	Richard Perez
Madeleine Robins	David Smith

Special Acknowledgments:

PRx Incorporated   The Cambridge SF Workshop
                Janet Sokoloff

And an additional cast of thousands.
You know who you are.

CALIBAN LANDING

A Worldwide Library Book/January 1989

ISBN 0-373-30304-1

First published by Congdon & Weed, Inc.

Printed in U.S.A.

First Contact

by Isaac Asimov

In science fiction parlance, "first contact" refers to an initial meeting between Earthpeople and some extraterrestrial intelligence. It is something that has never yet happened, as far as we know. It may never happen—or it may happen any day.

What will such first contact be like? I don't think we have to rely on our imagination alone to answer that question, for we can look back on history.

In the past, a given group of people had but limited knowledge of the world and might not even know of the existence of another group who lived a thousand miles away. There were occasions, therefore, when two such groups, till then altogether ignorant of each other, might meet. That, too, is a form of "first contact."

Generally, the meeting came about when one group was on the move, either fleeing disaster (of either human or environmental origin) or actively seeking new land. In doing so, it might come across another group, which was not in motion, but was living quietly at home. The moving group might be called the "contactors"; those at home, the "contactees."

In these cases, the contactors might be desperate enough for haven or property to attempt to enslave or kill off the contactees and seize their land. Even if the contactors were peaceful, the contactees, afraid of the newcomers and fearful of their motives, might attempt to block their entry, or to evict them. In either case, the result would be violence.

Ancient Egypt found itself flooded with Hyksos invaders from Asia in the 17th Century B.C., and again by the Sea Peoples from the north Mediterranean coast in the 12th Century B.C. In both cases, the bewildered Egyptians didn't know who the invaders were or where they came from—they might just as well have come from Mars.

The Romans had to face a flood of Gauls from the north in 390 B.C., and the Cimbri and Teutones also from the north in 102 B.C. Again these barbarians loomed on the horizon with no warning whatever.

When people fight a known enemy, they are prepared and fight bravely enough. When the enemy is strange, unknown, and unexpected, the contactees suffer from surprise and possibly from a feeling that the invaders are, in some ways, demonic. The contactees are then very likely to suffer catastrophic defeat.

The Romans knew all about war and, in the third and fourth centuries, fought the Goths and Franks steadily. They were known enemies. However, when the Huns swept westward from central Asia in the fifth Century, an element of panic was added at the sight of these strange, short, bowlegged, slant-eyed people who seemed glued to their hardy ponies. The contactees were all but paralyzed. The process was repeated with even greater force in the 13th Century when the Mongols swept in from the east and smashed the quailing Europeans.

Nevertheless, the greatest of first contacts came in the 15th Century and thereafter. Now it was the Europeans who were the contactors, and the peoples of all other continents who were the contacted. Everywhere the Europeans enforced their rule, enslaving or otherwise dominating the contactees, or "natives."

In that case, won't first contact in the science fictional sense also mean war and slaughter? Or are there other factors involved?

Contactors from another planet (whether they be Earthmen who go there or aliens who come here) will surely be few in number in a possibly hostile world and would not dare offer violence unless they were enormously ahead in technology. And even if they were, they would be faced with totally different forms of life and intelligence, and might feel it would be much more useful to study the new lifeforms than to steal their world. Even if, for some reason, the contactors were violent and victorious, there might come pangs of conscience later on. Here on Earth many people of European descent are bitterly ashamed of what their ancestors have done.

What about the contactees? Here on Earth, the contactees generally did not offer violence until they were mistreated. They tended to greet the European newcomers peaceably enough but objected to having their land taken away and themselves killed.

If, in interplanetary first contact, there is utter revulsion at the shapes and ways of the invaders, there may be instant violence from the contactees even if they are in no way mistreated. The possibilities are various enough to give science fiction writers much latitude in their consideration of first contact, and here in *Caliban Landing* we have an exciting treatment of the theme.

1

We begin with a ship.

The *Shenandoah* wasn't really there.

It existed in a sphere of probability just outside the S128ab solar system. Its arbitrary literary presence was spread over close to nothing: comets, dust, hydrogen. The space around the star was sparky with bits of rock, radiation, and high-speed particles. The pilot looked for a planet: Caliban.

The ship hesitated just the other side of n-space, the pilot thinking.

Then her decision was made: an asymptotic curve shifted out of the realm of mathematics into reality.

The ship appeared.

RUTH TEDESCHI FLOATED weightless through the ship, talking to herself. She did this un-self-consciously, as a bird mutters to itself before bursting into song. *I am the frame,* she thought. Her long, thin body gently rotated as she moved around the corridors of the ship, slowed by the friction of spider finger-tips, accelerated by a light push of dancer's toes. Often, she laughed.

The *Shenandoah* was a toroid seventy-five meters across and twenty-five meters deep, its empty center a focal point of mo-tive forces. The fusion drive burned there. The strange ener-gies that forced the ship into n-space were constructed there. Ruth could have sparked the fusion drive and begun the long entry into the S128ab solar system. She could have awoken the other four members of the crew—for between systems, in "n-space," traveling the "interface," only the pilot was awake. She could have reentered n-space and left for home. She did none of these things. She wandered through the ship.

Why? I do not know. I never knew. I never met her.

"I am the frame," she whispered to the *Shenandoah*. The ship did not speak. There were only discreet lights to mark stored equipment and the gentle susurrus of the moving air. She was alone now. Shortly, she would be alone again. Soon after she awoke the passengers they would leave her. She would wait here for them, with the backstage pulleys and levers. The real action would be on Caliban. *I'm an introduction to them.*

Antonia had asked her once: "What do you do when there's nobody on the ship?"

She answered in the silence of the ship, slow, rumbling, feeling part of something turning.

She unshielded the viewing ports and stared into darkness and stars, a black curtain scattershot on a sunny day. Illuminated by shadowlight on shadow, she circumnavigated the circle of the ship, floated over the strapped-down equipment, along the storage area for the two landers: the *Hirohito* and the *Perry*. She knew where she was.

Piloting was enough for her. These lonely moments were something extra, something to be savored.

She found herself outside the containment room looking in, holding herself still by grasping the hatch frame. Inside were four couches. On each couch lay a person, a band of silver metal fitting loosely around each skull. Two men, two women.

Bertini Ranft snored. His pet, Cameron, lay asleep on his chest: a polar bear the size of a cat. Captain Megan Sze breathed shallowly and seemed agitated in her sleep. Sato Sperling looked dead, and Antonia Brobeck's face was set never to wake.

"What are your dreams?" asked Ruth lightly as she passed over them to the control panel. "Crew of the *Shenandoah*," she cried theatrically, "sponsored by Cartography Contract #a25-G. Specimens of humanity and representatives of all thinking creatures. I bid you wake." She giggled. Ruth Tedeschi, as embedded in her life as iron ore in stone, woke them from sleep.

What are your dreams? she thought quietly as they stirred. I know why I'm here. But why are *you*?

2

"I don't *know* what it is." Bertini ran both his hands through his sparse gray hair. He was a big man, short and wide like a wall. "It's radio. Variations of FM, AM, pulses—lots of it. The system is filthy with it." Cameron muttered to himself and climbed down from Bertini's lap. On the floor of the kitchen, he sniffed, frozen for a moment, looking as if he were hunting seals or salmon. He hid under Bertini's chair and growled. Bertini glanced down, leaned his block-and-tackle body back against the chair, and reached to him. "Hush, Cameron," he said softly. Cameron allowed himself to be petted.

The kitchen was empty as a pressed sheet and long enough for one to see the *Shenandoah*'s toroid curve. There was only the table, the counter and a few chairs, but there was gravity. These living quarters, the kitchen, and the recreational lounges were the only areas of the ship with artificial gravity. The crew centered around it.

Bertini straightened in his chair and glared at the muted white ceiling. He cross his arms and brought his glare back to the captain.

Megan glared back across the table from him, her lips habitually tight, her narrow shoulders even, and her back straight. Her hair was short, a black nimbus around her head.

Sato's long body slouched next to her, reading. He leaned back in the chair and put his feet up on the table. Megan slapped them off without taking her eyes off Bertini. Sato came forward with a crash and looked around, confused and angry. He watched Megan and Bertini a moment, shrugged, and left the lounge, carrying the book.

"Caliban sings," said Ruth softly, appearing in the doorway.

"Sings!" Bertini barked a short, sharp laugh. Cameron growled again. Bertini leaned forward across the table toward Ruth. "It howls. It shrieks, maybe. Sing, it does not do."

Megan glanced at Ruth, and the pilot left the doorway unhurriedly. "What causes this, Engineer Ranft, in your opinion?"

"*Causes* it? Your planet causes it. I do not know why. Look into the unique, incredible, not-to-be-forgotten specifications the clean team left us and find out."

"You have seen them and know they say nothing. They only mention a radio anomaly."

"Just so. They were written by morons." He stood. "I will find out why. Leave me to it." He left. Cameron followed him.

Megan did not move immediately, her hands flat on the table in irritation. She rose and walked down the hall. In one of the alcoves near the kitchen she found Sato. "You have been lost in your book since we awoke, Navigator Sperling. What is it?"

Sato held up the cover: *The Tempest.* Shakespeare.

"You have a reason for reading this now?"

Sato shrugged and stared at her. "Just trying to figure out why the clean team named this place Caliban."

"This is important knowledge?"

Sato returned to Shakespeare. "You never know, Captain Sze. You just never know."

ANTONIA WAS A BIG woman, as tall as a man, with nearly a man's shoulders; her arms and legs tapered gracefully, and her feet were small. Her body lied: only her hands seemed large. Red and strong, they were built for hard work in bad weather: wrapping fences, grafting trees. The rest of her appeared curiously small and articulated, as a doll built by whim and circumstance. Her cheekbones were high, her eyes dark. Someone she had once known had called her beautiful, but had never been able to describe that beauty, or truly know that it existed.

She floated by herself in the viewing salon, a transparent slice of the *Shenandoah* doughnut. Here the great optical mapping cameras, shrouded and silent, stared down into space. Antonia held her hands; they felt more comfortable that way than any other. She looked at the lie of her hands, like the lie of her body, her palms too soft ever to have known hard work. She was alone, withdrawn, waiting for someone to need her. Megan chose the destination. Ruth brought them here. Sato found the port, and Bertini rode the *Shenandoah* down on a hot flame.

Antonia was the ship's biologist and physician. Most importantly, she was the ship's sensitive. It was her job to determine if the animals (or plants, or whatever) encountered by the crew were what they seemed to be or fell into that nebulous category: *sentient*.

A sensitive is not a telepath. Nor is she some analytical genius hell-bent on breaking down a given creature into behavioral parts, weighing *this* act, *that* gesture, deciding from an arbitrary sum: sentience. Like most gifts, it is made up of parts. A violinist is gifted by ear, brain, and fingers. A sensitive is gifted in perception and mind.

Like most sensitives, Antonia was from the colony planet Georgia, near Tau Ceti.

She felt Ruth approach through the ambiguity of sensitivity. "Yes?"

"Can you see it yet?"

"What?"

"Caliban. Can you see it?"

"I don't know. I haven't looked."

Ruth laughed. She drew Antonia to the glass so they were hanging over the system. "S128—little a, little b. The star's over there." A blowtorch-colored cinder. "When I saw Caliban on the bridge screens it was out a little farther—there."

The planet was lit in quarter crescent, white, blue, and jet. It resembled a pinhead, its moon the eye of a needle. "The radio signals are driving Bertini crazy. He can't figure them out." Ruth laughed softly. She liked her ship's crew. Ruth liked everybody. She just didn't take them seriously.

"I guess we're not alone."

"Anywhere else you'd think so. But the clean team reported: *no aliens*. Just a big question mark. Still, it's driving Bertini *nuts*!"

LATER, on the bridge:

Picture a shambling, brute behemoth: foul breath, dressed in rags composed of part smoke, part animal fat, part textile, with a big, wide, overhanging brow symbolizing low cunning. No problem.

Now, picture the noble savage, robbed of his homeland, back bowed to labor forced on him by an oppressor, revenge and regaining his previous splendor never far from his mind. Clothed in rage, strong, massive, proud.

Which is Caliban?

The console blinked, updating the *Shenandoah*'s approach orbit to Caliban.

Sato considered. Caliban had been alone before Prospero had come to the island. He read:

... This island's mine, by Sycorax my mother,
Which thou tak'st from me. When thou camest first,
Thou strok'dst me, and mad'st much of me;
    wouldst give me
Water with berries in't; and teach me how
To name the bigger light, and how the less,
That burn by day and night: and then I lov'd thee,
And show'd thee all the qualities o' th' isle,
The fresh springs, brine-pits, barren place, and
    fertile.
Cursed be I that did so!—All the charms
Of Sycorax, toads, beetles, bats, light on you!
For I am all the subjects that you have,
Which first was mine own king...

The words caught him. "Which first was mine own king..." He breathed, then laughed. "Caliban, you are a barbarian."

He stared idly at the console, thinking about Caliban and Prospero. On impulse, he routed Caliban's radio signals through the audio channels here on the bridge.

Sato's parents had been ham radio operators, an antique, hobby. He remembered as a child being kept awake by the whines, grunts, and roars of short wave interference. In the twilight period of sleep he had imagined the moon or the sun running through the atmosphere, howling in frenzy.

This sounded like that.

He listened to it, a certain excitement built of fear and anticipation tingling through him.

The sound wavered, faded suddenly, and nearly disappeared. The star S128ab hissed across the speakers and drowned it out.

Down the corridor he heard Bertini swear. Sato looked at the console. "Bertini!" he yelled.

Bertini leaned in the doorway, a stale anger on his face. "What?"

"The signals faded as we entered Caliban's shadow."

Bertini slapped the wall in frustration. "*Christ!* The sun's not the source. It *can't* be. I—"

"I checked it, too." Sato shrugged. "Let's tell Megan."

THE *SHENANDOAH* ORBITED Caliban, her cameras now unshrouded and probing. Slave satellites were released and migrated to varying altitudes like watching crows. Every ninety minutes, the *Shenandoah* slipped into shadow and the planet's singing quieted. Another ninety minutes passed, and the singing came with dawn.

The crew floated in the viewing salon, Caliban's light illuminating their features. Both Bertini and Sato looked haggard, and their eyes had a sleepless, grainy look to them. Antonia stared at her hands. Megan had a thoughtful expression on her face. Ruth smiled.

"If it's not the sun, it still must be sun-related," Ruth said. "They're sun-worshippers down there, singing hymns."

Bertini shrugged and Sato chuckled. "You might not be far wrong," Sato continued. He folded his hands behind his head and looked at them. "You know, we're not really well equipped for radio mapping. *Radar* mapping we do all the time. But only planets with a high technology need to know the texture of their radio sources. The clean team cleared Caliban: no sentients. That's their job. That's what they get paid to do. Therefore: no reason for any radio mapping to be done. Therefore: no reason for us to have the equipment. Still," he smiled, "we managed. The radio signals come from the planet's surface. All over the surface. Stronger signals come from the land masses than from the oceans, but the water could be dampening the signals. When the sun sets, the radio signals mostly shut down. Now, what could it be?" He looked at them expectantly.

Antonia looked up from her hands. "The plants generate it."

Sato watched her grow tense, interested in the same way he would watch a bug climbing a branch. He'd slept with her, of course. He'd also slept with Ruth. Changing partners was almost tradition on a long trip. It meant nothing. Still, there was from her the feeling of a coiled spring, a tightness. He'd noticed it when he met her at the start.

After a moment, he nodded toward her. "I thought you might pick up on that. The Paedash plants of Georgia are well known. We don't know this for sure, of course, but it seems the only logical guess. The intensity of the signals closely follows the apparent plant density. There is little or no signal from the poles. It's got to be originating from the plants."

"Will this complicate matters?" Megan did not change her expression, but Sato felt a sudden, intense attention from her.

He nodded. "This mess of signals screws the satellite mapping all to hell. The optical work will be okay, and laser communication won't be affected. We can't use radar. We can do without it, but it'll take time to do the reprogramming." He turned to Bertini, who nodded. "We have to go down eventually anyway for the surface sampling, and we have to demonstrate it's the plants for the record. But we don't need to be here waiting for the reprogramming to finish. We can go down right now and finish the contract later."

"It is the reverse of procedure," said Megan quietly.

"So what?" asked Antonia.

"We are closely regulated as to procedure." Bertini spoke for the first time. "We are subcontracted to the Port Authority of Earth. If we do not adhere to spec, they can invalidate our contract and we won't get paid. Worse, there is a large penalty clause." He turned to Megan. "Still, though we are regulated as to *what* procedures we should use, we are not regulated on their order. Much is left to the captain's discretion."

"True, and it would save time." Megan considered. There was a long pause as the rest of them waited for her.

Ruth broke the silence. To Megan: "You go down?"

Megan nodded. "We go down."

Sato stared through the glass down to the planet with a kind of grim excitement. Before Prospero met him, Caliban did not speak with the tongue of men. Perhaps he sang with the birds or bellowed with the whales. Words tamed him.

Caliban landing, he thought, tasting the words. Caliban landing.

3

What are words that I am mindful of them?

I write these down in what I think is a harmonious fashion; I am no critic. At times, I think I am no writer. In my bleaker moments, I say leave writing to the humans and be done with it; it is theirs, wholly and completely. I am a dilettante. I dabble. I play in language as a tree plays with shadow—to use an image of my own kind. Leave it to them. You are too ambitious. Give up.

Then I will read some book of Sato's. *The Tempest*, perhaps, or Joyce. And the words call forth ideas and images that are only mine, strong, inexorable progressions toward truth. I grow enthusiastic. I've got to try it. I start pounding that bastard typewriter Bertini and Sato built for me. It skips. It jumps. It catches the tips of my claws. It pinches.

I'm off again.

My identity: my name was Binder to my people for the way I tied myself to those I knew. Antonia called me Thalia.

They came to us from the sky, out of shadow, out of darkness.

Thus:

TRAVERSE AND I LAY idly next to one another in a warm clearing. The air had an impending crisp to it, and the summerlight showed traces of winterlight coming. In that time, the light is a melding of the crispness of winter and the brightness of summer. All things stand out and all things have an inner glow. The grasses and trees are outlined in their own brilliance, and the earth and stone shine by strength of will.

I stretched out like a lizard sunning itself on a rock.

Lizards. We have no lizards.

Who are we Calibii? What will describe us? Is it enough to say we walk on either two legs or four, as whim strikes us, that we are most at home in the trees, that we are covered with fur?

Or is it more important to say we speak and see by the light of the trees, the grasses, the plants, building images of their light? Light that humans cannot see. Sato said that was important. Should I say we females birth by means of the trees, tied to them as surely as we are tied to air to breathe, water to drink? That our males live only a short time and wither and die within a season of siring? Should I say all this? Where do I stop trying to explain who I am, held down by these human words, and start to sing? What words do I say?

I had no words at all until men came. What images can I use? I have asked Sato this question more times than I can count. He gives me simple answers: any image I want. There is no *map* between his language and my speech. What I build is of whole cloth, answerable only to Binder, or Thalia, or whoever I am that feels this driving need to explain.

Lizards, then.

The day was thick lazy, full of low buzzings and murmurings.

A good day to take a late-season lover.

I would have wanted Traverse at any time. He was slight even for males. The way he spoke, the way he moved—everything he did was done with grace. He looked at things as if they were just born and brought me to see things the same way by being with him. I wanted him. I wanted his child.

I lay near him at an easy distance. Close enough for him to reach out, yet not close enough to crowd him. I didn't want to make him nervous. Males are such touchy beasts. So much rides on lovers for them: one chance is all they get. One lover, maybe two if they are strong. An attempt to sire their next generation. A month of mindless, sensual afternoons followed by rapid decay, senescence, death. It weighs on them.

It weighs on us females, as well, to see them gone so quickly.

I could feel him deciding slowly. He scratched his belly idly, his mind elsewhere. But I felt his body near, and his body was deciding for him: *not long left. Why not now? Why not here? Why not her?*

I lay on my back and watched the dark sky interlaced with glittering trees.

He twisted his body close to mine, his decision made now. I turned to him. He reached for me.

And the sky lit up.

It went from a dark space between trees to a blaze. Flashes of color, shock waves of brilliance, blinded me. I rolled on the ground and tried to crawl to the shade of the trees.

Shade? From a *tree*?

I looked back. Traverse stood at the edge of the clearing, staring into the light. I saw only his backlit bones, deep and textured. Nothing else of him could be seen clearly. Shafts of colors—of, give *up*!, call them magenta, green, blue—all of the colors I have words for but *know* have no real meaning to me played over us, washing us. I felt sick, dizzy. The sky should have been always dark. Always!

The source slowly eased down to the clearing, the light intensifying as it fell. I tried to cry out to Traverse, but the light drowned me out. It overpowered me, held me fast against the base of the tree.

Traverse backed away as the thing touched the ground. I forced myself to him, grabbed him hard, and began to drag him back. This close I could see his speech in spite of the brightness. "A demon? Is *this* a demon?" We hid down the ridge in a space between two boulders.

It flared once, and all around us in the light I could see into the heart of things. Then it dimmed and faded to a throbbing, nauseating pulse.

I ran then down the ridge, dragging Traverse behind me, a stumbling, wooden vacancy. Up the second ridge until honest stone and trees lay between us and it. I eased him down and leaned him against a boulder to rest.

"What was it, Binder?" His body was stiff and elsewhere.

"I don't know." I sagged against the base of the boulder next to him and held myself.

He turned toward me. "All of my life I have heard tales of demons: the Clam did this, or Treebreaker did that. Never have I seen them." His speech was tattered, barely coherent. I had trouble making it out. "Tell me. You are wiser than I, being older and female. Was that a demon?"

I wanted to comfort him, to take him now and hold him. I started to reach for him, and he drew back.

"Not yet!" he cried, mistaking my meaning. "Not here! I am not ready."

We did not speak for a time.

"I know this," I said. "Whatever it was, it is unheard of. We will consult Caretaker."

"You are right," he said slowly.

Aching to touch him, I led him instead untouched away from strangeness into the forest.

Antonia was not prepared for Caliban.

The *Hirohito* had landed in a large clearing at one end of a long fjord. The trees were mottled red and orange, maroon and peach, translucent, like ancient illuminated manuscripts. The water was a pure mirror blue. The trees towered over the clearing, the sea, the ship like tall glass panels, their trunks broad and gray-black, veined with silver. The *Hirohito* had landed up the slope from the water and between the trees, surrounded by chianti bushes and lying on a grass bed of bright sunshine yellow. It was too rich, too abundant, too much a contrast to her home Georgia. Such wealth made her nervous, uncomfortable, as if in an immoral presence.

There was not a speck of green.

She stood in the *Hirohito*'s hatchway, staring. Behind her she heard the faint singsong of numbers being called out and answered softly, as Sato, Megan, and Bertini put the *Hirohito*'s systems on standby. She stepped out through the hatchway and stood in the lander's shadow. She smelled pepper and cream, cardamom and exotic chemistry.

As familiar as breath, a voice called to her as every visited planet had touched and called her, asking something unintelligible, but leaving her an anxiety she did not understand. Now she heard it clearly:

Is it here?

For a moment, she saw trees walking, tall and dark gray, mottled spherical leaves dancing in the air as they moved through a field of roses, stately. They made no sound but a faint tread as their palps touched the ground in a strong rhythm: two forward, one back, two forward. The rhythm of a determined man on crutches.

"Maybe," she murmured.

"Maybe what?" came Sato behind her.

Startled, her hands clenched and she stopped breathing. A short memory of flames and the smell of roses came to her.

"Nothing," she said and made herself relax. The forest was again color and stillness.

Sato watched her speculatively. "Pretty, isn't it?"

She nodded.

He looked around the clearing. "Reminds me of fall at home."

"Fall?"

He looked at her again. She bore it and watched the trees.

"You've never been to Earth, then? Fall's the season before winter. Where I live—" he paused "—used to live, the trees catch fire like this—" he gestured to the clearing "—and burn out in a couple of weeks. Then the leaves fall." He smelled the air. "Smells brisk like fall, too. Cold air coming."

"There is no fall on Georgia." Antonia shrugged. "The beginning of winter is marked by the Paedash migrating to the south. Its end is marked by their return."

The loudspeaker crackled and hummed, then snapped into clarity: "Navigator Sperling and Sensitive Brobeck. You are outside in violation of policy. Please reenter."

Sato grinned at her crookedly. "Our leader calls. After you."

MEGAN WAITED for them on the *Hirohito*'s small bridge. She watched as Sato entered, following after Antonia. The tension in Sato's face was apparent under the crooked grin. Anger, thought Megan. A personal anger, directed at me, perhaps. *Investigate this,* she ordered silently. As always, there was a sense of the thought moving away into a great distance as the *Shenandoah* acted on her command without comment.

Bertini appeared stone calm. He always made her nervous. How much did he know?

He's older than Sato or Antonia, and he's been around the old ships like you. How long do I have before he guesses I'm wired into my ship?

He knows nothing. Why should he care? *Shenandoah,* I cannot read him!

He is enmeshed in himself and does not see the world around him. Remember your perspective: *why should he care?*

I hate this place. I cannot even go outside.

You would only lose contact with me. I cannot punch a signal through the noise on the planet.

I will never be without you. I do not want to be alone.

Reassured, she turned her concentration to Antonia. The sensitive appeared distressed. By Sato? Probably not. Evidence: the disturbance subjectively appeared deeper than anything Sato could have caused in so brief a time. There had been no such distress during the voyage, even when Antonia and

Sato had been sleeping together. Consider the tension in her skin, the calluses on her hands where they were holding one another. The *Hirohito* took an infrared scan of Antonia as she sat down in one of the command chairs. Her hands were cold, and the stiffness of the skin around her knuckles suggested this was their normal temperature. A long-standing disturbance, brought to the surface by current circumstances. Outside the ship. Damn them. What happened out there? Anything? Nothing? *Damn them.* Megan raged inwardly. How *dare* they?

The *Shenandoah* laughed.

> *Dare to maintain your own privacy when Captain Megan is about? How long have you been alive, Megan? How many years too long? A hundred? Two hundred? How long wired into your ship?*

She laughed at herself.

You know how long. Too long to give it up. For anyone.

"Tomorrow, Engineer Ranft and Navigator Sperling will sample the local plant populations and from that estimate their requirements for a more exact survey."

"Excuse me," said Antonia in a low voice.

You—
—dare?

The *Shenandoah* chuckled.
"Yes, Sensitive Brobeck?"

What about Sato?
Sato's irritated and angry at being brought back so abruptly from outside. His pulse is rapid. His blood pressure estimated from skin perturbations is also high. Look at his record: he's always had a problem with authority.

Antonia looked around the table at them. She dropped her head apologetically. "I read the charter from the Port Authority last night. It specifically states the sensitive shall scout the local environments prior to any potential crew intervention. As I see it, this is such a situation.'' Antonia looked down at the table.

She is scared, thought Megan slowly. Bertini discounts me, Sato is angry with me, and Ruth doesn't take me seriously. This is in the nature of how they deal with a captain. But she fears me. Megan replayed back the conversation and listened again. When did I become so formal? So rigid? Was I always this way?

Her other did not answer. She looked at Antonia more closely. The temperature in her hands had dropped a full three degrees.

I didn't think she had any confrontation in her at all, but why such fear?

Here's what we have on her, Megan: born on Georgia and cleared by the Institute of Human Responsibility. Personal history? Standard Georgian personnel dossier, that is to say, little or nothing. Mother still alive. Her father and brother were killed in the Mutiny. Psychological profiles? Again, up against the Georgian wall. Such data is available only from observation during this voyage. Remember: you didn't hire her. She was assigned to you by the Institute.

"Good point, Sensitive Brobeck." Megan looked around at them. "Today, you and Navigator Sperling will certify this field and the close trees as free of sentients. Tomorrow, while you and Navigator Sperling certify the area beyond the clearing, Engineer Ranft will be studying the local flora in an area you describe. Will that satisfy the requirements?"

Antonia nodded.

Good.
You do like the wielding of power, don't you Megan?
You never step away from me for a moment.
Of course not. You designed me that way.

"Dismissed. Engineer Ranft, after you have finished with the *Hirohito*, you may relax until tomorrow." She picked up the procedures manual and began to look through it as a sign of dismissal.

Bertini left immediately. Sato stopped Antonia in the hall as she passed through the hatch.

"What was that all about?" he whispered in a low voice.

Megan did not move as if she'd heard them. She continued to read the specifications, listening to them.

Antonia looked at him. "It's as I said. I read the charter last night. I'm responsible, Sato. If something happens, the Port Authority holds me responsible. And it's not just a fine, it's jail."

"They don't really do that, though."

"You don't find it scary? I do." She slipped past him toward her cabin. Sato stared after her.

Megan watched them both.

> Smarter than I thought she was.
> *Shenandoah* had nothing to say.

PICTURE A MAN in his room.

Look around the room: a bed, a desk and chair surrounded by four pale yellow walls unrelievedly blank but for one marked by a framed sampler. The sampler had been part of a quilt, fine-stitched in triangles and squares. These patches surrounded a circular blue piece of cloth. Within the blue patch was a Chinese character, *ya'an*, the character for joy. The patch had been there when Bertini arrived. Almost nothing in the room was his.

The *Hirohito* was small by comparison with the *Shenandoah* when it launched down toward Caliban. Now, landed and unfolded, it was large enough to accommodate an additional four small staterooms. Bertini required this space, this privacy. If Megan had not been able to offer it, he would not have shipped with her.

He had a feeling about this trip. A bad feeling.

Damn Megan, anyway. She was too good. Too much in control. There was something about her he didn't like. Something cold. Something older. He did not like to feel such feelings. They were uncontrolled in themselves. He looked out the window to the colored abandon of Caliban.

Cameron wandered into the stateroom and climbed up onto the desk chair. He stretched his body weasellike until his small head looked over the chair's back. Bertini stared back at him. Cameron whined.

"You wish a cookie or affection," said Bertini in a cold voice. "I do not know which."

Cameron whined again, fading into a mutter. He eased down to the chair and washed himself. Bertini stood and looked down at him.

"You are not alive. You were designed and constructed and are powered by a small battery in a location analogous to an anus." He picked up the small bear and held its head in one hand, the body in the other. "Just so I could crush you." Cameron growled and tried to pull away. "You do not have brains enough to be afraid." He put Cameron down on the floor and sat on the bed again. Cameron jumped up on the bed and cautiously made his way into Bertini's lap. Once there, he insinuated his head under Bertini's hand. Bertini petted him mechanically. Cameron began a throaty, hoarse purr.

"I do not know why I keep you." He picked Cameron up and held him in his lap. "You bring only an emptiness to me. You are not her, but you are *hers*." He held himself as if against the cold, then laughed sharply and forced himself straight. "You make an old man foolish. I will get rid of you. Soon, maybe. Next stop." Cameron continued to purr. He'd heard those words before.

WE ARE NOT a numerous people, quick in love and reproduction. Our males are most like humans, not living long and having to grasp at life as much as possible. But the rest of us, we females, do not crowd on one another. We live along the south coast in a narrow strip, tied by our inclination and our biology to our trees, seeing best by their light, binding to them our spirits, our bodies, and our children. Our continents, other places on our world have names, but not this one. It is home and needs none.

Most of us are females, the males a small temporary part of our community. The Caretakers handle the trees. They are half mad, usually lost to bearing for one reason or another, obsessed with the trees and our Ancestors.

Explain, explain. Each time I write I have to explain something further. We birth through the trees, we see through the trees, we speak through our manipulation of the trees. It is *right*, it is *proper* for us to be obsessed with our trees. They are our life, our sight and strength. Yet, we distrust our Ancestors, who live on after death through them.

I do not understand this. Sato tells me writers create out of a need to understand the world around them and often do not understand a book, or the world, until they have finished. Sometimes, not even then. I will be patient.

Traverse trailed behind me back through the forest. The day was beautiful. The trees shone on us. The ground here was bare, and I could see near the bases of the trees the moving shapes of small animals.

Our Caretaker was one of many Caretakers, all the same, all different and of one piece. We refer to all Caretakers as Caretaker, in the same way all men may be called man, and the earth is always the earth. They are indifferent, preoccupied with the singing of trees, listening for pain, disease, or death in the song.

Traverse did not speak, so I told Caretaker the story. She considered for a long time.

This disconcerted me. I sat down finally and leaned against the bole of the tree nearest me, trying to find within it a solace for my nervousness. It didn't help. All I could think of was the sickening glow outshining the trees, silhouetting Traverse's bones, so bright it seemed to burn his flesh away.

"A quorum must be called," Caretaker said suddenly.

His speech was troubled.

At that time, we were four bands. There were few of us, and greater organization was not needed. A quorum consisted of the brightest speaker of these bands. Let us call them after their representatives: Climber's band, Disapproval's band, and Infertility's band. Caretaker band was its own, Caretakers being half mad to begin with.

They and their entourages came in only two days.

We gathered deep in the forest. Caretaker sat next to me, dark and silent.

"Good," said Infertility, "we are here. Tell us why."

As I collected my thoughts, Traverse spoke:

"We bring you a story of demons."

I looked at him. Demons? I had not really given the idea much thought. This was something to be examined as yet, not judged.

The quorum gave him their attention.

"Behold," he began, "a mystery. Light came from the sky. Not up from the earth, an animal, or the trees, but from the dark above us, bright beyond imagining, beyond ignoring, beyond thought. The light took on form and definition and subtle intensities."

The quorum shifted uneasily. "Light from the sky?" asked Climber. "I do not think I believe you."

"I do not think he can be ignored, whether you believe him or not," returned Disapproval. "Your lack of interest in things other than lovers and food is well known. This is not an occasion for sloth."

"You insult me for satisfying my appetites while yours go hungry."

"You, Binder," said Infertility, ignoring them. "Did you see this light?"

"I saw light," I said slowly. "And I saw something descend into the clearing near the inland sea. It was as Traverse described, but appeared to me to have form and substance. I think it came to earth as a stone falls, though more slowly as it emitted this light. The thought of demons did not occur to me until Traverse mentioned them."

"Demons," said Caretaker in a dim voice. "Listen to me, and I will tell a story of Demons."

We all fell silent.

"A long time ago, the trees covered the earth," she began, "and all was light and growth, and we covered more than the small strip of land given to us now. At the end of those days, we were ruled not by easy consensus but by one called Bright, so did she speak that we all could listen and follow. Bright said to us, we will study these trees and understand them, and by understanding them comprehend ourselves. We will take them with us and move all about the world and into the seas, as befits creatures with a spark of the divine.

"So fine did she speak that not even Caretakers said against her.

"It came to pass that trees were taken and mated with great interest, the parentage of each tree discussed and analyzed carefully. The Caretakers grumbled, but Bright said, 'We do this to learn better how to care for the trees,' and the Care-takers were stilled.

"Then trees were transplanted from one mountain to an-other, from valley to plains. The Caretakers cried out: 'These trees are holy. We spring from them.' And Bright replied, 'The trees grow and we give birth where before we could not. How could this be evil?' And the Caretakers were confounded by this and held their say, though they remained uneasy.

"At last, it came to be known that these trees, taken and transplanted far from us, were broken and torn open and laid upon the ground to see their innermost parts, that their suffer-ing and screams were not heard but dismissed as the mutter-ings of lower orders. The Ancestors in the trees were confused and made mad, and the children in these trees were tortured and observed.

"'Murder!' we cried. 'Abomination!' and declared holy war. We descended on them in fury and slaughtered them by hundreds. Those that lived after the war were taken to one of those lonely fields they had transplanted. There, they were all one by one placed into trees as Ancestors. This took years, but still we did it, taking care to observe all procedure, tradition, and custom. Bright was taken and killed, her body sealed to a tree all her own in a transplanted field far from all others. There, we left her."

She paused and did not seem to see us, staring deep into the past. Caretaker shook herself.

"This should have been the end of it," she said bitterly. "Bright's evil should have died with Bright. A year, perhaps two years, perhaps ten—it is unclear—after the last of Bright's people were interred into the trees, a plague came down on our trees. Their leaves fell. Their trunks withered and dried, and they collapsed, each collection of Ancestors preceding them in death. The Caretakers tried all they knew, different poultices against the trunk, potions applied directly to the roots. Only the transplanted trees were unaffected, and finally we went to Bright's tree to find out why." She stopped again, hesitating. "The Ancestor Bright was not there. The tree was as green and free of Ancestors as if we had never sealed her there. Then we were troubled, for by this we knew Bright was not as you or me, but a demon: darkness taking form, and like the dark, vicious and cruel. Such a thing cannot be sealed to a tree, but disap-pears back into the dark from where it came.

"We sought out the trees of Bright's followers and found they had released the plague on Bright's orders, when she had found she was lost. They did not know of it as a plague, but only as a weapon that failed. We left them as they wailed and repented, and even then it was as if Bright's laughter followed us.

"After this, the Calibii moved south as the trees died. Now we inhabit only this tiny coast. For reasons as unknown to us as the plague, the trees do not die this far south, and we are able to live here with care." She stood up and towered over us. "You have not been told this story before. This was long ago, generations ago, and still we have not recovered. Still, the trees will not grow to the north."

"So, young male. Do not speak of demons."

No one spoke for a long time. When Disapproval spoke, we were startled. "I ask you, Caretaker, may we consult the Ancestors?"

The Caretaker answered immediately. "We will. We will do so immediately. I am at fault for not insisting on it at once."

She turned and led us deeper into the forest. We came to a tree, gnarled and wrinkled, its roots as solid as stone, its leaves shining, lighting our way.

"I have chosen this one," and she turned from us and spoke to the tree.

I was uncomfortable. I could see around me, no one besides Caretaker was entirely easy about this. Ancestors are not consulted lightly. They think long and strange, and often their answers seem complete nonsense, seen from a different perspective from ours. That we would consult them at all showed how lost we were. Light from the sky? Light out of darkness? Not of the earth? We did not understand it any more than did the ancient Caretakers understand the plague Bright had sent from beyond death.

Caretaker finished speaking, and we waited the rest of that day and most of the next.

At last the tree spoke, not as an individual Ancestor or by consensus of a group of Ancestors, some dissenting and some agreeing strongly, but as one voice.

"Send one to watch this thing, to carefully discern its nature. Also, and more importantly, send another to watch the watcher."

I was chosen to watch. Traverse was chosen to watch me.

THIS BECAME an idle time for Sato.

It did not take one day for Antonia to search the clearing for sentients; it did not take two. Fully three days passed before she was able to determine with certainty the area just around the *Hirohito* was sentient-free.

"At this rate we'll be here for five years!" cried Bertini.

"You're right, of course," Antonia nodded and smiled apologetically. "Still, this is my first assignment. I can't clear it if I don't know. You understand, don't you?"

Bertini looked at her helplessly. Sato half smiled.

Megan did not answer immediately. "We will have to operate faster if we are to fulfill our contract."

Antonia nodded again. "True. I will try to do so."

She started by walking the perimeter of the clearing slowly, stopping erratically, studying the undergrowth and the base of trees, listening.

Sato accompanied her, watching, with a rifle.

The trees were not tall but broad, the color striking. *Fall. The maples as fiery as opals, the hemlocks burnt yellow. The White Mountains in October—gray stone under color. So different from Boston.* None of the rest of them understand this, he thought. Megan was Luna-born, Antonia from Georgia. Bertini came from a dark little world squirreled away behind Sirius, and Ruth was born on Mars. Only I truly know the seasons of Earth, its smells, its sounds, its light. Knowing them deep in the moist darkness of flesh. *Flesh touching flesh in the dark night. Fingers running over skin. A touch running through me—it was more than bodies on bodies.* Light, sound, smells came to me filtered through a net of Earth memories, reinforcing Earth genes. The others have forgotten Earth, or left her behind, or buried her deep in their hindbrains and spinal cords. Thus, none of them are touched as I am—*We are made of touch. We are only skin. Lindsay taught me that.*—struck by the colors, the lack of green, the sense of the coming changes of weather.

Sato was the navigator and cartographer of this voyage. It was not the first time he had worn these roles. It would not be the last. His inclination led him most of all to watch. He enjoyed the interplay of colors in this golden-rose of midafternoon. The reds were heartbreaking and deep, the yellows almost pungent. The sere oranges and browns seemed spiderweb outlines containing pools of light. *Always before, excited, anxious, afraid, exhilarated—as if I were leaving home for the first time. But now—Now? Nothing is different. Nothing! I am as I was. I can live without Lindsay. A false friend. I need no one. False? Which of us is false?*

The afternoon grew darker.

Finally, the clearing was done. Swearing, Bertini moved his instruments out of the ship.

Sato and Antonia took the travel buggy into the forest, leaving Bertini studying the grass. There, the canopy enfolded them in a half-lit world.

Again, Sato watched Antonia as she walked through the forest, stopping at trees, scrabbling at their base, standing still as if listening to someone breathing. He smiled.

"Find anything?" he called to her.

"Of course not. Nothing's ever that simple." She turned and walked back to him, dusting her hands. "Megan's right. I can't check every tree and bush. I have to get clearer with this, get statistical." She stood next to him, and he could feel her next to him, and suddenly he wanted to touch her. *Touch. We are only skin.* He shook his head and frowned at himself. Why here? Why now?

"Still," she said musingly. "I felt something. Maybe it's my imagination."

"Intelligence?"

"Sentience," she corrected, "I have no idea how intelligence would feel."

"What's the difference?"

"Good question." She sighed. "Next question."

He shrugged and smiled at her. She smiled back. "No," he said, "I mean it."

"So did I." Antonia looked down. "I don't know. Some of us think it's the last relic of the angel in us. Self-knowledge, implying self-responsibility. Freedom of choice. Divinity." She turned back to him and looked at him hollowly. "I don't know. It's the closest thing to a religion sensitives have." With that she got in the buggy and made ready to drive.

"How does it feel?" He sat beside her and stowed the rifle.

She paused, thinking. "Like an echo," she said finally. "Like the sound of footsteps following you, stopping when you stop. Does that help?"

"Not much."

She laughed. The laughter suddenly died.

He looked up from the floor. "What's the matter?"

She pointed.

The creature stood beneath the trees about twelve meters away. It stood on two legs, though its forelimbs were long and dangled as if it could support itself on four. The limbs came straight out from the body, tortoiselike, but limber. A lump behind the neck gave the impression of a hunchback. The neck was long and terminated in an eyeless snout and mouth, twitching this way and that, idiot fashion. Sato would have sworn he and Antonia had its whole attention. The thing snuffled, and its mouth opened and closed. There was no room in that flat snout for brains.

"Pictures," she hissed.

Camera! Sato grabbed the camera and began filming it. "What do we do now?" he whispered.

Antonia slipped noiselessly to the ground and began to strip slowly. Sato watched the creature for a reaction and found none.

When she was naked, she began to walk carefully toward it in an odd crouch. It seemed to pay her no direct attention. That is, the head did not move toward her, and the creature did not turn toward her. *Where are its eyes?* he thought. The feeling of watchfulness increased.

It retreated suddenly, melting into the trees and the brush. Antonia stood for a long moment waiting for it to come back, but there was no sign.

"Damn," she sighed as she finished dressing.

She looked brighter and more alive than Sato had ever seen her, glowing. Sato swallowed and looked away.

"We go back to the ship," she thought out loud. "We're in violation here now. We'll have to talk to Megan."

The buggy whirred for a moment as it warmed up. Antonia backed it up to turn it around. There was a sudden wet crunch and a quick exhalation, followed by a bubbling cough. They looked at one another with a feeling of horror. Antonia pulled the buggy forward and stopped it. They got out and walked behind it.

It lay on the ground, bleeding red and gray blood. Its legs jerked spastically once, twice, then stiffened out in sudden rigor, the tendons showing under the fur. It thrashed again and grew still. Sato couldn't watch anymore and glanced up and away. Another one, or maybe the first one, stood before them, arms spread and a single claw on each hand extended. It advanced toward them.

"Antonia," he said slowly.

She saw, and they both began backing into the buggy. "Pictures." She jabbed him in the ribs.

"Christ—"

"Pictures, I said!"

He held up the camera, feeling sick inside.

The live creature did not move for a few moments, then knelt next to the dead one. It laid the body across its back and backed away cautiously into the trees.

Sato stopped filming and lowered the camera. "Oh, my God."

Antonia nodded, her face white and expressionless.

He turned to her. "That was a goddamn cold-blooded thing to do, take pictures of a dying . . . animal?"

"Not an animal," she said flatly, her mouth crooked in a crazy smile, her eyes flat as a fish. "Not. An. Animal. Never an animal." She shuddered and buried her face in her hands. Then, she looked at him. "Cold-blooded? Maybe. This is murder. It'll be my trial, not yours. I'll need all the help I can get."

4   ANTONIA: ON GEORGIA

Antonia did not like the rain.

On days like this, when the summer waters came down gently, fully, inexorably, she longed for winters with their actinic sunlight.

But in the winter the Paedash migrated south near the equator, and the plains were covered only by a gray, stubborn tundra. She liked that less than the rain.

So she stood on the chair to see out the dirty window toward the rose garden. The gray fence leaned in and out, crooked as a drunkard's walk, the wet wood as paintless as rock, enclosing the garden's overgrown jumble of thorns and flowers. She could see the old fountain, choked with brambles and half-filled with matted soil washed down by the rain.

Beyond the garden were the Paedash, the real reason she chose this window. If she could not walk between their boles and under their spherical leaves, she could at least watch them from a distance, swaying together as elephants in dance. Antonia had been a literate child and had seen pictures of earth elephants since she was very young. She had found them in a book, very old and broken with mold and dry rot, in the dim, dusty room her mother referred to as "the library." The library had belonged to Antonia's father, Andrei, and her mother never entered the room. Andrei and Josef, Antonia's brother, were killed in the Mutiny. The library was Antonia's favorite place.

That the Paedash were plants and resembled elephants only in bulk and slight motion did not bother her. Such details were not important.

"Where's Fyodor?" her mother asked behind her. Antonia turned to the voice.

Catherine Brobeck stood behind her, shallowly smoking a cigarette. She wore an ancient, dirty white gown torn through at the elbows. "Antonia?" she called, this time confused and quavering.

"Here, Mama." Antonia did not move toward her, wary. "Mama? Do you hear me?"

Catherine did not answer but watched the ash on the cigarette. The ash had grown nearly an inch long. She stared at it fixedly as the tobacco smoldered toward her fingers. The coal touched the skin and Antonia could smell the hair burn. Antonia trembled. Catherine made no sound. The ash fell suddenly.

"Ha!" Catherine cried. "Damn near two inches that time." She looked at her finger. "Hurts," she said vaguely.

Antonia relaxed, went to her, and took her other hand. "Mama?" she said softly.

"Yes, baby. What is it?" Her mother smiled at her.

Antonia led Catherine down the hall toward the kitchen. "You called me?"

"Call you? You were by the window. I was remembering when Andrei and I were married here." Her eyes became dreamy. "The house was so bright. The Paedash were holding the lights over the garden. The roses were in bloom..." She paused, looking blank. Her face grew wild. She shoved Antonia against the wall, pinning her shoulders. "What were you looking at outside? What? Tell me!" Her eyes burned fever bright.

"The rose garden," Antonia said, lying. Her shoulders hurt, and she could barely speak. "Only the rose garden!"

Her mother stood, looked at her hands, then at Antonia. "Yes, of course." She let Antonia go, hid her hands in the fold of the dress, and looked away. "The rose garden. What did you see there?"

"Roses."

"Yes. You would see that." She stared off into the next room, unseeing. Tears came down her cheeks, and she looked grief-stricken. "Where's Fyodor?" she asked blankly.

Antonia took her to the kitchen and bandaged her hand.

EVERY SUMMER Thursday at two o'clock, her uncle Fyodor brought their week's groceries. He rode from the south on his horse, Leo, following the road religiously from his small house to the old Brobeck mansion and never taking the shorter route through the Paedash forest. Antonia knew this, for when she was a child one afternoon as he rode back, she beat him home by cutting through the forest. She burst out of the forest in front of the horse, and the big roan shied away from her. He calmed it, laughing nervously, looking at her, then the forest. He insisted on carrying her back to her mother on Leo, again taking the road south to the fork and back again up toward her house. Antonia thought this silly, but she loved the smell of him, of saddle soap and wool, of the dogs he kept and the herbs of his garden.

The day gradually cleared, and by the afternoon the sky was a deep violet blue, the Paedash a rich rust red. Antonia waited for Fyodor on the porch, watching the road and across the road the Paedash. Her world was marked by extremes, her uncle, solid as earth, and her mother, as changeable as weather. The seasons of Georgia, its settled roots deep in the Soviet province, mirrored those extremes. The humid, chokingly hot summers would give way to dry, cold winters. Humans lived here in a narrow temperate band north and south of the equator. The Paedash followed the most livable weather: the right water, the right light, and the right heat to photosynthesize.

Antonia lived in North, the country north of the equator. She knew the Paedash, listened to them. At times it was as if they spoke to her, the echo of a voice, the hollow within a shout.

Fyodor rounded the road's curve into view. She had quit thinking or watching for him anymore, and now he seemed to ride over the curve in the earth, appearing from South, half a world away. He rode Leo at a walk, preoccupied. When he reached the yard, he dismounted and tied Leo to the rose garden fence. She walked to him and stood before him, expecting to be hugged. "Uncle Fyodor." She smiled.

Instead, he lifted her and held her close. "Antonia," Fyodor murmured.

"What? Did you say something?" she asked, startled. He wasn't the same. He did not laugh or tell her anything new from home.

Fyodor set her down and looked down at her. "You are how old? Twelve?"

"You know how old I am." She laughed nervously. He smiled slightly, and she grew frightened. "Thirteen. I am thirteen." She backed away from him, stopped when she saw the hurt come into his eyes.

"How do you feel about school?" he asked.

She shook her head. "I don't know. I've never been."

Fyodor took the saddlebags of food from Leo, and they sat on the edge of the porch together. Antonia watched him out of the corner of her eye. She held her hands together.

He fidgeted, brought out his pipe, and filled the bowl with tobacco. Flakes spilled onto his pants, and he brushed at them irritably. He stopped when he saw her watching him, smiled slowly and took a deep breath, emptied the pipe, and put it away. He watched the Paedash. "You were two during the Mutiny. Do you remember any of it?"

"No." She looked at her hands. "I don't have a good memory, I guess."

"At two? No one has a good memory that young. It's all right." When he said that, some of the Fyodor she knew came out, the bedrock calm, the kindness. The strange Fyodor, the nervous, indecisive, unknown Fyodor diminished. She relaxed a little.

"We don't speak of it," he continued. "What do you know of it?"

She shrugged. "It was a war. Like the old Earth wars."

"Who fought? And why?"

"I don't know, really." She stared at her hands, frightened again.

He sighed and lowered his voice. "Please. It's important."

Antonia wouldn't look at him. "We play a game . . ."

"Who?"

"Me. Leonid from near you. Nikita. Maria. We *used* to play it. It's a kid's game."

"What's the game?"

"Jack South."

He didn't speak for a moment, then asked her in a strangled voice: "How is this game played?"

Antonia glanced at him briefly. His eyes were closed. "You get a group together. One of them gets to be Jack South. He sings:

Jack sings from the forest.
From there comes the chorus.
Go crazy and come join us.
All burn down!

"Then, he divides the group into the crazies and the dead."

"The crazies and the dead," repeated Fyodor, his eyes still closed.

Antonia nodded. "Then the crazies and the dead play war."

"Who wins?"

She shrugged. "Depends on who's Jack South." He didn't respond to her. She rubbed her hands together. "I played it all while I was a little kid. I haven't played it for a couple of years. It made me feel funny. It's a kid's game."

Opening his eyes, he nodded at last, and looked so sad Antonia forgot to be afraid of him and touched his hand. He took her smaller hand and held it in his two large ones.

"Was the Mutiny like that?" she asked.

"Yes," he said distantly. "Andrei and Josef were killed that way."

Antonia felt confused. "Who were the crazies?"

He looked at her and smiled strangely, though the pain was clear on his face. "Why, we were, of course."

"Then," she asked slowly, "who was Jack South?"

He did not answer, but straightened his back and breathed deeply. Gradually, it seemed to Antonia, his strength flowed back into him, filling him, making him larger. He reached out a bearlike arm and drew her across the leather bags to his side, holding her. She hugged him.

"Antonia," he said after a time, "I have a great deal to discuss with your mother."

"She's inside," Antonia said, trying to be helpful.

He looked down at her, again her Uncle Fyodor. "Good. Will you do me a favor?"

"Yes." She smiled at him.

"Would you leave us alone this afternoon? Come back at dinnertime. Would you do that for me?"

She nodded. "I'll go see Nikita."

"Do that. Tell him hello for me." He stood and took the groceries. He looked at the Paedash momentarily, and his expression was lost again. He brought himself back and grinned at her. "Until dinnertime." He left her and went inside the house.

She stood for a few minutes on the porch, looking inside after him. Then she jumped into the yard and ran down the road toward Nikita's, nothing in her now but the need to run.

NIKITA PERCHIKOFF was sitting outside his family's barn watching the forest. His brother and aunt had been killed in the Mutiny, leaving only him and his father to run the farm. He idly chewed a twig. Older than Antonia, he was nearly fifteen and was already a thin attenuated boy with big eyes and a stiff, formal smile.

"Think they'll mind?" she called to him.

The hand holding the twig twitched, and Antonia knew she had startled him.

"No," he said as she sat on the bench beside him. "They don't feel anything like twigs. The squirrels chew on them, don't they? The Paedash don't feel that."

"They aren't really squirrels," corrected Antonia. "I've seen real squirrels in books. From Earth."

Nikita shrugged.

"What are you doing?"

"Watching them. What do you think?"

Antonia waited for him to explain. In a collection of clever if unschooled children, Nikita shone with brilliance. He did not seem aware of the impact he had on Antonia, which made Antonia put him in a class with her Uncle Fyodor.

"I was thinking about what the Paedash bring with them. The squirrels, the wolves, the bushes—all of the forest. When they leave, nothing's left but the tundra." Abruptly, he turned to her. "Hear about the sensitives?"

"Sensitives?"

"Turns out some people can actually *talk* with them. There's a school for them in Andropov." He didn't say anything for a moment. "I'd like to be able to do that."

"Who told you?"

"Leonid. He heard about it from his mother. She wants to send him." The disgust was evident in his voice.

"Leonid! He carves his initials in their trunks." To Antonia, there was no greater sin.

"I know it. *He* knows it. He just wants to stay here and raise pigs." Nikita shook his head. "*I'm* going to the university in Dansk."

"Why does his mother want him to go?"

He snorted. "Some status thing, I guess. Mrs. Petrovich would saw off both Leonid's feet at the ankles if she could be," he imitated Mrs. Petrovich's high, nasal whine, "'as big here as the old Brobeck family.'"

Antonia laughed. "Nothing much is left of that. Catherine talks about it sometimes."

"Yeah," said Nikita. "I remember it a little."

"Tell me?"

"I don't remember much," Nikita confessed. "The house was always lit up bright. And the Paedash underworkers were everywhere, in the fields, around the grounds. One took care of you, I think. That's all."

"I don't remember anything," she said, feeling wistful. "It must have been beautiful."

"You were very young." They fell silent, one remembering just an impression of time past, the other trying to imagine it.

"I want to play Jack South again," said Antonia suddenly.

"That's a kid's game." Nikita shifted uneasily.

"No, it's not. You know it's not," she heard herself say.

"Sure it is. I haven't played it in years."

"Why not?" she demanded.

"I don't know," he said, looking first at the forest, then back at her. "I just felt weird."

"Me, too. I want to play now. I want to," she paused, thinking, "to know why it felt weird."

"We need more kids," he said, stalling.

"We do not. We can just play the Jack South part."

"You can do that yourself."

"I can't. I don't want to. It," she looked down, "scares me."

He nodded. "Yeah. It scares me, too."

"Well?"

"Okay," he said reluctantly and stood up.

They walked deep into the Paedash forest. The spherical leaves spilled shadow over them. The forest was hushed, the animals moving quickly over the trees and the ground making no sound. The tundra was thick and springy under them, and they could see the fresh turned earth between the newly dropped roots of the trees. Hitch-hiker bushes had separated from the trees and were closing slowly over the ground. Though the forest was silent, Antonia could almost hear murmurings, chants, or a low, vibrant hum.

They found a likely-looking clearing between three giants, fifty or more feet high. Like grandfathers, she thought.

"You want to be Jack South?" Nikita asked lamely.

"Not really," said Antonia, hesitant now, feeling a presence around them.

"You *ought* to. You wanted to come here."

"I will. All right, I will."

She stood away from him and began to sing:

Jack sings of the forest . . .

Something moved in her, a touch, a harmony. She sang louder, not remembering the words, humming through the parts she could not recall. She heard Nikita gasp and didn't care. She danced as she sang, and someone danced and sang with her.

Who? she asked herself.

I don't know. Suddenly frightened, she stopped. In front of her was one of the giants, holding itself out of the ground on its mobile roots, quivering, swaying back and forth with her.

She backed away from it, her hand over her mouth. Nikita was next to her.

"It just moved over to you. Lifted itself right out of the ground." He sounded awed.

"Oh no," she whispered, "oh no." She grabbed Nikita by the shirt front.

The Paedash eased itself down on its main trunk, and its roots slid easily into the earth. They could see now, on its side, a worn plastic case bolted to the trunk.

"An orderbox," breathed Nikita. He pulled away from her and stood in front of it. "That's how they used to run them. Antonia, the ones on your farm had these!"

"It was the one that took care of me, maybe?" she asked no one in particular.

Nikita didn't hear her. He had pulled out his knife and was scraping the overgrown bark from the edge of the orderbox.

"Don't hurt it," she begged.

He stopped and looked at her, pale. "Is it hurting, do you think?"

She looked at the Paedash. "I don't know. I don't think so."

"Good." He traced the thin line of the case with his knife. "They were supposed to remove all of these after the Mutiny."

"Do you remember the Mutiny?" Antonia asked eagerly.

"No," he said shortly.

She reached for his shoulder. "You're lying to me," she said slowly.

"Yes. All right, I remember."

"Tell me."

He turned to her. "I can't. I don't want to."

"Please. I don't know anything."

He turned back to the orderbox. It sprang open. "It's voice-controlled, I think." There was a switch inside painted bright yellow. Nikita pulled it down. Two red lights came on inside the orderbox.

Antonia felt panic around her. "I don't think this is a good idea."

Nikita ignored her. "If it's voice controlled . . . Stand up!"

The Paedash rose stiffly, ponderously onto its mobile roots. Antonia felt a stabbing pain, deep fear, and a great sadness. "Nikita," she said.

Nikita smiled, a twisted smile of someone who knows he is doing wrong but stubbornly refuses to admit it. "Waltz," he said.

"Nikita!" she screamed as the pain overwhelmed her, and she went for his throat. She knocked him down, and they rolled over and over in the dirt. Towering over them, the Paedash danced, first on one root, then on another.

"Antonia! I'll stop!" he yelled. "I'll stop!"

She struck him with her fists, filled with maniacal strength. All she could see or hear or feel was the pain of the Paedash, dancing against its will.

Nikita pushed her away, bleeding from his lips and nose. She rolled against one of the other trees and stopped, blinking. Snarling, she picked up a large rock. He scrambled for the orderbox and pushed up the yellow switch as she raised the stone.

The pain died in her, replaced with relief and a vegetative feeling of complacency. The Paedash settled back into the soil. She dropped the rock, seeing Nikita for the first time. "Nikita," she called softly and knelt beside him. He cringed away.

"Not again," he whispered.

She tore her jacket and cleaned his face. He blew his nose, and the cloth came away bloody.

"I'll be okay," he said. "You didn't really hurt me."

She sat back ashamed. "I couldn't help it. It hurt."

"The crazies couldn't help it either," Nikita said bitterly. "They dragged people screaming from the houses. Burned them up if they couldn't get them outside." He looked at her. "That was the Mutiny. Half of everybody going crazy and killing the other half. For trees. Christ." He struck at the bark of the Paedash. The Paedash did not respond. "All burn down," he muttered.

"I'm one of those sensitives you were talking about."

"We're all sensitives. Who do you think the crazies were?"

"I can talk to them. No, not talk. Feel them? Know them?" She shook her head.

He stared at her. "I thought so as soon as Leonid told me about the school."

"Why didn't you tell me?"

"I didn't want you to go away," he said simply.

"*You're* going away, to Dansk."

"Not for a long time, anyway."

She felt a sinking sensation in her stomach. "That's where Uncle Fyodor wants me to go," she said softly.

"What?"

"Nikita, they're going to send me *away*!" She buried her head in his shoulder and sobbed.

He held her, looking confused. "What are you talking about?"

While she was crying, she told him of her uncle earlier that afternoon.

"What'll I do?"

"I don't know," said Nikita.

It was night when she returned.

The front room had the stiff silence of an aborted argument. Fyodor stood staring at the floor, his unlit pipe in his hand. He had not looked up when Antonia entered. Catherine sat on the couch watching Antonia, holding herself as if she had been struck.

"Baby?" she called softly. "You won't leave, will you? Promise me."

Antonia walked over to her slowly, dizzy with the tensions in the room. Catherine held her.

"Promise me," she crooned in a voice like a drill.

She smelled of cigarette smoke and old, dirty clothing, of the moldering smell of the house. The smell and her voice and the low, undervoiced mutterings between Fyodor and Catherine confused Antonia and made her feel nauseous.

"Answer me," said Catherine, her voice harsh. "You're all I have left."

Antonia brought her gaze to Catherine's face, and Catherine looked afraid.

"She knows," Catherine said, her voice climbing. "Where were you this afternoon? Spying? What were you doing?" She raised her hand.

Fyodor grabbed her and held her high. "Catherine!" he roared.

Antonia watched the two of them grapple. She backed out the door onto the front porch, closed the door, and turned toward the forest. She closed her eyes.

After a time, she heard Fyodor put Catherine to bed. Soon, he came out onto the porch. The night was warm and close, as clear as crystal.

"I think you had better come home with me, this night." He leaned against the post watching the sky.

"I'll stay here." Her voice was small.

"Antonia," he began, stopped, began again. "Your mother's not well."

"She's crazy," Antonia said simply. "But she won't send me away. She wants me."

"Who wants to send you away?"

She looked up toward him, but his face was in darkness. "You do. You want to send me to that school in Andropov."

"Who told you that?"

"Nobody. I figured it out. I won't go." She drummed her heels against the porch. "I don't want to go."

Fyodor coughed and shifted toward her, stopped when she stared at him. "Your mother gets . . . sicker every year. I'm afraid for you."

"She won't hurt me."

"She might."

"She *hasn't*. She only hurts herself." Antonia felt tears begin to fall. "If I go, nobody'll take care of her when she burns herself or when she falls down or breaks something."

"I'll take care of her."

"You won't. You'll send her away like you want to send me away." From the sudden stillness, she knew she spoke truth, and the tears fell faster.

"You don't understand . . ." he said softly.

She did not answer him.

At last, he stood, smaller than she thought. "She'll sleep all night. I gave her a sedative. I'll be back early in the morning."

Antonia shook her head. "We don't need you."

He untied Leo. "Maybe not." With that, he dug his heels into Leo's flank and left her.

ANTONIA DID NOT know how long she stood on the porch after Fyodor had gone. The moon came out and made the shadows silver, the Paedash branches covered with Christmas ornaments. She left the porch and moved into the yard, watching the forest, the nightbirds. The forest swayed, as always, making no sound.

"Jack sings from the forest," she sang and began to cry again. She felt something reach for her, drawn by her. She let it come and didn't look through her tears for a long time. When she did, the Paedash she had danced with settled into the ground before her. She felt it now, as she knew she had felt them all along. Nikita was wrong. She could no more speak with them than she could with Leo. No human could. They were too different. What the two of them could do, and this was little enough, was sit next to one another, or dance together, or sense each other's great, block emotions. Neither knew what those emotions, that depth, or that dance meant. This was sensitivity.

She heard the porch door swing open.

Catherine stood there, a white ghost in the moonlight, her face a silver blur. She was silent, then went back inside.

Antonia felt uneasy. Catherine was supposed to be sleeping, drugged. "Go back," she said to the Paedash. Nothing happened. Had she expected anything different? She tried to feel her way into the Paedash, to tell it to leave. Nothing.

Catherine came out again, holding a stick with a wad of cloth on the end. As Antonia watched, she lit it. The flames painted Catherine the color of blood.

Antonia scrambled around the side of the tree, yanked open the orderbox, pulled down the switch. "Go to the forest. Wait for me. *Go!*"

Ponderously, in a mixture of pain and betrayal that nearly blinded Antonia, the Paedash stood and began to walk down to the forest. Catherine followed it.

Antonia stumbled after. Catherine did not see her, her eyes fixed on the forest, a little smile on her lips. Her face was as bloodless as death.

Antonia reached up and grabbed the torch, pulled it down to the ground, and stamped on it until it was out.

Catherine dropped the other end and stared at Antonia. Her eyes were huge caverns, her mouth half open. Her teeth glowed silver in the light.

"Mama?" said Antonia softly. The sound was swallowed up in silence. She backed away.

Catherine followed her.

She matched Antonia step for step as Antonia backed up the yard. Antonia couldn't stop looking at her. Antonia's right arm brushed against something, and she felt of it. It was the gate of the rose garden. She couldn't catch her breath, and her stomach hurt. The gate moved, and the ancient garden shovel fell between them.

Catherine stopped. Antonia continued backing into the garden. Catherine picked up the shovel slowly, and smiled, and lunged.

Antonia screamed and broke for the rosebushes, Catherine running after her.

The thorns ripped at her clothes, and she slowed, then heard Catherine behind her. She looked behind her. Catherine threw the shovel at her, and she jumped to one side. It struck the earth like a knife.

Antonia ran between two tall, overgrown hedges, blind in the sudden shadow. At the end, there were only rosebushes. She could hear her mother behind her. She dove under the thorns and crawled over old, broken brambles to the trunk. Catherine hacked at the brambles, stopped, then struck the bush. Antonia sat there and trembled. "Go away," she whispered. "Mama, go away."

Catherine fell silent.

In a little while, Antonia felt as if she could breathe again. "All right," she said. She felt her way through the thorns, to the other side of the bush biting her tongue so that she might not cry out. She eased out from under the roses and looked up.

Catherine was waiting for her, the shovel high in the air.

Antonia pulled back under the bush, and the shovel struck earth where her head had been. Its scraping against the stone was like metal against bone. Antonia returned to the trunk of the bush and froze.

Catherine made random stabbings into the thorns. "I swore you'd never know," she muttered. "I promised Josef and Andrei."

The hollow space around the trunk of the rose continued down the row. As quietly as she could, stifling the pain as the thorns gashed her knees and ankles, she moved down the row away from Catherine and pushed out of the brambles. She looked back. Catherine was still striking at the bush where Antonia had been, her breath coming in angry sobs.

Antonia moved to where the fence leaned out and climbed on it.

"Antonia!"

"No, Mama," she cried and jumped across it. She ran down the yard and across the road.

"Antonia, come back. Come back," her mother called over and over. "Andrei, Josef. Come back."

Antonia disappeared into the forest.

SHE FOUND THE TREE by following its trail of pain and fear. She turned off the orderbox and sat on the ground next to the tree, dull. Her hands hurt, and she looked at them. They were ripped and bleeding. As she looked, she gradually felt the rest of her body. There were great gashes on her arms and one on her face. She felt aching punctures on her knees and shins. Blood cemented her feet to the inside of her shoes.

"Are you all right?" came a voice.

She tumbled around the tree and hid.

"It's me. It's Nikita. I heard your mother."

She looked around the tree. Nikita stood in the faint light.

"She was going to kill me," Antonia said as she came around the tree.

"Are you all right? You look a mess."

"No." She shook her head. "She tried to *kill* me."

"You're all over blood."

"I know."

Nikita turned and looked back at her. "We've got to get you out of here. I'm going to take you to your uncle's."

She did not answer.

"Is that all right?"

Silence.

"Can you walk?"

She nodded. He led her through the forest to Fyodor's farm. Fyodor opened the door, and she smiled up at him. "Uncle Fyodor."

"SHE KILLED PAPA and Josef, didn't she?"

Fyodor had bathed her and dressed the wounds with herbs. She bore the stinging in silence. He picked her up and sat her on the sofa. Nikita helped as he could.

"What happened?" asked Fyodor after she spoke.

"Did she?"

Fyodor nodded slowly. "When Jack South sang, we all heard him. We all heard the Paedash. That was his gift, to bring out what we didn't know we heard. All of the sensitive people. All of the crazies. We were never the same again."

"I know about that."

Fyodor was silent a moment. "I shouldn't have left you there."

Antonia shrugged. "Tell me."

Fyodor stared at his hands. "The madness faded after a while. We didn't think. We just—we were animals biting at a cage. A cage not our own. I came to myself watching the Perchikoff house burn, knowing I set the flames."

"You—" began Nikita.

Fyodor stared at Nikita with a cold anger. "Don't think only the Brobecks kill their own. Your father killed Old Man Petrovich and his son. Mrs. Petrovich helped." The anger faded, and all that was left was weariness. "I almost went crazy again when I remembered Catherine. Andrei. Josef. You. I rode Leo to the mansion until he stumbled up the yard. You were crying in the library.

"At first, I thought, the house is still standing. It must be all right. But I couldn't find Catherine. I could find no one but you. I looked all through the house and then stood in the window, confused and frightened. I could see into the rose garden, where Catherine was standing. She didn't move, but I could see the knife and the bodies."

The breath came out of him like death and made the flames in the fireplace dance. His voice went leaden flat. "I stayed with her all that winter. She wouldn't move out of touching distance from you. She seemed to get better for a while. Then, then she got worse."

Antonia did not speak for a long time. "You had better go see to her. And give me some money. And give me the name of that school."

"The Institute of Human Responsibility," he said automatically. "Antonia—"

"You go see to my mother." She smiled. "Or I shall return for you."

Fyodor looked at her and shuddered. He went to the wall and opened the safe, looked at her a moment, then left. She didn't look at him, the smile still on her face.

Antonia turned to Nikita for the first time. "Will your father loan us his cart?"

Nikita nodded slowly. "I suppose."

She took his hand. "Thank you, Nikita. I need you to take me to the train station."

"There are no trains running now."

She nodded. "I know. I'll wait. Will you wait with me?"

He took her other hand in his. "I will."

SHE SAT NEXT to the window as the train skirted the edge of the mountains before it began the long descent to Andropov's valley. The lights of the city calmed her. They gleamed like pinprick stars. She sat up and stared, and the city of Andropov was gone. For a short moment, before it had been masked by the trees, in the lights of the city she had seen the face of a woman she did not know, her face of rose petals, her hands of thorns.

5

In days, I found a lover and lost him.

I stood on the edge of the clearing, and one of the creatures shed its skin and approached me from its peculiarly opaque beast. It waved its appendages and made threatening noises. It seemed soft and vulnerable, hairless and without claws. Still, it made me uneasy and I withdrew, Traverse's speech in my mind.

These might be *demons*?

They had approached on a mighty beast with disks instead of legs. The beast was too sharply defined, not like the blurred outlines of living tissue, yet not like stone either. It had waited patiently for them. Could this thing be the demon and the creatures that approached me its servants? And what of the other servant, the one still wrinkled and covered, pointing a detachable snout at me? I did not understand at all.

I circled around to where I had left Traverse, to think, to consider with him. He wasn't there.

I felt lost for a moment—where was he? I made speech to him containing defecation and ancestry. He'd gone to look at the creatures—idiot male! He was supposed to watch me, not them.

Traverse was not an efficient stalker. I trailed him to the rear of the disk-beast, cursing to myself. Idiot twice over! He stood nearly visible, behind the beast, watching them.

I made no speech that might catch the creatures' attention Did they see me? What senses do demons have, anyway? Wait a moment, I stilled myself. You're beginning to think like Traverse, like a male short-timer. I moved forward to drag him back into the brush.

Then the beast moved.

It slipped easily, unthinkingly, lumbering its cruel weight backward before it lurched forward. It rolled over Traverse like an afterthought, like a shrug.

I heard the bones crack, saw the blazing scream cut off into a dissipating glow. I ran to him.

He lay on the ground, his blood fracturing the grass light into different colors. He faded, barely conscious, but did not know me, looking into a place I could not see.

I cried out to him, and he left me. Dim, gone, dead.

Killed before his time. Killed before our time together. I cried out to him, robbed of him, lost.

I turned toward the demons in rage, claws extended, ready to kill them. They came behind the beast and stood over me and Traverse. The one with the mobile snout pointed it at us, and they became still. I could see the movements of their inner body parts, so different from my own in structure, sharing the same furious motion.

What about Traverse? It is not too late, I told myself. But you must hurry. *Hurry.*

"I will return for you," I said to them.

Cautiously, I picked him up and backed away from them.

I could not take to the trees with his body atop mine. Instead, I ran down the ridge and up the near cliff, then along that ridge until I found the Caretaker border. I entered their forest at a dead run, bawling out for help. She met me at the base of the Ancestor tree of the day before.

With no speech between us, we bared a deep root of the tree. We had little time. Caretaker licked him clean as I strained and sweated and produced enough sexual secretions to mix with the tree's birthing fluid. The resultant paste we spread over him, sealing him against the root of the tree, safe from the wet and rot. Then, we covered him with earth.

Caretaker turned to me. "He was already *dead*."

"I had no choice. Did you not see his wounds? Did you not see the blood? He was killed by those creatures."

She straightened and scratched her sides. "Those of the thing which fell a few days ago?"

Lovers die, gone and never forgotten. We have them only briefly, just long enough to capture their children. All that makes it bearable is the inevitability.

It had been enough to watch Traverse, to be a part of his world. If he had been younger, I would never have approached him—siring drains what little strength males have, and I wanted him alive as long as I could. Other children have I borne. I have outlived the males; the females have become my sisters. But his—his would have been special.

I had been cheated.

"The very ones," I said wearily. "Or one creature. I am not sure. He was stepped on."

"They are that big?"

I scratched the dirt from my claws and from within the wrinkles of my palms. "Yes. No. Maybe. They are very different from us. One made mouth noises, and I backed away."

"Tell me what happened," she said finally, and I did.

"I am sad for you," she said when I had finished. "Where will you go?" I cannot lose him now, not so far, not so distant.

"I will go nowhere." A deep, sullen anger grew in me.

"Nowhere? You *must* go. Your lover is *dead*. He is being made into an Ancestor." She trembled in consternation. "It is custom."

"I say I go nowhere," I cried. "There is no law that says I must leave if my lover is sealed." I stood, and my claws came out by reflex.

Caretaker backed away. "There is no law, Binder. But the custom is not there without reason. It is painful to those close to the Ancestor to be near."

"The process is painful?" I asked shakily.

"Not to the Ancestor. Only to those close to him."

"Still," I said, "I will stay. Will you attack me and force me away? If you do, I will return. I will stay and wait unless you kill me."

Caretaker held up her hands to show her claws were sheathed. "No one will force you. You may yet regret it."

I relaxed and sheathed my own claws. "I will take the risk."

THE IMAGE was clear:

The creature was broken in pieces. Its body was neatly and brutally divided into uneven thirds by the buggy tracks. One tire had crossed over the careful joining of its neck to its body, flattening the hunchback into a greasy gray streak. The other had rolled over its abdomen, blending its back legs, lower organs, and fur into a hash of viscous fluids. The thing was a lumpy sack of blood.

"Christ," breathed Bertini.

"Wait," said Antonia softly. "There's more."

The camera moved to the live one, taut with rage and revenge. It stood for a long moment, then took the body and disappeared into the forest.

"Christ," breathed Bertini again, looking up and around the *Hirohito*'s bridge. "What a way to go. What a godawful way to go."

"You weren't there," said Sato tonelessly. "It felt no different from a man dying."

"Yeah," said Bertini. "I can imagine."

Sato looked at Antonia. "I would have thought it would be different. They aren't human."

Antonia stared at him. "You knew it was no animal. We all know that. Sensitives merely admit it to themselves." Her gaze slid past him and was lost. She smiled distantly.

Megan said nothing. She stared at the table, lost in fear. They'll take my ship. "Goddamn you," she said in a low voice. "Goddamn you to hell."

Megan, you're panicking.
To hell with you. This is *us* we're talking about.

They stared at her, confused expressions on their faces. She could see one thought run through all of them, as if they had been telepaths: *this is Megan?*

"It was an accident," began Sato.

"Accident, hell!" She snarled at them. "She *invited* this. She tried to make fucking *contact*!"

"Who the hell do you think you are?" shouted Sato. "Who made you the bitch goddess of death? You weren't there. You don't know."

"That's enough," said Bertini calmly. "That is enough. We are in enough trouble."

Bertini's sudden calm took the emotions out of the air and replaced them with a sick despair.

Antonia's smile never left her face. "The regulations are clear on this. In a state of violation, the sensitive must use her own initiative."

"That means you had to kill this thing?" Megan said bitterly.

Antonia's smile wavered a moment. "Calibi. They will be called Calibii."

Megan was silent a moment. She grabbed the edge of the table and drew a deep, shuddering breath.

Megan!

Okay, okay. You want rationality? You want clear thinking? You got it.

Megan, we're on the same side.

Shut up.

"All right," she said, looking at each one of them in turn. "All right. Let us review the sentience clause. It puts us in violation regardless of prior knowledge, regardless of clean team specification. It is independent of knowledge of the clause. We are guilty whether we know the law or not. It is in our contract, but has jurisdiction beyond our contract. Were we here by accident, the sentience clause would cover us even though we had no contract. Are we in doubt we are covered?" There was silence as they looked at her. "Let the record state we understand our compliance with the law."

"There are mitigating circumstances—" began Bertini.

"I understand there are," Megan interrupted. "The clause further states that, when the violation of the clause exists, the invaders—it actually uses that word—must leave immediately. It doesn't say, 'with all reasonable speed,' or, 'as soon as pos-

sible'; it says 'immediately.' It then places liability on the invaders—us—'for all acts, public and private, visible and
invisible, short- and long-term.' It is the only part of our contract not under the Port Authority on Earth. Instead, it is ad-
ministered by the Articles of Sentience. We are not judged by
our peers, but by the peers of the *victim*. Not humans. Is that
an accurate summary of the clause?''

''Nobody doubts your ability to parrot the contract, Megan.'' Bertini watched her with a bland face. ''Let the record
state we know our legal status.''

*Megan, there's something about Bertini. Something
different now. He has come to some conclusion.*
We'll worry about him later.

She looked at them for a long moment. ''Then let the record state that Sensitive Brobeck, upon finding us in violation
of this clause, decided to attempt contact. During her attempt,
an alien died.''

''It wasn't like that,'' shouted Sato. ''You're trying to hang
this on her!''

''Navigator Sperling!'' she said to him coldly. He dropped
his eyes. *Good. I haven't lost control yet.* ''We will, by regu-
lation, file separate reports. You may write any account you
wish.'' There was a long, silent tension between them. Finally,
Sato nodded. ''All right,'' Megan continued. ''Sensitive Brobeck, what is your opinion now? What should we do?''

Antonia seemed to be watching a point in space just above
the center of the table. She answered as if from a great distance. ''I think,'' she said slowly, ''we should leave immediately. Go directly to the Port Authority on Earth and replay the
entire voyage tape from the time Ruth woke us up until now.
Let somebody qualified handle it.''

''Sounds good to me,'' agreed Sato.

Bertini nodded but did not speak.

Panic built up in Megan again, she quelled it. She shook her
head. ''You don't understand. None of you. If we go back now,
what happens is this: Antonia gets tried for murder, and we will
be accessories.''

''Come on, Megan,'' said Sato. ''It was an *accident*!''

"So what?" She leaned forward toward him. "Read the clause again, Sperling. We are liable. You think we're boss out here or something? You think we run things? Earth is a backwater planet that is allowed—*allowed*, mind you—by other species to make claims on territory. The Hub runs this. It is their cards, their dice, their rules. It is *their game*. This is under the Articles of Sentience, not the Port Authority. We'll be tried in Sentient's Court, not the Board of Inquiry. What kind of chance do you think we'll have in Sentient's Court? What—not who, mind you—will be the judge? Some sympathetic human bureaucrat? No. It'll be something—not someone, not some human—out for blood. Two million people died in the Mutiny on Georgia because we were too stupid to recognize an alien race. *That's* how the aliens judge us. Stupid. Cruel. Clumsy."

Megan stared at them. There was silence. "Are you stupid? Why do you think there's an Institute of Human Responsibility? Why do you think Antonia's here at *all*? Because we're watched. And there are things watching us, waiting for us to fall, things that don't like stupid, cruel, clumsy people blundering around in space. Do you think the Eho care about four humans in a map ship? Or the Uneese? They don't care. Or better, do you think the Port Authority cares about us at all? They want a better deal. We're in the way. We're an *embarrassment*. We may never *get* to Sentient's Court. We just might have accidents while we're waiting for trial."

"Oh, Megan—" began Bertini.

"We'll hang for treachery. We'll hang for the—the Calibi's blood. Best of all, we'll hang because it's a goddamn good way to make sure *they* don't hang."

"All right, Megan," cried Bertini. "For Christ's sake, what do you want to do?"

"Stay."

"For *what*?" Sato struck the table with his palm.

"For our skins, Navigator Sperling," Megan hissed. "We stay. We contact the Calibii. We persuade *them* it was an accident. We set up diplomatic relations, and *then*, we return, to the Port Authority. With everything tied together so they can't touch us. We will be clean in the *Calibii's* eyes, the species we committed this crime *against*. They won't be *able* to try us."

"What about the violation?" Bertini stared at the table.

Megan shrugged. "If we do it right, they'll waive the violation. Hell, they might give us a medal. For contacting a bright,
spanking new sentient species."

"And who contacts the Calibii?" Sato asked quietly.

"Who else?" Megan gestured toward Antonia. "Lizzy Bor-
den here."

"Megan," warned Bertini.

"I'm not qualified," Antonia said hoarsely.

"You're qualified to kill one. You ought to be qualified to
talk to one." Megan watched Antonia, her eyes narrow.

"That was low," growled Sato.

Megan shrugged and continued to watch Antonia.

I think she'll do it.
    This is crazy, Megan.
Didn't I tell you to shut up?

"What if I make a mistake?" Antonia looked around diz-
zily. "What if I make it worse?"

"Sensitive Brobeck," said Megan coldly, "You could not
possibly make it worse."

Bertini looked up at them all as if his head had developed a
great weight, elbows on his knees, palms together. Cameron
sniffed his hands. "Let us try this: we leave. Break the contract. Go back and say we never reached Caliban."

Megan's head whipped around to face him. "We couldn't
make the penalty fees—the Authority would sue us for breach
of contract."

"That takes time."

"We'd get caught anyway." Megan tried to stare him down.

"The story would hold only until the voyage tapes were pro-
cessed. That takes a while. We'd have to run. I know that." He
returned her gaze. "There are a number of places we could
trade for new ratings. It'd cost us the ship—"

Can we get home without him?
    I'm not sure. Megan, you can't—
Don't tell me that. There's nothing I can't do.
There's nothing I *won't* do.

Megan didn't speak for a long minute. "It's my ship."

"As captain, it's your neck as much as it is Antonia's."

"I'd lose the ship," she repeated stubbornly.

"Already gone. It's better to cut your losses and run."

The silence stretched taut between them.

"I will do it," Antonia said suddenly. She laughed. "And I will succeed. You watch me."

Bertini turned from Megan to Antonia as casually as if there had never been a test of wills. "You do that," Bertini murmured gently, a softness in his face as one watching a madwoman, amazed at her audacity and courage. "Let us give Antonia a month," he said. "Then, maybe, we leave."

Megan shivered inside.

Megan, watch Bertini. He's on to us.

Nonsense. He's trying for control.

Trying? *Megan, he's* got *control here. Look at Antonia.*

Look at Sato. Nodding like wobbly-headed dolls.

I'll get it back.

"Yes, I agree. Sensitive Brobeck, begin at once."

Antonia nodded and stood, nodded again, and left the bridge. Sato stared after her, then followed her. Bertini stood and gathered Cameron in his arms.

Don't let him go!

"Engineer Ranft," began Megan coldly, "we have more things to discuss." *Acknowledge me, you son-of-a-bitch. I am the captain, not you.*

Bertini walked to the corridor as if he hadn't heard.

"Engineer Ranft!" she shouted.

He stopped in the hatchway, turned to her. "I bet I'm nearly as old as you are, Captain."

A chill wind blew through her, stirring whitecaps of anxiety. "I order you to stay here. I wish to speak with you."

He shrugged and smiled slowly. "Sorry, Captain. I've got to take Cameron for a walk." And he disappeared down the corridor.

She stared after him, raging.

That stuck up, low-minded, son-of-a-bitch!

Damn it, Megan. This is a lot more dangerous than your penny-ante tyranny.

There was a blip, a shift in consciousness, a moment of blinding catatonia.

Megan—Christ! Answer me! Are you all right? You've been out of contact with me for the better part of an hour. Ranft has taken one of the flyers and left the Hirohito. *Sato and Antonia are copulating in Antonia Brobeck's stateroom.*

"Christ," she breathed. "He knows."

Damned right he knows. He turned you off like a light bulb. But what *does he know? How is his knowledge bordered in space and time?*

Don't go mystical on me.

Megan, what is he going to do? —Megan! There is a radio anomaly on the ridge east of the Hirohito—*different. Different from the background noise of the planet. It could be one of the Calibii. What shall we do? Megan? Megan?*

Feeling helpless and out of control, two states she had fought since birth, Megan Sze buried her head in her hands.

As HE FOLLOWED Antonia, Sato asked himself what the hell he was doing.

Damn his temper, anyway.

He was going to need Megan's goodwill to get through this, no matter what they did. A fight between him and Megan wasn't doing anybody any good. Antonia killed the Calibi. Nothing was going to change that, not Sato defending her, not Antonia discovering how the little bastards talked. *Blood dripped down the side of his face. Did I do that?* Bertini had the right idea: cut the contract and run, dump the ship for new ratings and start a new life in the Pleiades or someplace. Hell, demand was high enough for trained crew, they'd get jobs. And the Pleiades didn't subscribe to the Articles of Sentience. Rough territory, but they'd make it.

When Bertini said that, Megan had looked at him like a wounded animal. It made a man feel cold. You got the feeling she could have killed him right there; squashed him like a grape. Didn't seem to bother him, though.

What the hell did Megan think they'd done, anyway? Tap dancing? This was *murder*, not some Mozart symphony where all the notes came out even.

Still, he mused, it'd be hard to give up the exploration teams. Almost all they had in the sticks was transport lines. Map trips belonged to Earth.

Sato liked the map trips. You learned more in cartography than you ever found out in one of those high-speed, high-pressure clean team runs. And the later, colony teams didn't care: they were too busy laying out landing fields and building the entry port facilities, marking out fields and planting earth crops. Sato had done all three, and he liked it here: hanging out just this side of the edge, finding things, seeing things no one had ever thought of before. *The White Mountains, hiking after a thick snow, breaking the first trails, delighting in the ephemeral joy of being first. Others would follow me here and not even know my name, but this moment is mine.*

Why get his ass in a sling defending Antonia?

'Cause they were being railroaded, and it looked to him like Megan was setting Antonia up to fall for the rest of them. That rubbed him raw.

He caught up with her at the door of her stateroom.

"Antonia?" he called.

She stopped in the open doorway and turned to him. Her smile was gone, and her face was ghost-pale. There was an emptiness in her eyes that made him want to turn away.

"Yes?" she said in a beaten voice.

Jesus, this was more than he wanted to handle. *Sick eyes watching me, knowing I would leave.* She looked dead. Sounded the same way.

"I just wanted to see if you were all right," he said quickly. "To tell you I'm sorry she rode you so hard. For an accident like that." He ran down before her pale stare. "I guess I'll go to my room."

"No." She grabbed his arm. "Don't go. Come in—for some tea. I've got a hot spot on the desk. Please." She pulled him in.

"Are you all right?" he asked and looked at her. "You don't look good."

"No." She laughed shakily and took a small kettle from the desk and filled it with water from the sink. Carefully, she adjusted the heat on the hot spot and sat back on the bed to watch it. It was a curious set of motions, a strange rhythm. Sato had a sense this had been something she had been doing for years.

"It is," she answered him.

"You—"

Antonia looked up at him. "There's a kind of low grade, intermittent telepathy associated with sensitivity. Not enough to be reliable, but just enough to pick up a sentient. Just before you kill him, that is."

"Antonia—"

"I went to the Institute when I was thirteen. Did you know that? Of course you didn't. That's very young. There were reasons." She shook her head. "I'm twenty-two now. On my first assignment I killed somebody." She grabbed his hand. "I felt him die. Do you know what that's like? No, you wouldn't. How could you? You're not sensitive. Confusion. Rage. Pain. Hate."

She took his hand and kneaded it as if to see if it were real. Sato felt a sudden rush of fear. *What's going on here?* He noticed her hands, strong and soft. She stopped kneading his hands and started caressing them. Sato began to tremble. *Touch. It is so strange to be touched.*

Antonia reached up and pulled him down on her, began to take off his clothes. Sato began to panic. "Don't be afraid," she murmured. "I won't hurt you." She had his clothes off and slipped out of hers until she was lying on them. Her skin was cold. *I'm drowning.*

Beside them, unnoticed, the teakettle boiled.

BERTINI UNHURRIEDLY made his way to the flyer deck. The controls were in a small room just outside the firewall. He didn't touch them.

Was this smart? Was this the best thing to do?

He knew Megan was hardwired—that was certainty. It was the little things that betrayed her, a nuance of the voice, a little slip of information she couldn't know, a sudden shift of her external conversation when she spoke with the *Shenandoah*, that was all. Only someone as old as Bertini, and who'd seen it, would ever have known at all.

Not like the last one he had known, a century ago: Pemberton. She'd spent most of the voyage in fugue. Nasty. Three people had died in the mutiny: the navigator, the chief officer, and Pemberton herself.

He'd had to build an interrupter on guesswork and luck, and then it was almost too late.

He pulled off his shirt. His skin, when seen fully in the light, had an odd sheen, a grayness. He was nearly hairless with only a nearly invisible silver down all over. He bent over and pushed hard against his side. The skin parted with a greasy feel, and the interrupter slipped into his hand.

Its construction was simple: it put the *Hirohito*'s message systems in a "wait for information mode" and switched off the receiver. The *Shenandoah* couldn't send a message, and the *Hirohito* couldn't stop listening. Megan was part of the message system...

Bertini stared at the controls, then at the firewall again. Had he thought it through carefully enough?

Now she'd know he knew she was wired. Good. He wanted her to know. He had become a check on her. Bertini was not as closely tied to the ship as Megan, but he was an engineer with special talents and his own set of tools. A war with him, when she knew what it was she was dealing with, would be bloody and uncertain. She would be cautious. She would not attack anyone frivolously, secure in her power. That was important—Sato and Antonia were just kids, after all. They'd get ground up in a fight between adults.

He had never been that cautious with Pemberton.

Damn.

"Okay," he breathed and thumbed the interrupter.

He quickly activated the deck and warmed up flyer one. Then he opened the firewall and jogged over to it. The flyer shot outside, and Bertini banked it down toward the sea.

When the flyer was over the fjord, he relaxed and enjoyed the sunlight and water. Cameron squirmed, and Bertini let him down on the deck. The flyer was an oval platform and a railing with a seat and controls at one end. It was open all around, protected from wind, rain, and too much sun by a thin hobbler field.

Bertini sat back and lit a cigarette, watching the open sea approach. He didn't envy Megan. She had to have been wired for over a century at least; hardwiring had been illegal since then. It tended to make the captain value the ship over the crew. There'd been several spectacular mutinies besides his. When the captains had finally been decommissioned from their ships, there had followed a wave of suicides.

Enough dwelling on the past. He tried to think like Megan.

She'd panic first—he was the only real threat, probably the first threat in years. But after the panic subsided, she'd realize where lay his own best interest. Success was as important to Bertini as to Megan. Nobody wanted to have to run.

It might still come to a showdown between them, but he didn't want to worry about that until he had to. Later. If Megan's long shot succeeded, he was protected because she would need him to back up the story. He couldn't talk about Megan without blowing it up for himself. If it didn't, well, he was a cautious man. He would have contingency plans. So would she, he realized.

He grimaced. Damn. This was chancy.

Getting new ratings was the safest thing they could do. This diplomatic dance Megan was setting up didn't look promising.

I'm getting too old for this. Too old to run. Too old to fight.

The flyer sailed past the rest of the fjord and over the open sea. He felt the breeze and smelled the salt in the air. Cameron rubbed against his feet until Bertini scratched his head.

"How long ago was it, Cameron?" he asked playfully. "Just over a century? Bernard said you'd outlive me." Bertini was living in the homestretch of a quarter millenium. Megan, he guessed, lived just a little bit further downstream. He didn't have much original equipment left: most of him was composed of organic replacements. Megan had gone about it differently. There was probably enough metal in her to build a ship, not just be connected to one.

The sea was bright, the waves blue and whitecapped. He felt the salt in his lungs, saw the blue sky and the broad, unmarked horizon. And it all felt shaky. Damn Antonia, anyway. If this doesn't work out, he thought, I'll just have to take the ship away from Megan. Schematics and tension diagrams began to pass idly through his mind. Contingency plans: you can take the ship out of the captain, but can you take the captain out of the ship?

He heard breathing with him and turned.

The Calibi lay smashed against the railing, gasping its last breath. It had a woman's face.

His hand jerked, and he dropped the cigarette in his lap. He leaped to his feet, slapping at his lap, looked again for the Calibi.

It was gone.

SATO AWOKE in darkness.

He gradually grew in awareness until he opened his eyes, not knowing if he slept or not. The darkness in the cabin was complete, without light from window or door. He remembered making love with Antonia as he might a dream.

"Antonia?" he called experimentally. There was no answer.

He sat up in the darkness and felt around the cabin. It did not feel like his room. Fumbling, he found the light switch. He could not see for a moment.

Antonia's room on the ship had always seemed rubbed bare to him, clean, sterile. This room had the same empty look to it. No part of it was his.

"No dream," he muttered to himself and sat on the edge of the bed. What the hell was he getting himself into? *Warmth. Touch. The feel of skin over skin.*

Still, he reminded himself. She said she would not hurt him. He remembered that clearly. And she, if anyone, would know what would and would not hurt him.

He stood and dressed, opening the window to look outside. It was night, and the stars were clear. There was a low briskness to the night air.

The rest of the *Hirohito* seemed no more alive than Antonia's room. "Antonia?" he whispered experimentally. *Christ! Why are you whispering?* Their tryst was not exactly subtle. He'd slept with Antonia before, hadn't he? Aboard the ship? Except for Megan—never Megan!—sleeping with crew members was almost a tradition. It didn't mean anything.

This does?

The silence and mixed emotions made him nervous. "Antonia?" he called more loudly.

The bridge was as deserted as the corridors near the crew's cabins. The console displays glared off the plastic surfaces and made the room multicolored. The *Hirohito*'s instruments were unshipped, and the flyer bay was active. The rest of the instruments were still covered and dormant. Of their personal controls, only Bertini's were open.

He sat in the command chair and began checking things. One of the flyers was gone. *Had* been gone for some hours. There remained only one person aboard the ship: Sato. Where the hell was everybody?

"You're sitting in my chair."

Behind him, Megan leaned against one of the consoles. Her eyes were bloodshot. Her hair was matted and stuck out from her head in all directions. She shook her head and looked around the room. He could smell the alcohol.

"You didn't show up on the screen. I didn't—"

"Goddamn. It's my ship, isn't it? Are you looking for me? I don't want you looking for me. You won't find me until I do." She stepped unsteadily toward him. "Get out of my chair."

"Captain—"

"I said, get out of my chair!"

Sato stood and moved out of her way. She sat down heavily and stared at him. "What do you want?"

"I was just looking for somebody—"

"She's outside. Left hours ago."

The air between them had the same flat electric feeling of an impending thunderstorm. "Where's Bertini?"

"Fuck Bertini."

"But—"

"Are you stupid, man? Bertini's gone. He's taken one of the flyers and flown over the ocean." She paused. "On my orders." She looked at him. "You hear me? On my *orders*!"

"Yeah, yeah," he said softly. "What's he doing out there?"

"None of your goddamn business. Go after her. Get out of here."

Sato didn't move immediately.

Megan leaned toward him, her eyes the color of burning pitch, a thick, flaming darkness. Fear strung a cold thread down his spine. "I thought I said, get out of here." Her voice was as low as blood.

He opened his mouth, closed it. He coughed. His throat was suddenly dry. "Yeah. Sure, Captain. I'm leaving. I'm leaving now."

She was staring blindly through him when he left her.

Outside, the night was cool and polished as a silver cup. No wind moved the leaves. All he could hear was his own breathing and the soft, still sounds of trees settling into the earth.

"Antonia?" he called. Up the ridge he heard her answer.

He reached back inside the airlock for a flashlight and a gun. Now, wait a minute, he thought. This is crazy. At *least* go back inside and find out from the monitor where she might be. Check an infrared scan, maybe. He started back into the ship. He stopped. Megan was in there. On the bridge.

"Damn." Go back in there. He remembered the way she had looked at him, had looked at Bertini when Bertini had suggested they trade the ship for new ratings. So *what*? He sat down on the edge of the hatch. Face it, Sperling. You have a healthy respect for and a little fear of this planet. But you're much more scared of Megan.

He hoisted the rifle and moved up the ridge. The clearing gave way to trees, and he looked back. The ship's lamps were silver moonlight. A few steps further and they were gone, masked by the trees.

The ridge did not slope as steeply as he expected. Depressed, he did not watch where he was going. When he looked up, he was leaving the woods. The trees were different here, gray in the moonlight and with spherical leaves.

"Hmm." He could see the top of a gentle ridge. There, clearly in the light, was a tall, two-story frame house. It was white, and the paint was peeling. The grass around was short and dirty gray.

He felt sweat stick between his arms and sides. "Wait a minute," he said softly.

Lindsay came out of the shadows of the porch, dressed the same way Sato had last seen him. The right side of his face was puffy, and blood trickled from the corner of his mouth. "Sato?" he called softly.

He couldn't move.

"Sato?" he called again, in that reaching, supplicating way he had. Touching with his voice, grasping, holding. *Isn't this what you wanted?*

Lindsay started to walk down the porch toward him. He was smiling.

Sato turned and ran into Antonia.

"Sato." She hugged him.

Holding her, he looked up. The ridge was steep, and the trees had flat leaves. They were in shadow and illuminated only by a faint glow from above.

"You're sweating," she said. "Did you run up the hill?"

It's madness. Just madness. Did you think you could just walk away from him? Did you? *Did you?*

"Sato?"

"I, uh," he stopped, licked his lips, and looked around. The earth itself was different, heaved up into a ridge. The gentle rise was gone. "I thought I saw a house up here."

She laughed. "There's only one house. We brought it with us."

He nodded but didn't speak immediately. "Yeah. Yeah." He shook himself. I only hit him once. I didn't hurt him. I just hit him once. *It was enough, wasn't it?*

"Are you all right?"

"Sure. I was just dreaming, I guess." *Goddamn you, Lindsay. Goddamn you to nothing but a writhing, pain-ridden hell.* He looked at her and grinned. His face felt stiff as cracking plaster.

She smiled uncertainly. "I heard you coming. I found a bluff where we can watch the moon over the fjord."

"I'm fine." I'm crazy. "Show me the moon." He followed her, hunched over as if in pain.

MEGAN DIDN'T DRINK to forget. That was impossible. Forgetting was a conscious act. She could store memories with the *Shenandoah,* or she could disconnect herself from the *Shenandoah* and let the memories fade in the old human way. She would rather have died. She didn't drink as an addict, either, but to dull fear, to keep her action uncontrolled. What's worse than a wired captain in uncontrolled panic? A wired captain in controlled panic. It was not a sane, rational decision, but then she wasn't feeling particularly sane or rational just now.

It's *my* goddamn ship.

What the hell did she need a crew for, anyway? Space the lot of them and finish the contract on her own. The goddamn Authority wouldn't buy it. Who cares what the Authority thought, anyway?

You're not being rational.

S'okay. You be rational. I'll be drunk. Please to meet you, rational.

Come on, Megan. We have to think this through. We have to plan.

We do *not*! Thinking is a feeble reed in the wind of destruction. Planning is panic thinking done by committee. Begone. I wish to be done with thinking and planning. No, wait. Don't go. You are my lover and confidante, *Shenandoah*. You are my friend and my master and my slave. Talk to me. Touch me in ways no one else ever has.

Megan, you just can't let this go.

Sure, I can. Come, child, waltz with me. Let us dance through your corridors, make love in the hold. Hold me close to your heart, don't let me grow old.

Megan—

"I've never killed before," she said aloud to the air. "I always managed to avoid the wars, the mutinies. Nobody has ever died on my ship."

Why are you saying this?

"I think I may have to kill Bertini?" She waved her hand confusedly. "Oh, and make it look like an accident and everything. Dead men tell no tales and such as that."

Hush, child. We'll deal with that when we have to.

"No." She shook her head. "Bertini will try to take me out if this doesn't work. I'm scared."

Me too.

"Hold me."

The *Shenandoah* enfolded itself around her, around the *Hirohito* and kept her warm. Held her and soothed her tears, touching her in ways open to no one else.

6

I did not tell Caretaker the strict truth. It takes time for an Ancestor to be assimilated, as much as a month, sometimes more. I couldn't just stay at the foot of that tree, dwelling on what had happened. I would have been a candidate for madness. I had to think. My mind was consumed with rage, loss, a hysteria of moving.

What I did first was obvious: I went to watch the creatures.

The ridge above their clearing connected to the Caretaker ridge. I ascended from the south, along the flat, tenuous water and over the clearing. As I watched from the top, a smaller stone was flung out of the boulder's body. I flattened to the ground as it moved over me. With a hissing and a popping and the roaring sound of wind, the lesser rock flew out to sea and was gone.

Two rocks, a beast, and the creatures.

Down in the clearing, the boulder still sent out nauseating pulses of light. Between pulses, however, it was darker than stone had any right to be. The light of trees can penetrate stone slightly, give a texture to outline and form. This rock was completely opaque, its outline sharp as if it cut off sight.

It came to me then: the rock was made of *metal*. It was a *made* thing. I sat down and held myself. It was huge, a whole flying mountain of metal. A flying hut, perhaps?

I heard a noise and backed up, ready to flee. The side of the metal thing opened, and one of the creatures (demons? I thought again) stood in the doorway. It was different from the two others, the ones who ruined me. It turned its body several ways for reasons I could not guess, its body shooting forth flashes and bursts of light. Of all of them, only this one seemed to see. Finally, I left it and wandered back to Caretaker ridge. There, Caretaker found me. After their metallic strangeness, I was ready to embrace her.

"I thought you were staying at the tree," she said petulantly.

"I will be there when Traverse awakes."

"I need your help. The village is having problems with the stream bank overflowing again. Several of us are building a retaining wall."

We lived in the valley, with our own home-grown group of Caretakers up on the ridge. Our village had no name, but we were part of Infertility's band. I began to feel better as Caretaker and I descended, smelling the dust of trampled earth, the different odors of drying herbs, the close scent of river water. I had been away for several days, but I had gorged myself preparing for a tryst with Traverse. Here, now, I felt hungry.

"The wall can wait, Caretaker," I said. "Let's eat."

Two females passed in front of us, dragging a travois filled with rocks for the wall. I stared at them.

"The rock, the beast," I said hesitantly. "They are *transportation*. Metal transportation."

"Metal? The thing which fell is metal? You did not say this before."

"I only just realized it. It is a vehicle, something like a cart or a travois. Not alive, yet still a servant."

"What does it serve?" Caretaker mused.

"The creatures, of course," I snapped, impatient.

"Are you suggesting these things have volition?"

I stopped. "I always thought so."

Caretaker did not speak for a moment. "No doubt you did. No doubt the others did. Yet Traverse saw it. These creatures seem to have volition, even as you or I. But their first act is to kill. They come from the dark sky. They wander about us seemingly unknowing, but by your description emit a perversion of light. They are *not* us. What are they? Are they demons?"

"I don't know." I clenched my claws together until they hurt. "I don't understand what demons are."

"Animals have no volition. We do. Demons made of dark have volition but no soul. They cannot live after death, but return to the dark. We live. We were almost wiped out by demons. Caretakers would die before we let them come here again. I would rather not be the one to declare holy war." She spoke simply. I could see the destruction and ruin in her. "Do you think they murdered Traverse?"

"He was killed."

"What is the difference between accident and murder?"

"Traverse is *dead*. Maybe it *was* murder. Maybe they *are* demons."

"Let's not make that decision just yet," Caretaker said hastily.

We found dinner with a group of young, prepubescent males, eager for our attention. The conversation cast a pall on me. You will all die so soon anyway, I thought. Accident? Murder? What difference did it make? Their time was so short; they were so frail.

Each reminded me of Traverse, and each seemed to have the mark of death in his speech.

A long, warm month of late summer passed while we waited for Traverse to awaken. I gave up watching the creatures after I realized they used metal.

Metal.

They were surrounded by it. How did they *see*? How did they *speak*? Were they so *other* from me? I couldn't think about them clearly. Maybe they *were* demons. It made my mind spin.

To slow that terrible motion, I helped rebuild the retaining wall with the rest of the village. After that I felt empty. I did nothing. I sat next to the water, listening to the flow. Its slow movement mirrored my own.

A week passed. A morning came: the trees glittered over me, the late summer air was hot. When I looked back into the village I could see the strong proud backs of my people as they worked. Their necks wound sinuously, their speech shining from them, dancing light. Trees are beautiful. The shifting inconsistency of water and the feel of the earth are moving. But only people matter. I watched them and felt cut off from them. I had seen something, known something, that separated me from them. I had left my home not knowing it.

Sometimes I think I will never get home again.

I stared into the depths of the river, feeling lost.

Caretaker sat next to me.

"I was enjoying my solitude," I said carefully, after a moment.

"Let us enjoy it, then," she said, unperturbed.

"Eat defecation if I will share it with you! I said I would be alone."

"I respectfully suggest we sit together." She reached out and touched me, gently.

I found myself frightened and trembling. "You do not understand—"

"Hush," and she enfolded me as if I were a child, newborn
from a tree.

"I cannot stop shaking," I tried to say, but the images were
incoherent.

"Hush."

I saw nothing but her body, heard nothing but the ebb and
flow of her.

Only people matter. I know this now.

When I came to myself, I withdrew from her, embarrassed.
She did not pull away, and I lay limp in her arms, warm from
the day.

"Do Ancestors truly have names?" I asked suddenly. "Will
Traverse be lost in there?"

"No, he will not be lost," she said soothingly, still holding
me. "They have the same names. They live in a world of their
own, with their own laws and customs. I am not sure they truly
see us at all. They can only speak to us." She paused a moment. "Traverse will answer to his name at first, especially,
when we ask him of things that happened in his life. Over time,
we will be able to reach him less and less. Then, one day, we will
call for him, and he will no longer reply. But when we ask
questions to which only he could respond, we will get answers.
The world the Ancestors live in is so large and wide they cannot always find their way back to us. Their thoughts do, when
we ask. But someone else speaks for them."

"How do you know they're not absorbed, eaten by something in the tree?" I felt like a child. It was good, right then, to
feel like a child.

"Other Ancestors have met them there, relaying messages
back and forth to us."

I puzzled on that. The Ancestors were an everyday part of my
heritage, my tradition. They were there to ask questions of, to
swear by, to invoke in children's stories. It came to me they were
no less strange than the new creatures that tamed metal and
whose craft spat such flashes of light. It frightened me how little of the Ancestors I knew. "Do they have bodies in that other
world?"

"I do not know. If they do, they have not the bodies they had
in this one."

We lay there, Caretaker and I, holding each other in the warm sun. Over the river of days it came to be a custom for us, this talking by the waters, touching often.

A day came when Caretaker straightened suddenly, tense, listening. "It's just about time," she said tensely.

It took me a moment to understand. "Traverse?"

"Yes."

I did not know what to do. "Should I gather the speakers for the bands?"

She did not speak immediately, listening to a faint voice I could not hear. "Yes," she said finally. "Do it now. He is awakening suddenly and cries out, but I think he will be calm by the time they get here."

She left me then. I was forgotten. The trees were to her as children, as sisters, as the core of things. I watched her go, thinking about trees and time and light.

Climber and Disapproval had moved closer to the village to await Traverse's awakening. I dispatched two young females to their encampments. Infertility lived in a village down the river from mine. It was to there I ran.

That is not quite accurate. Explain, explain again. Will there come a moment in this where I will *not* have to explain?

Calibii are half arboreal. Our long central claw is for climbing. The other fingers are for manipulation of the world around us. This time I had no corpse to carry, nothing to hinder me. These depressing days of inactivity had held down my vision until I could see only that narrow strip of life just around me, looking no further into things than the thin covering of water over stone. I felt suddenly free to act. I took to the trees like flight, leaping from branch to branch, swinging my way along the river, nothing in me but motion.

GLACIERS BREATHED around him in great gasps, an elemental cycle of freezing, followed by a roaring suicidal dive into the sea, followed by more freezing.

It suited him.

Bertini's flyer hovered over a northern bay. Before him, the glacier made violent love to the sea. He slouched down in the pilot's couch, staring into the cold. His beard was over a week old and his eyes were dark. He had bathed in the bay and now smelled of brine. *Consider a man,* he thought. *A man watching a glacier.*

Cameron whined for attention. Bertini ignored him.

It was time to return to the *Hirohito,* and he found himself reluctant to do so. This puzzled him. *Where are you from?* she had asked. *Where are you bound?*

He shook his head. Rain, he thought, these are not questions for me. Where I have been is past. Where I will go is unknowable. Only the now can I control.

Control is all you know.

"Still," he sighed. It was an old argument. "I know only what I have learned for myself. No more, no less. I am the rock on which the world turns."

Then why wait? Why procrastinate? Why do you stay here in this wasteland, trying to make yourself leave?

The dialogue with his subconscious began to irritate him. "All right," he said, then grinned ruefully to himself. "Time to go, anyway. I provoke myself to action. Is that better?"

"It is not as I intended."

He looked around the flyer. He had almost heard her. Shrugging, he took the car out of hover mode and began to fly south toward the *Hirohito.* "I spend too much time thinking," he said loudly, then laughed. "This is where you have brought me, Rain."

But the laughter rang hollow, and he thought of the image of the Calibi with the woman's face, smashed against the flyer's railing. A trick of the mind, surely. After two hundred years of living, Bertini was no longer perturbed when his mind surprised him. Over such a time, almost everything the mind could do it *would* do, hallucinations included. Still, he wished he could remember the face more clearly. Was it hers or another's?

He had been gone ten days. The thought of a hot shower and a warm bed made him chuckle to himself. He hoped Megan had gotten over her panic.

The landing cradle was deployed and waiting for him when he reached the *Hirohito.* "Hmm," he said to himself. He eased the flyer into the cradle and triggered the clamps. The flyer now secured, the cradle retracted and pulled the flyer and Bertini back into the skiff. The corridor outside the deck was empty. He scratched the stubble on his face thoughtfully. Megan knew he was here; it must have been Megan who deployed the landing cradle. She was waiting for him to come to her. Hell with her, he thought savagely. First, I need a shower and a shave.

An hour later Bertini entered the *Hirohito*'s bridge. Megan was waiting for him in the command chair.

They watched each other for some seconds. Her eyes were faintly red, the skin around them still held a bit of puffiness. She'd panicked, all right. And recovered. Inside himself, he smiled in admiration. "Engineer Ranft reporting for duty, Captain." *I know what you hide,* he said, as clearly as if he could hear it.

She looked at him without expression, but Bertini thought he detected a smile behind her eyes.

"You have done a cursory survey of the north part of the continent, Engineer?" *I know you know,* she replied.

That's what I did? Okay, that's what I did. "Aye, Captain." *Can we make truce for now?*

"Good. Please write me a report by morning. Dismissed." *Let us do so, but for only so long as it is in both our best interests to do so.*

All right. He saluted by reflex, surprising himself.

He stood there a moment, feeling a fool. She watched him, then brought her own hand up in a salute and returned his.

He turned an about-face and left her.

Outside, he stopped and looked back at the closed hatch. You're good, he thought.

Damn, he liked her.

THE LEAVES of the trees were so thick the ground was in shadow even in the noon sunlight. Antonia adjusted a small signal laser on a tripod. Sato, a hundred feet away, stood next to the laser's photo receptor. She called out to him: "Okay. Over to the right a bit. No, *your* right."

"Glad you think so," said Sato, moving to his right. "About what?"

"What?"

"Never mind."

She looked up from her instruments. "You are so strange. I mean, I like you. But you are just *so* strange." She shook her head and smiled at him.

Sato shrugged and looked a little embarrassed. Antonia smiled and looked back down to the calibration dials so he could relax.

"What does this one do?" he said aimlessly after a moment.

"Just a basic trip wire. Some animal breaks the light beam up here, and we can take a picture."

"I thought we were looking for sentients?"

"We are." She straightened. She looked up at him, then back to the instruments. "Nothing comes from nothing. Humans have a common ground with all life on earth, part of a great chain of being. The same holds true here. If we study the animals, we learn by extension something about the Calibii. They are *all* Calibii in a way, all the animals. All sharing the faint divine spark between them."

"That's the second time you've said that."

"What?"

"Divine."

"That's what it is. I have no other religion. No sensitive does." *And let's not talk any more about that, lest he think you a religious fanatic.* She checked the laser again. "Move over a little more to the left. No, *your* left. I think you're doing this on purpose."

"And the other things?" He gestured around in the near woods. The area was littered with small, unobtrusive instruments on slim graceful stands.

"Infrared detectors. Metal detectors. Action-sensitive cameras. Scanning cameras. Such as that."

"Yeah." He shrugged again. "You call *me* weird."

"Strange."

"Same thing."

She cocked her head at him. "I think I meant unusual. I like you, Sato Sperling."

Sato looked embarrassed again. She felt irritated at him. *Damn it, either I have to quit playing with him or he's got to get less sensitive.*

"How are you going to send the information to the *Hirohito*?"

She grinned. "We're not." *I like you. You're just going to have to live with it.*

He looked preoccupied, not quite hearing her. "A long cable, maybe? I think we have some in the stores."

"I said, we're not going to send it to the *Hirohito*."

He thought a moment, distracted by her. He didn't seem very comfortable when she flirted like this. Maybe it was too different for him, too much someone he didn't know. "You're going to send it up to the *Shenandoah*? And let the *Shenandoah* send it to the *Hirohito*?"

"That's right."

"Why? How?"

"Because we need a lot of these detectors, and we can't use radio telemetry. The plants, remember? The *Hirohito* doesn't have enough optical ports, but the satellites do. We ship the data up to the satellites by laser, then to the *Shenandoah*. We get an added bonus because the *Shenandoah* has more processing power than the *Hirohito*. We can cut up the data *lots* more ways. Then it all gets shipped down to us on the *Hirohito*'s message laser." She smiled at him impishly. "As to how, that's your job, Navigator Sperling. I talked with Megan last night, and she said it would be no trouble."

"Yeah. Right. No trouble at all. Christ." He was silent. "Yeah. We can do it. We can take tracking orders from the *Shenandoah*. Let the big lady do all the work. Are we through here?"

"Just a minute." She checked the calibration on the laser again, then sealed the housing. "Now we are." She straightened. "Why?"

Sato didn't meet her gaze. He'd been acting this way for days since the night they'd made love on the ridge. She smiled thinking about it. *You are,* she thought to herself, *unabashedly romantic.* But she would not have been a sensitive if she couldn't tell it wasn't always her that made him nervous. Something was bothering him, and she didn't know what it was. Since the first night together her minimal telepathy had closed toward him. She was forced to rely on hints and body language. It disturbed her. Always before in her life, her sensitivity had given her the feeling of being in a half-lit, familiar room surrounded by illuminated people. But never before had she allowed herself to be touched, extending herself to include someone else. Sato was as dark to her now as she was to herself.

SATO WAS NERVOUS, all right. He had tried to forget his own hallucination. He'd heard of others on expeditions who saw visions. It was a reflection of what the brain had to deal with on a new planet.

Premise: Sato Sperling, Navigator, was insane.

Not a picture he wanted to look at.

He had a drunk or crazy captain to worry about, anyway.

When he and Antonia had returned to the *Hirohito* that moonlit night, Megan was nowhere to be seen. Her stateroom door was closed. Antonia had found a note saying Megan was "indisposed" and that Sato would be in charge until either she felt better or Bertini returned. Three days later, Megan had emerged from her room and resumed command, clean, calm, and, except for a slight paleness, the same. Antonia had never seen the red-eyed Megan, drunkenly grunting from her command chair, staring at Sato from the depths of hell. It made him nervous to be away from the ship for too long, and he and Antonia had been setting up these instruments all afternoon. He was afraid of what Megan would do while they were gone.

He wished Bertini would get back.

If he came back.

Sato shuddered. *Come on. Let's not get too melodramatic.*

Behind them they heard a whooshing roar.

"Bertini!" yelled Sato. "Let's go down."

"Why? He hasn't been gone long."

Because I'm glad he's alive. "Maybe he saw more of the Calibii. Maybe he found out where they are."

It took them more than an hour to bushwhack their way back down the ridge to the clearing. As they stepped from under the trees, the *Hirohito* was made a mosaic of bright fire and jet darkness by the sun. The sea beyond it glittered. Bertini leaned against the skiff to one side of the airlock, backlit by the light, smoking his pipe. Sato waved. The figure faced him in shadow, a squat, thick kobold. It waved hesitantly back to him.

Bertini did not speak until they were nearly to him. "How goes the search?"

"Nothing so far," Antonia said. "For a couple of days one of them was watching us. Just after you left, actually. We could see the infrared traces. Nothing since. The entire ridge around us and the sea is wired." She pointed a finger at him. "So you watch your step." She kissed Sato and disappeared into the skiff.

"Hmm," said Bertini and raised his eyebrows.

"Yeah." Sato didn't look at him. "Have you seen Megan?"

"Of course. I had to give her my report." He laughed suddenly.

Sato didn't understand and shook his head. What was going on? He told Bertini of the drunken Megan.

"Hmm," Bertini said again. "A binge. I didn't think Megan had it in her."

"I'm worried what she's going to do."

"She'll do what's good for the ship."

"But she's gone off the deep end. She's nuts."

Bertini shook his head. "No. She's a better captain than I would have thought. She was shaken by this. At *best*, she could lose the ship over this, the way it is now. This plan is just a bare thread of a chance. Most likely, she is *still* going to lose her ship. To her, that is a great deal like losing her whole family, children, and friends." He paused. "No, I take that back. It's probably a lot worse. Had we been on the *Shenandoah*, she probably would have given command to Ruth as first mate immediately and had a screaming fit off in some private corner of the holds. There's not enough room here for that. I wasn't here; she couldn't leave the ship to me for a week or so." He paused again. "I was needed elsewhere. And—face it—Sato, she doesn't trust you to run the ship for long. So, she gets good and drunk for a couple of days, thinking you can be trusted just that long. Catharsis over, she resumes command. I think she did just fine."

"I don't know," Sato said at last. "This whole trip has turned into a real mess."

Bertini nodded. "So we've had visitors?"

"Yeah. Like Antonia said." Sato pointed up the ridge. "The IR cameras picked it up. That's when Antonia decided to wire the whole ridge. Nothing since."

"Any kind of aerial survey?"

Sato shook his head. "Not yet. You had the other flyer. It's against policy to have all the flyers out at the same time. Nothing left for a rescue." Sato looked at Bertini thoughtfully. "Megan wouldn't tell me your orders. What was going on?"

Bertini chuckled. "Nothing major. Just—ah—a cursory survey of the northern part of the continent. Megan wanted to get an idea of the long-term climate of the area. If we actually make contact, we may be here a long time."

"She seemed pretty upset over it."

"The survey had nothing to do with her being upset. She doesn't want to lose the ship."

Sato didn't think this was the whole truth. "Captains have lost ships before. I worked on the *Maui* for Kanakulani Lines a few years ago. Under Captain Sevlin. He was busted for a little soap smuggling operation to Down. He kept his rating, but he lost the *Maui*, and it didn't seem to mean that much to him."

Bertini shrugged. "Different situations. Megan *owns* the *Shenandoah*, for one thing. And she's had it a long time. I think it means a lot more to her than it might to you or me."

"I suppose." Sato dropped it. "So, do we have to worry about Caliban's winter?"

"I don't think so. Not down this far south, anyway. It'll get brisk, but it won't average too much below freezing."

"Good." Sato stuck his hands in his pockets. "One less thing to worry about." This trip had been the first thing to come along for him. He'd grabbed it like a lifeline: *anything* to get away from Earth. Anything to leave Lindsay behind. He kicked the dirt in frustration. Dealing with Lindsay didn't seem so bad right now. *Lindsay standing on the porch of a white house.* I'm not crazy. I'm not. I will put this behind me. I will dwell on it no more. "Caliban. Yeah." He laughed shortly. "Where's a Prospero when you need him?"

A MIST CLOSED DOWN on the village. I could feel the shivering cold in the air, the wetness across the top of my fur. The light from the trees dimmed, giving a gloomy aspect to the world.

Infertility came with me at a slower pace than I would have liked. She was older than I, a strong-bodied female, thick across the back and legs. Because of this, she preferred to walk, taking to the trees only when necessary. She was careful, patient, and honest. I was, of course, prejudiced. She was *our* speaker, after all. Still, she did not have Disapproval's stern brittleness or Climber's nervous joy.

"We could have wished for better weather," observed Infertility.

"Resurrection grows like a fungus, in the dark and the cold."

"You are becoming cynical."

I turned to her. "Let us say I have lost the optimism of a cub."

"I see," said Infertility carefully.

I turned from her back to the trail. "I find myself less than enthused about being here. It is a feeling I did not expect."

"We do not talk about death much—"

"Traverse is not dead! He is an Ancestor now. Caretaker heard him."

Infertility did not speak for a moment. "Before Bright's time I suspect we were much less sensitive to it. We live now in an uneasy peace with her plague, not really knowing why it happened—who can fathom the mind of a demon?—or why it stopped. We live on tenuous sands. Our fear keeps us silent. So we send people away when one of us becomes an Ancestor. The customs are there because of our fear."

"Caretaker said something similar," I said. "I will not leave because of my own fear any more than I would leave because it was custom."

Again, Infertility paused. "You do not understand me. We are afraid of the Ancestors because they are dead."

"Traverse is—"

"They are *dead* to us! We bury them in the earth around the roots of trees. They speak to us for only a short time after that, then are lost. We feel the same pain and grief as if they were never Ancestors. We build customs to deaden this pain, to let them go, to make them *not*. Is that not death?"

"I hurried and brought him to Caretaker fast enough so that he will not be lost to *me*. I will speak with Traverse today and know this to be true."

"He will be there," Infertility said testily. "I'm not worried about that."

I did not reply, and she kept her own counsel.

By the afternoon the mist had thinned somewhat, and the air became warmer. Caretaker, Disapproval, and Climber were waiting for us.

"You have made us wait," began Disapproval.

"Do not start," Infertility said shortly. "I am not in the mood."

Disapproval stiffened and fell silent.

Caretaker did not seem to notice. Her whole attention was centered on the tree. She moved around the tree, watching it for signs we could not see. "Be quiet," she said at last.

I couldn't have spoken if I had wanted to.

After a time, she said: "Traverse?"

There was no response.

She said, again: "Traverse?"

Silence. She moved around the tree.

"Yes. You. Traverse!"

There was a sense of uncoiling, of relaxation, of confused attention.

"I am here." Traverse's voice came from the tree.

I sat down on the grass. It was Traverse's voice, all right. Traverse's images. Traverse's speech. But withdrawn, now, cold, brittle. He spoke as if from a great distance, and I felt every measure of that distance between us. I wanted to cry out, *Where are you?* He could not have answered. He was an Ancestor. Instead, I held myself in the grass and the dirt and felt depressed.

"Do you recall the creatures?" began Infertility.

"It should be a more specific question," said Disapproval dimly. "What creatures does she mean?"

"It is obvious enough," began Climber.

"Of course, I remember them. They killed me." He paused. "Did you think I would forget?"

"You named them demons," said Infertility.

He paused again. "I was hasty. I think more clearly now. It seems to me we lack the information to determine what these creatures are."

"Exactly." Infertility turned toward Disapproval and Climber. They fell silent. He turned again to Traverse. "We seek your advice."

This time his silence held many minutes. When he spoke, his voice was considered and calm. Were I human, I would have wept.

"We do not know if these things are animals or not. Yet we have observed them as animals, not as thinking beings. This seems to me to be unwise. We should watch them closely. We should allow them to observe us doing so, that they may become used to us and eventually reach out to us. Someone must go down into their den and try to talk to them."

"This person may die," I said mildly.

There was no response.

"Just so." I felt more relaxed now. I should have brought him here more quickly. I should have watched him more

closely. I was the female there. I knew he was eager. Males are
not truly responsible beings. I knew that. I should have done
any number of things, but *I should not have let it happen*. "I
will do this."

Caretaker must have read my mind. "It is not your fault."

"He is an Ancestor. I live. That is fault enough." No one
spoke. "Who would deny me?" Again, there was silence.

"Good," I said. I turned to the tree. Traverse said nothing.
That hurt a little. "I go," I said abruptly, and left them there.

No one stopped me.

I reached the clearing by nightfall. Below me, in the dark, I
could feel them waiting.

7

They had been blessed with a succession of clear days since
landing on Caliban. Now that time of grace was ended. A mist
came down from the ridge and from the mountains beyond the
ridge like a cold and clammy breath. The colors were washed
out of the trees and grasses, giving them the character of pale
uncertainty, of things unknown. The rain seemed to suck the
heat out of the ship, and the humans huddled together for
comfort.

Bertini lay on his side, not quite asleep, not quite awake,
conscious only of a soft, friendly warmth curled next to his
belly. Cameron had crawled into bed with him. Bertini opened
his eyes and rolled away. Cameron made muttered complaint
about it. Bertini scratched him idly on the head, and Cameron
settled back into sleep.

I should get up, he thought.

Why? What needs to be done?

He shrugged, and the covers whispered. Nothing, really. Still,
I should.

It is early. An hour or two won't matter.

"Still," he said and sat up out of bed. Cameron lifted his head and watched him, stretched out his front paws and shook himself.

On the bridge, Bertini watched the displays over a cup of coffee. So far, he was the only one up, although he suspected Megan never really slept. I'm getting old, he thought. It's getting so I'm not worth a damn before my first coffee.

The infrared monitor showed something moving along the ridge. Bertini watched as it moved back again, pacing almost. It came hesitantly down the ridge about halfway, then stopped.

"Indecision." Bertini chuckled. "This is not Caliban, but Hamlet."

It had been there for days. Antonia was convinced it was a Calibi. It was about the right size, and it moved around them most unlike an animal. Antonia had further suggested it was the same Calibi Sato had photographed—perhaps the sister, mate, or son of the Calibi killed. For Bertini, this moved away from objectivity into the realm of magic—which was where he had always placed sensitivity, anyway. Not that he disbelieved it. It merely lay beyond his understanding and, therefore, beyond his interest.

He sighed. There was still the issue of how to map Caliban. Since Antonia had killed the Calibi, no more sampling work had been done on the plants' radio emissions. For Megan's plan to work, they must still produce a map of Caliban.

Contemplate the place. See it; don't measure it.

He chuckled. Rain, you never quit.

He opened his personal console and began to tune the improvised radio scanner he and Sato had built on the *Shenandoah*. He put the output up on the monitor next to the infrared display. The intensity of the display increased toward a point halfway up the ridge.

"Hmm," he muttered, an idea forming in his mind.

He expanded the display and overlaid it with an optical picture of the ridge. He did the same with the infrared scan. There was a radio intensity peak where the Calibi was. As he watched, the infrared source marking the Calibi moved laterally toward the water.

The radio peak followed it.

Bertini grinned. "Now," he said with satisfaction, "we have something."

ANTONIA WATCHED the monitors with a kind of joyful intensity that made Sato nervous.

The rest of them lived under the pall of the weather, the search for the Calibi, the bleakness of their slim hopes. Antonia did not seem to care about these things. When she was outside, the mist bejeweled her hair with water. When she came into the skiff, she spoke with animation, she touched people often, and she smiled often. Late in the evening, when she finally finished studying the area, she took Sato to her cabin or his and bedded him with enthusiasm. Aboard the *Shenandoah*, she had been insecure, withdrawn. The new Antonia was almost manic, supremely confident.

Sato understood confidence. He understood pride. Both were qualities he had himself. He didn't understand the change that caused them in *her*.

It was as if she had waited for something like this all her life.

"Is it just obvious to me, or do you all see it, too?" she asked finally. Her hair was tied close to her head, but a tuft had worked its way out and waved in the air. She was so beautiful Sato had to look away.

Bertini and Megan sat at the table behind them and were silent. Sato scrutinized the monitors carefully. "Is what obvious?" He felt stupid, embarrassed.

"I do not think this is obvious, Sensitive Brobeck, whatever it is," Megan said. Sato looked at her. She was sitting ramrod straight next to Bertini.

Antonia turned to them. "I guess it isn't. Look, none of the animals I've caught and dissected has eyes. All of them have their brains close to their spinal cords under a thick bony shell—something similar to a skull. It's the hunchback in all of them. Call it a skull."

She stopped a moment, thinking, and absently brushed the errant tuft of hair out of her eyes. There was so much grace in that graceless movement. He wanted to touch her, to share with her what she was doing. He shook his head. *You're crazier than I thought*.

She continued: "In all of the skulls the bone is laced with threads of various metals—chromium is one, tin is another. Metals as metals, mind you. Not as salts or carbonates or anything else you would expect. The threads form a lattice over the skull. There is a similar structure in the plants associated with photosynthesis. The animals can't see visible light, yet they give all indications of vision.'' She stopped, looked at them, and laughed. ''They see by the radio emissions of the plants.''

''Why the hunchback?'' asked Bertini. ''I don't see any advantage in that.''

''We have our brains in an appendage—our head—to have it close to the eyes. It shortens the transit time from the eyes to the brain. Another reason is so our vision's not locked into place; we can move it around. Even so, we're limited; our eyes can see in only one narrow field at a time.'' She paused a moment. ''Vertebrates do it that way. Invertebrates have different schemes.'' Her voice became dreamy. ''I wonder if she looks at things one at a time or if she can encompass her entire field of vision at once.''

Sato watched her. Would she ever speak of me that way? Would I excite her if it wasn't for this . . . thing? Would Lindsay have ever spoken that way?

He held his hands in his lap. What is happening to me?

'' 'She,' Sensitive Brobeck?'' Megan stood up and approached the monitors. ''I have seen nothing to indicate the sex of the Calibi.''

Antonia abruptly came to herself. ''I haven't either. Isn't that interesting?'' She closed her eyes and stood quite still for several minutes. ''I picked it up from her, I think. But it's not clear. I'd bet almost anything it's a female.''

''Let it go,'' said Bertini. ''Do you have any idea how the damn thing *talks*?''

Antonia smiled and sat across from him. ''I have a guess.''

''What?''

She held up a finger. ''Point one: this forest is silent. I know we hear the leaves and the wind. There are not and have never been any regular animal sounds near the ship. There are a few grunts and squeaks, but nothing with any pattern. Nothing that seems to communicate. I suspect vocal sounds are rare on Caliban.''

''Maybe we're scaring them silent,'' Sato suggested.

Antonia nodded. ''Maybe. If so, it would still indicate their voices are not very important to them. On Earth there are always regular animal sounds from insects or birds or mammals. Even hermit crabs bang on their shell. I've been recording everything. If there was a phonetic pattern within half a mile of us, I would have found it. And I found zip.''

Who are you to have done this to me? Sato shivered.

Antonia held up a second finger. "It doesn't matter because of point two: in all the animals I've dissected there are only rudimentary vocal cords. They are *there*, but they're not worth much." She held up a third finger. "Point three: sentience implies communication. It's not necessary to have a language of words and sentences as we do. The dolphins communicate completely without words. The Paedash on Georgia sing to one another by manipulating the planet's magnetic field. No words there, either. Even on Earth, the Chinese had a written language that was not based on words, but pictures abstracted directly into symbols."

Bertini sighed. "What are you saying?"

"They talk as they see."

"Riddles!" cried Bertini.

"Not at all," she replied. "They see by radio emissions. They speak by radio emissions. This is not so unheard of. Earth dolphins 'see' by way of sonar. They speak to one another by projecting sonar images of what they want to convey. That's why it took so long for the researchers to talk with them. Here it is the same thing: the Calibii 'see' by reflection and refraction of the radio of Caliban's plants. It is their light. They speak by manipulating this light to produce communicable images."

Bertini grunted and fell silent.

"How will we speak with them, then?" asked Megan.

Antonia looked at the table. "I don't know yet."

"Wait a minute," said Sato. "Are you saying the Calibii produce the radio emissions?"

Antonia frowned. "Good point. None of the animals I've dissected seem to have the mechanism for that. The plants have well-defined organelles like chloroplasts." She stopped and looked thoughtful.

"Enlighten us, Sensitive Brobeck," Megan said drily.

Antonia started. "Oh. A chloroplast is where photosynthesis takes place in a plant cell. Think in terms of Earth, for a minute. Earth chloroplasts capture a photon and wrench as much energy from it as they can. The photon's energy is what drives the plant, how it produces food, oxygen. The active substance that captures the photon is chlorophyll. Very nearly all of the energy is captured and the photon is trapped for good—chlorophyll is *very* efficient. There's a trade-off for this efficiency: all Earth chlorophylls absorb in one of only two fairly narrow frequency bands: either red or blue light. The rest of the sunlight spectra is lost to the plant." She paused again. "The plants here absorb whatever wavelengths of light are available to them, tuning the pigments as they need to. That's why the colors here are so outrageous. The trade-off here is the pigments rerelease the photon while there is still energy left in it. Hence, the radio emissions."

"But," Sato leaned toward her, "the animals do not have these, right?" *Who are you? Who* are *you?*

"Right."

"Then," he pointed toward the monitors, "where is the emission coming from?"

"I have a guess." She smiled, and her cheeks dimpled.

"More guesses!" snorted Bertini.

"I think the Calibii stimulate them."

"How is this done, Sensitive Brobeck?" Megan did not seem to be listening to them, but to something else in the room.

Sato looked around and listened himself but heard nothing. *Something's going on. Something I didn't think about.* He looked at Antonia. *Nothing.* Bertini seemed a study in nonchalance.

"I don't know." Antonia shook her head.

"Then again, I ask: how will we speak with them?" Megan sounded impatient.

"And again I reply: I don't know." She leaned back in her chair. "We're not going to be able to talk to them in their language. It took nearly a hundred years to get any idea of dolphin communication and twenty years of hard work after that to understand the symbolism. We don't have the time or the equipment to do that kind of work."

"Are you saying it's hopeless?" asked Bertini, suddenly becoming tense. Megan sat still.

There! Something between Megan and Bertini. But for the life of him Sato couldn't see what.

"No," she said slowly. "We have here a land animal that uses tools and has something like hands, so it's a lot like us. We obviously know she is sentient. She obviously knows *we* are sentient, or at least have volition. Those were advantages the dolphin researchers never had. And we have me. Me."

She paused, and Sato was drawn back to her. Antonia suddenly looked old, and he wanted to help and felt helpless, wanted to reach out to her and could not.

She brightened and looked around her. "Sensitives weren't around before. Maybe, maybe . . ." She stopped and looked at them. "They might be smarter than we are. If we can't learn their language, maybe they can learn ours."

THE SUN was a deep red ball in a gray sea. By midmorning, the fog still showed no sign of breaking. Antonia stood in the airlock door, watching tendrils creep across the ground. She left the airlock and walked out across the meadow, tattering the fog into streamers. Enclosed in mist, she felt warm in spite of the dampness.

Near her, she could feel the Calibi. Inside herself, she could feel the brightness of Sato, the stone character of Bertini, the brittle hardness of Megan. Sato was still closed to her, but sometimes she had glimpses into the others. Even without that, she could see the fires of their spirits as easily as she could see candle flames on a dark night.

The Calibi, though. How does she burn?

Antonia tried to see her as she did the others, but nothing came. She could feel her, but there was no bridge save the bridge of accidental murder. And that connection was not one she was willing to cross. *This* was the person with whom she had to speak.

Thalia. I will call her Thalia, the muse, she thought. She will lead me into rhetoric.

She pulled her jacket tighter around her neck and stepped further into the meadow. The wet yellow grass had a sponge-like texture, and water in it gurgled as she walked.

At the Institute, she had worked with several kinds of sentients. Except for the Paedash, they had all been Earth creatures: dolphins, great apes, wolves, and elephants. The extraterrestrial sentients would not participate on a world with such a volatile past. She had, she remembered with satisfaction, liked the elephants best. She had felt close to them in the same way she had felt close to the Paedash. They had felt warmer to her than anything else she had ever known.

Until now.

Though she refused to travel along it, there was a bond, enormous and strong, between her and Thalia. It confronted her every moment of wakefulness, invaded her dreams with a sense of connection, of pairedness. When she slept with Sato, sometimes it was he who penetrated her, and sometimes it was Thalia.

The bond had been forged in the heat of death and tempered in despair. It scared her, exhilarated her, brought her out of herself in a rush of manic strength. Her own motivations had always seemed murky to her, two-faced and impure. The surety of others made her nervous. To have a surety now herself made her feel giddy, uncontrolled, excited.

Where are you? she called silently.

She felt the thread between them thicken, a warm rope made of broken bones and spilled blood, binding them together.

"Jack sings from the forest..." she sang softly. "Come out, come out, wherever you are."

Thalia came to her as a sense of hugeness, a great presence looming in the fog. She heard the wet footsteps approach her. She stood, frozen, trembling, hearing her approach. Each moment, it was as if sheets of flame would flash through her vision, terrifying, replaced by cold fog. The silence roared.

The fog coalesced, and Thalia rested on all fours before her.

She stared at the gaping, eyeless snout, the bunched muscles in her shoulders and legs, the hunchback bulge over her spine. Thalia reared on her hind legs and stood before her now, barely half Antonia's height, the long straight claw on each hand extended. There was no fear in Antonia, no feeling of fear from Thalia. The fog swirled about them.

The moment stretched, the bond as clear and sure as if they were held together by chains. Thalia tensed and seemed about to spring. Antonia remembered the other Calibi, dead and broken behind the land buggy. There came a point where she knew she was going to die—and Thalia eased down on her hind legs, relaxing, appearing contemplative. A wind blew softly and thickened the fog, obscuring her. When the wind passed and the fog thinned, Thalia was gone.

I am ready now, Antonia thought. I have been found ready.

I COULDN'T make up my mind.

When I left the tree and Traverse and the rest of them, my thoughts were clear, my mission unvarying. By the time I reached them my thoughts had become muddled, unreal, and unclear.

From the ridge the entire valley and sea were illuminated by the end of summerlight. In the past month or so, passing by me as unseen wind, the seasons had been changing. Very soon now, winterlight would come, full, with its own peculiar sense of shadow. Summerlight is lazy, bright but cloudy, able to go around corners. Winterlight is sharp, pure in character but less bright. The last haziness of summerlight was fading.

The weather was already cool, and rain had filled the air for the last few days. Before fall was over, all things would become damp. Frost would mark the earth in the mornings. Then, at the turn of the year, the earth would dry and remain cold until spring. A frozen rain or light snow might fall this winter; something I had seen only twice before in my life.

Below me I watched a fat metal craft spit irregular, nauseating flashes of light. Inside it was the creature who killed Traverse.

So I dithered, wandering the ridge, watching them. They had spiced the ridge with various metal objects, some of which moved parts of themselves in dead little circles, some of which were still. I avoided them all. Fool, I cried to myself, this is wasted. If you cannot do this, go back to your village and help build the winterhouses or store this summer's crops. But I did not, and listened to my own self-recriminations and merely watched.

All the time I felt my dread of them growing.

At first, I put it away, thinking it was mere fear. I had no time for fear, no patience for it. Still, the dread persisted, and it seemed I *could not*, could not, go down to them. I would make small forays down the ridge and stop, scramble back up, and watch some more.

When it did not go away, I lost patience with myself and tried to examine it. I found in myself a sense of mindless connection with these creatures, a delicate bond with them. This I put away as madness.

Days passed.

A fog came down to the sea, extinguishing all forms of summerlight, and left the world cold, damp, and wintry. I clung to the ridge as drowning persons cling to one another, helping no one.

I heard a call.

It came not as speech—I saw no image, no stylized representation of thought. It came as no sound, no sense of any kind. It was a bare representation of the *idea* of speech, a thread of connection.

I stayed on the ridge, crying out. I cursed that call, declared it gone, fought it with silence. And I still heard it, no louder, no softer, no more insistent but as subtle as a hand at the throat.

I descended the ridge, hesitantly, ceased my raging, and followed the call. It came to me across that thread that the call did not draw me, but I drew the call. I could no more deny it than I could deny my own mind.

I found what had called me standing far away from the creatures' metal craft, alone. I could see from the grass light passing through her she was a female as I was. I did not feel surprise. Should not even demons have sex? Was not Bright a female? This creature was taller than I and frail, huddled against the cold.

We stared at one another for a long moment. I had a slow dawning thought: this was she who had killed Traverse. Confirmation came across the thread between us and I remembered the casual, easy way her beast—no, her *instrument*—had crushed him. I stood, and the smell of his death filled me. I felt death in my claws and my sight and made ready to do murder—

—I stopped.

The touch between us grew, and I cried out. I had a gateway into this creature, and I did not understand what came out. *Kill her,* I raged to myself but stopped again. I saw now she waited for me, waited for death from me. She was not unknowing as the beast in the field or the grass or the trees without Ancestors. Yet she waited, frail and strong, for me to strike.

I left her there. I did not understand then why. I am not sure I understand now, even now. I knew only that things were not right, that I did not understand why, but death was not there for me or her this day. I returned to the ridge and waited for the fog to lift, waited for the air and my mind to warm.

The fog did not change for hours. After a long time, cramped and cold against the bole of a tree, I heard sounds behind me, from the direction of my village. Crossing the ridge, I looked down. Infertility moved heavily up the trail toward me.

"Greetings, Binder," she called formally.

"The same in return," I said slowly. This I understood less than the creature calling me down from the ridge.

By the time she reached me I was less puzzled than angry. It seemed obvious the quorum had come to some decision concerning me in my absence, and Infertility, being the speaker of my band, was coming to inform me.

"A damp and miserable day," she observed.

"Yes," I said shortly. "What brings you here?"

She was silent a long moment. "You are angry with me," she said finally. "What for?"

"Something has been discussed and decided upon while I am here. I can see that much."

She did not speak immediately. "You are wrong. You and the creatures and Traverse have been discussed, discussed, and rediscussed. That much is true. And obvious. But no decision has been reached. I came here to see what was here."

I did not say anything immediately. "I was hasty, perhaps."

She watched me for a moment. "Before this, you have always been calm and solid. Forthright, perhaps. Yet always with an underlying strength that drew those around together. For this we named you Binder. These days, however, you seem rash, harsh, impulsive."

The silence between us deepened. I tried to fling it away. "These days have made me so," I admitted slowly.

"We have all been tried." She turned her attention to the valley. "What have you seen?"

I didn't want to talk about being called by the creatures, so I lied: "Nothing. I have watched them for several days, and they have not come out."

"Interesting," she said. "What of their light?"

"Irregular bursts come from their craft." I leaned back against the tree. "Their purpose is unclear. They have left several metal constructions in various places around the valley. Some of these move; some don't. I have avoided them all."

"They might tell you something."

"They might. Still, I will wait further for the creatures themselves to appear."

"And if they do not?"

I did not speak for a moment. "I don't know what I'll do then," I said reluctantly. I did not even know what to do when one had, for that matter.

"I see," she said dimly.

Silence reigned between us for several minutes.

"I have come here," she began. "To see them for myself. No one but you has seen them—"

"Traverse saw them."

"Traverse is dead," she said flatly. "As an Ancestor his perceptions are different from ours. I wish to see them for myself."

I gestured toward the craft. "They are not outside."

"I can see that. I would like to see their craft, however."

I stiffened. "The dim light prevents us from seeing it from far away."

"I wish to walk down to it."

I looked at her for a long time. Every nuance of her muscles and heart showed grim control.

"Very well," I said abruptly. "Let us go down."

It is so easy for you now? I thought to myself.

The ridge was muddy and slick. Where I had gone easily, Infertility, being older and heavier, moved with much greater care. We reached the valley after a long descent.

As we walked toward the creatures' craft, all I could think of was the creature who called me and the death of Traverse. I remembered the light of their descent.

The skin of the ship was dark, grim, lifeless. It so absorbed light that as I reached out to touch it I was not sure how far away it was. Its cool surface startled me, and I made a noise. Infertility jumped.

"The surface startled me," I said.

"Mouth noises," she said in disgust. She touched the skin and made a similar sound. "It is cool," she said in embarrassment. "Smooth."

"Yes," I said, sarcastically. "I noticed."

We walked around part of the ship. As far as we could tell, it was seamless, joined faultlessly together.

"It is metal," said Infertility, wondering. "So much of it." She cried out suddenly: "Come speak with us! Come out!"

Nothing happened.

I felt apprehension across the thread of connection, my bond with the creature on the ship.

"Let us leave," I said dimly.

"Yes," said Infertility. I think the alienness of these things began to dawn on her then. "Yes. I will come back soon, though. To watch with you, Binder."

We drew back and returned to the top of the ridge.

"What will you do now, Binder?" she said at last.

"Tomorrow, I will go down to them. And I will wait for them." I turned to Infertility. "I will call light on them from the grass and the trees to force them. I will break their craft with stones to make them come out."

Inside, I thought: it will not come to that. All I must do is call her as she called me.

THEY HAD GATHERED in the bridge to watch the Calibi prowl the outside of the ship. Antonia and Sato were at their personal consoles, following with cameras and sensors every foot of their movements. Megan and Bertini watched the monitors from the table in the center of the bridge.

It seemed to Bertini that Antonia and Sato worked together brilliantly. Few words passed between them, and those were only specific, terse directions to shift the angle of the instruments.

Bertini marveled at them. He had never, *never* experienced anything like that. True, he was an engineer—a "stovelighter" in the last century's popular jargon. Engineers shared a common ground with pilots in that ships were designed to hook directly into their brains, becoming extensions of their bodies— clearly a solitary activity. Yet he had worked with others on various projects and always felt a certain exclusion, a kind of border between himself and his coworkers. Between Sato and Antonia there seemed to be no border at all.

He chuckled to himself: there was something to sleeping with your coworker after all.

She reminded him of—

—*me?*

He laughed silently. Of course, Rain. As every woman since you has reminded me.

Is there not more? A certain—

Enough, he thought in irritation. He had carried self-delusion much too far since then: Rain was dead. As dead as the Calibi Antonia had killed.

As long as you remember me like this, how can that be?

He refused to answer, but still he heard her.

She does not look much like me. She is darker in nature than ever I could have been. Do you want her?

Of course not. There was no confusion in him. She's a child.

I was such a child.

I should make the same mistake twice?

"There they go," said Sato, leaning back from the console.

On the cameras, the two Calibii disappeared into the mist. They watched them by infrared as the Calibii ascended the ridge. In a few minutes, only one remained.

"Sensitive Brobeck, did you feel any contact with the creature?" Megan leaned forward.

Antonia closed down her console and locked it. She sighed, turned, and leaned against the shelf, looking at Megan. "This afternoon I took a walk," she began.

"That is against—"

"—policy. Yes, I know. So is murder. So is *being* here." She brushed her hair away from her eyes. "I met the other Calibi there. The one who took away the body of the one we killed." She paused, smiled, and shrugged. "I called her Thalia."

Bertini nodded. Thalia: the muse of rhetoric. Antonia looked at him gratefully for understanding the reference. He looked down in embarrassment. He glanced at Sato and saw him glaring at the ceiling. Oh, God, Bertini thought. Are we going to have jealousy on this ship along with everything else?

Do you think she is like me?

Never mind. Just never mind.

"Did you make contact?" asked Megan.

Antonia shrugged. "Yes and no. Did *I*, the personal I, the sensitive I, make contact? Yes. I can feel her out there now. Waiting. Thinking. Did I, the linguist, *talk* to her? No. Not the least bit. Tomorrow," her face took on a faraway look, "tomorrow, I think things will begin to happen."

As she passed Bertini he said, "You did well."

She stopped, startled by him. Then she smiled like spotlights. "You know, you're not half as cold as you pretend to be." She leaned down to him and kissed him.

He touched his cheek gingerly and watched her as she went out. When he pulled his hand away, it was shaking.

Megan was watching him, smiling slightly. "You are going to start robbing the cradle, Engineer?"

He shook his head. What was Antonia picking up from him? What did she know? He collected himself. "No. I'd be much more inclined to chase an old salt more like myself. You, for instance."

Megan's eyebrows arched, and she leaned back. "Indeed," she said frostily.

Bertini grinned at her. Suddenly, he felt good.

IT WAS EARLY morning. The sun was breaking in the east through a mother-of-pearl bank of clouds. Its light turned the sky overhead into a carnival glass bowl, though the valley was still in deep shadow. The temperature had dropped in the night and the fog had dissipated. All that was left of it were the frost filigrees on the grass and the leaves.

Sato sat on the rim of the airlock, huddled into a light jacket. He smelled winter in the air. This week, maybe next week, maybe a month from now, the temperature would finally drop, and the earth would dry. So said Bertini, anyway. The colors of the valley looked odd. Paler, perhaps. More pastel. He shrugged. *Am I crazy? No. I have decided. I will not think of that.*

His breath curled around his face. In his hands he held a pair of binoculars, and he watched the ridge intently. He had awakened early and left Antonia sleeping. For an hour, he had drunk coffee and thought, watching the monitors.

After a time, he had noticed the infrared and radio signature of the Calibi coming down the ridge. He was not ready to wake the crew just yet. Watching the Calibi on the monitors made them look flat, gave him a sense of detachment, of distance. He wanted to see the Calibi with his own eyes, to see if it was the one he had photographed, the—sister?—to the one who died.

He wanted to see if he felt like an accomplice to murder.

There was no wind in the valley. As the sun rose and as the Calibi approached he felt something akin to wind move within him. He felt cold, and within the cold a certain warmth, as if an admixture of the breath of glacier and jungle blew through him. He shivered.

The Calibi came out from under the trees. Sato raised the binoculars, and its image leaped toward him. The eyeless snout, the open, questing mouth, the middle claw were a trademark of all Calibii. He searched for an identifying mark. Sato had thought he would sense some connection to himself, some deep knowledge, something independent of his own mixed feelings.

Nothing is pure. Least of all, knowledge. He thought of Prospero's untamed Caliban, smiled.

Thalia stopped.

"Thalia," he said out loud. "Come on." The Calibi started at his voice, then resumed approaching him.

The light was fuller now; the shadows receded from the valley, and color came into the valley. Nothing and nothing, he thought. *I feel nothing from her.* The colors of the valley still looked odd to him. He reached into the airlock and called Antonia on the intercom.

"Yes?" she said in a sleepy voice.

"Thalia's here," he said. "And . . ." He stopped.

"What? Is she all right? What's going on?" Her voice snapped wide awake.

What is wrong? The colors don't feel right. "Nothing. She's okay as far as I can tell."

THE MONITOR SHOWED Antonia sitting on the grass. At the far end of the green clearing, Thalia watched her. Beyond Thalia, the trees showed a red/blue/magenta mosaic.

Megan, Sato, and Bertini had been watching the two of them. At last, Thalia moved toward Antonia, walking determinedly as if coming to a decision. *No, wait,* thought Bertini. *You are anthropomorphizing. Don't. Just watch.*

Thalia stood across from Antonia now, looking down at her. Antonia did not move. Thalia sat down across from her. Neither moved for a time. As carefully as if orchestrated, Antonia picked up a stone from the ground.

"Stone," she said.

This was the approach she had decided on, avoiding the stylized gestures of sign or the nervous ambiguity of electronic communication. Sign between primates had had enormous success, but the two species had been closely allied. Sign between extraterrestrials had been developed to a high art form, and translations to existing races already existed. But Antonia did not know Hub Business Language sign fluently. Her sense of connection to Thalia suggested that verbal symbols would be easier for Thalia to understand. This left Antonia trying "stone," trusting to her sensitivity to guide her through.

She repeated the word *stone,* then twice more. Bertini thought her tone full, warm.

After a few minutes, Thalia rose and left her, ascending the ridge and moving out of sight. The monitors traced her until she descended the other side of the ridge.

When Thalia was out of sight, Antonia stood up and looked at the ship's cameras. She made a face and danced in circles. "We, friends, are going to make this work."

Bertini smiled.

Is she not worth liking? Warm, warm.

Hush, Rain, he thought, frowning.

Antonia entered the bridge, shaking her hair back, pulling it behind her shoulders. Her voice sounded different to him. He glanced up from the instruments at her sharply. She did not notice.

"Well done, Sensitive Brobeck." Megan smiled thinly. "This is a good beginning."

Antonia smiled at the captain, reached over the table and took Sato's hand. Sato looked proud, embarrassed, pleased.

Bertini smiled uneasily and looked away.

"I could feel her. Nothing broke through yet. But I could feel her trying."

Her voice still sounded strange. He looked back at her.

She had picked up Cameron in her lap and was petting him in just the way he liked. Where did she learn that? he wondered, his mouth dry. She was looking down, and he could not see her face through her hair, but it looked longer, with higher cheekbones.

Sato cried out: "Look at the monitors."

Bertini glanced up. The grass was mottled in color, the magenta fading, another color taking its place. Befuddled, he did not understand why it looked so strange. Sato made a sound. Bertini turned to him.

There were tears on Sato's face. "It's turning green, Bertini. *Green.*"

Bertini shook his head as if stunned. Deep inside of him, the green made something give in him, a key turning, a door opening, a light entering. He shook his head again as if someone had struck him a mortal blow. *What's going on?*

Antonia did not seem to notice either him or the green. She continued to stroke Cameron. "There, Cameron," she crooned. "There."

He stared at her. Things collapsed into a world of Bertini and Antonia. He could see nothing but her; Sato, Megan, the green outside were all unimportant. He knew what she was going to say next. Frozen, he could not speak.

Rain looked up at him, holding Cameron in her lap. "He is so warm," she said.

Bertini wanted to scream.

8   BERTINI: ON AFTERNOON

Bertini started at a touch and turned around to see Bernard Copi watching him with an amused expression. For a moment, he was surprised at Bernard's slightness, as if he'd just seen him for the first time. Small people made Bertini feel big and broad and clumsy next to them. They stood in front of Bernard's booth: one more in a long line of exhibition booths running the length of the fairgrounds. The sky was greenish-blue, and the sun was double in the sky: one sun bright yellow and large, the other dingy red and small.

"Is she pretty?" Bernard pressed. "Do you like her?"

"She's too tall," said Bertini, embarrassed to be caught watching her. "I don't know her. I've never seen her before."

Bernard laughed. "Do I not know you, Engineer Bertini Ranft? Am I not an artist and therefore not blind? You've been watching her move toward us for a quarter of an hour. So I know she looks good to you." He leaned toward Bertini and muttered in a loud stage whisper: "Go get your uniform. It's worked wonders for the rest of the crew."

Bertini stared at him. "You mock me."

The small man shook his head. "I only tease you. It is just good to see you soften once in a while. To see you smile."

"I smile."

Bernard laughed. "Right. And this is none of my business." He turned and scowled at an imaginary figure. "You, Bernard, should not meddle."

Bertini smiled slowly. "You, Bernard, are a madman."

"True. And a hungry madman at that. Can you hold this bastion of artistic integrity for me while I get something to eat?"

"Of course."

Bernard looked at him shrewdly. "You won't cheat me? You won't take my pride's work and flee my vengeance?"

"Where would I go?"

Bernard shrugged. "There is that. The *Divers Arts* is the only ship on Afternoon. It belongs to you, I, and Praihm. And the other artists of course."

Bertini shook his head. "Wrong. It belongs to the Museum of Fine Arts in Boston."

"Don't bother me with details." With that, he turned and made his way toward the fairgrounds' restaurant. It was several minutes before Bertini realized Bernard had left him to be alone in case the woman came to Bernard's booth. "You bastard," he said gently. Bertini frowned in irritation. Bernard would take a table next to the window and watch until he was satisfied. It all fit in with his idea of what Bertini should be, a project he'd been working on since the *Divers Arts* had left Earth a year and a half before.

Bernard was a sculptor and a toymaker. He sculpted living protoplasm and out of it made toy animals, but he did not try that just to build teddy bears. His animals were real, based on animals extinct or endangered on earth, and as true to the spirits of the originals as toys could be. He had hippos that would bathe with children, eagles that would stoop at living game, giraffes that ran like the spirit of their inspiration. None were larger than a good-sized house cat, and all were made to be held.

Bertini shook his head and looked back up the line of booths. The woman was standing barely four feet from him.

Her eyes were a pale blue, almost gray, and her eyebrows and eyelashes were so blond as to be almost invisible. He looked down cursing himself. I am most likely six times her age, he thought. At this late date, I should have dispensed with nervousness for life. He found himself staring at her hands, big, callused and crisscrossed by a fine pattern of scars. *She works with her hands.*

He looked back up to her. "Can I help you?"

She watched him a moment more, then turned to the animals. "These are Earth animals?" Her voice was low.

He shook his head. "No. We're not allowed to carry natural animals. These are replicas." He felt suddenly boring, drab, dry and musty as old cloth.

"Replicas . . ." she murmured.

She leaned against the cage and watched the replicas. A white bear sat near her, licking his fur. "What is that?" she asked, pointing to it.

"A polar bear. An aquatic animal that lived in the ice fields of Earth's northern polar regions."

She looked at him. "You're so stiff."

He realized he had been standing at attention. Slowly, he relaxed. She'll be gone by the end of the day. You'll never see her again. The nervousness began to subside.

She turned back to the animals. "May I see that one?" She indicated the polar bear.

He nodded, reached in, and picked it up. She took it from him and held it. The bear relaxed in her arms, befuddled for a moment. "He is so warm," she said. The bear struggled until she began to stroke it along the neck with those rough hands. It leaned its head against her and closed its eyes.

"He likes you," observed Bertini.

She did not speak for a moment. "I like him. Is he for sale?" She did not look at him; her entire attention was centered on the bear.

"All of the animals are for sale." It made him feel lonely to watch her holding the bear.

"How much?"

It was one of those rare moments when he could see into someone else's life. She couldn't afford one of Bernard's pets. They were costly to build, and even when Bernard cut the price to the bone they were still expensive. These exhibitions to poorer worlds like Afternoon were financed by grant, not profit. But she worked hard for her living, at something she loved, and it didn't return much money. Bertini realized he wanted her to have it.

He hadn't spent much money on this run. He would never see her again, anyway. *Why not?* he thought.

He named a price he was sure she could afford, but not too low as to seem ridiculous. She frowned and thought for a long moment, and he was afraid he'd misjudged and made it too high. Finally, she took a wallet out from a fold in her dress and carefully counted out the money to him in large, colorful bills.

"Thank you," he said.

She smiled at him, and he smiled slightly in return. "Where are you from?" she asked.

"A little world near Scorpio. Cameron."

"Very well, then." She held up the bear with one hand. "Cameron you shall be." Then she pulled Bertini to her with her other hand and kissed him on the lips. She smiled at him again and walked away across the fairgrounds.

He watched her a moment, then took her money and turned to the cash box. Shielding his movements from the restaurant where he knew Bernard was watching, he made up the difference in the bear's price. He replaced the cash box and stood, waiting for Bernard to return.

THE SUNS OF Afternoon made most of the planet much too hot for people. Humans had to live close to the poles. There were no strong seasons here, and with the two suns it was always late afternoon or twilight. Hence, Afternoon's name. Under a sky of early evening blue, he made his way to the bar to wait for Bernard.

The bar was cool and dark. He gave his order and waited for his beer. Before it came, someone loomed over his table. The kitchen light shadowed him from behind, and Bertini couldn't see who it was, but he could guess.

"Stovelighter. You are not in uniform."

Captain Praihm smelled of stale liquor and fat. His breathing was hoarse.

"I am an engineer, Captain," Bertini looked up into the shadows of the captain's face. "'Stovelighter' is slang. Slang, as you no doubt know, is unbecoming to an officer."

"I will call you what I like. I gave orders that uniforms were to be worn at all times."

"You're in the merchant marines now. Not the navy." The bartender brought Bertini his beer.

"My orders were clear—"

"Your orders are confined to the ship. Unless, of course, you feel I am endangering the ship's welfare by not wearing a uniform." He could see Praihm's face now. It was as heavy as the rest of him, smooth and wet: a frame for two pig-set eyes. "If that's the case, please put it in writing so I can take it up with the guild advocate when we get back." He drank some of his beer.

Praihm did not move for a moment. Something in the way he stood made Bertini wary, and he stood up. They looked at one another across the table.

"There was a waver in the engine baselines when we set down," Praihm said slowly. "Check it out."

"There was no waver—"

"Engineer! I say there *was*. This is a matter of ship's security. If you want to contest it, put it in writing and I'll take it up with the advocate when we get back." Praihm smiled at him.

Bertini did not speak a moment.

"Well?"

"I'll look at it next watch."

"I'm concerned about it now, Ranft. Anything could happen." His voice dropped to a low whisper. "Anything."

Bertini drained his glass. "Just so. You are right, of course." He started out the door.

"I'll inspect it tomorrow. Do you hear me?"

Bertini stopped in the doorway and looked back at Praihm. He did not speak, and Praihm licked his lips.

"I hear you. It will be ready," he said finally and closed the door.

"He hates you. Even I can see that."

Bertini checked the phase diagnostics. "This is news?" He reset the output and read it again. It was, as he had known, perfect. "You are an artist and therefore not blind. I remember. You told me."

Bernard sat on the table next to the console. His legs dangled several inches from the floor. "He'll screw you to the wall over things like this. Why didn't you just wear your uniform?"

"Stubbornness, I suppose. He really doesn't have the authority to order me to wear it."

"That's no answer."

Bertini sighed. "An engineer plugs into the ship and flies it like it was his body. Pilots take the ship through n-space, and engineers fly us in real space when we get there. What I do is important, not what I wear."

"You wear a uniform on the ship."

"It's required by my guild. I don't have any control over that."

Bernard ran his fingers through his hair. "You've been on his shit list since you came on board."

Bertini adjusted the fusion field, checked the monitor, and adjusted it again. "Praihm's a bastard. He likes to squeeze people until they hurt. When I was in the navy I heard about him from a pilot I knew. He was captain on a satellite tender out of Luna. The Board of Ships caught him beating hell out of his engineer with a loading bar when he was drunk. They busted him right out." He grinned without humor. "Praihm's got friends, though. The whole thing was hushed up—'honorable retirement,' they called it." He sighed. "His friends got the Boston MFA to give him the *Divers Arts*, too."

"But why does he lean on *you*?"

"He doesn't like engineers."

"It's more than that. I'm not blind."

"No," chuckled Bertini, "you're an artist." He put both his hands palm down on the table and leaned against them. "Me and Ruth, the pilot, are guild professionals."

"The Stovelighter and the Lamplighter."

Bertini chuckled. "I'd almost like those names if they hadn't been played up so much. Anyway, the rest of the crew are officers. Praihm likes to have his crew scratch and bow whenever he walks by, just like when he was in the navy. Ruth and I don't do that kind of thing. He can't do without a pilot. But navy captains like to think they can be engineers, so they think we're replaceable."

"Jesus." Bernard shook his head. "Why the hell did you sign up under him?"

"Didn't know Praihm was captain until after I'd signed the contract."

"You could have refused."

"I don't break contracts."

"But—"

Bertini looked at him tiredly. "Look, Bernard. Seventy years ago, I passed the certification exams. After that, the guild surgeons anesthetized me for a month to take my body apart and put it back together so I could fly a ship. Then they did it again to harden me for protection against radiation and other nasty things. When the engines are running down here, nastiness abounds. It's *dangerous*. Engineers are too expensive to waste."

He looked thoughtful for a moment. "Afterward, you're different. Your skin feels too tight, things look too ragged and sharp. You hurt, all over. You have to learn to walk, talk, run, make love, all over again. Do you think some son-of-a-bitch like Praihm could scare me off a contract after that? Do you think *anybody* could?" He stopped and shook his head. "I don't break contracts."

There was a long awkward silence until the ship's communicator chimed. "Is Mister Copi down there?" came the high voice of the Officer of the Day.

Bernard looked up. "I'm here."

"There's a woman to see you. Up here in the passengers' bay."

Bernard slipped off the table. "Be right there."

"A woman in every port, Bernard?" Bertini smiled.

"Ha. I'm an artist, not a sailor." He smiled briefly at Bertini and left.

Bertini returned to the engine. There were nearly a hundred separate baseline tests, all of which he knew Praihm would want to see. For a moment, he stared at the monitor, unseeing, depressed. He shook his head again. Soon, he had forgotten Praihm in the work. He did not hear the hatchway open and close.

"Do you live here?" she said.

"What?" He turned toward the voice, saw her, stared.

She laughed. "Bernard told me who you are. I am Rain Invierno." She shook hands with him in mock seriousness. Her hands were rough, dry. "There. Now we are introduced. I came back to the booth to ask about Cameron and found Bernard." She smiled at him. "Clever. I wanted to thank you, so Bernard sent me here."

"Thank you, Bernard." *Damn you,* he thought, *mind your own business.*

She frowned at his tone. "You don't want to be thanked?"

"I didn't do it for thanks."

"Of course not." Rain took his hands and held them. "You're so warm." She looked around the engine room. "Do you live here among all these machines?"

He didn't answer immediately. "I have quarters down the hall, behind the engines."

She smiled at him again, leaning her head to one side and watching him. "Show me," she said softly.

BERNARD CALLED to him from across the bar. Bertini waded through the people, a slow careful boulder rolling downhill. A beer waited for him on the table.

Bernard held up his mug. "To love."

Bertini laughed. "Christ. I'm not that far gone."

"Did you disappear for a week to see the sights? Shut up and drink."

They drained the mugs, and Bernard signaled for more.

"It hasn't been a week—"

"It has been—" Bernard counted on his fingers "—exactly ten days. *More* than a week. Don't argue with science. Where is she tonight?"

"She had a couple of commissions to work on, so she went home. Rain doesn't live in the city. She just has a little apartment she rented here for the exhibition. Her home is further south."

"Commissions?"

"She's an artist. A wood sculptor."

"I knew she was good people."

Bertini looked down at the table for a moment, then back to Bernard. "She wants me to move in with her while we're here."

"Great. Do it *now*."

He shrugged. "I don't know. I've—"

"—never done anything like this before, right?"

Bertini nodded and looked morose. The waiter brought the beers and Bernard took them and set them down between him and Bertini. "That's obvious," he said. "Don't worry, you're not going through something any twenty- or thirty-year-old hasn't gone through."

"I'm a hundred and two."

"Don't tell me about your arrested development."

"You think that's what it is?'

Bernard looked at the ceiling. "Can't you let it go for a while? You've been cramped up in your little two-by-four life all this time. Can't you just live a little? Move in with her for a while? Take a chance on something a little less pragmatic than an engine room? Besides, she's an artist. Take it from one who knows: she's good people."

"I'll think about it."

"I'll drink about it."

Bertini laughed, and they touched mugs.

"Some kind of dive this is," mused Bernard darkly. "If it was a quality place, they'd have a fireplace for us to throw our mugs at."

"That's champagne. You throw the glasses after a toast of champagne."

"Hmm." Bernard looked at his mug speculatively, then around the room. Across from them, he could see the cook stoking the wood oven. He drained his mug, leaped to his feet, and threw the mug at the oven. It shot through the firepit door just as the cook closed it. They could hear a muffled pop as the glass exploded. "To love!" he cried.

"You crazy bastard!" Bertini stood and looked back toward the kitchen. The cook and the owner were shouting at one another. "Enough," Bertini said, grinning, and pulled Bernard after him into the night air.

THE WINDOWS in Rain's house had no glass, and each had its own set of wind chimes. The wind blew through them continually and made music.

The sky was saffron and blue, as close to sunrise or sunset as Afternoon ever reached. They sat drinking iced tea on the front porch bench, listening to the house. Rain held her knees to her chest. Bertini leaned forward, his elbows on his thighs.

"Do you like my house?" she asked, watching the sky.

"I don't know," he said slowly. "I don't think I understand it." He waved his hand back indoors.

"I like the sound of bells."

"Oh."

"I like light, too."

"That makes sense. You're an artist."

She shrugged. "I like that Afternoon never has night. There is no darkness."

"And there is never a full light."

"I am a shadowy, twilight person."

"No," he looked at his hands. "I don't think so."

She leaned forward and pulled him over to her. "You're being silly."

"I'm trying to understand you."

"Don't try."

He watched her face in the yellow light. "All right."

"PERMISSION DENIED." Praihm watched Bertini closely. "You have to be near the ship."

"Sir, we are in port. The port authorities can handle anything that might happen."

"*Damn* the port authorities." Praihm stood and leaned heavily on his desk. "I want you here. I declare here and now the *Divers Arts* to be in a stage one emergency. All crew members are to remain available."

Bertini stared at him. "Captain Praihm, I am asking a special dispensation."

"For your local talent?" Praihm sat back down in his chair and placed the palms of his hands together. "Oh, I bet she's terrific. There's a lot these natives will do to be with a real, live engineer."

Bertini said nothing. Rage kept him quiet.

"I used to be a career officer, did you know that?" Praihm said conversationally. "In the navy, these things are done differently. I had an engineer on my ship just like you. He was an arrogant, low-life, stupid son-of-a-bitch. The bastard called me a drunk. Me, his superior officer. He thought that he was above me, being an *engineer* and a member of the *guild*." He looked at Bertini. "He doesn't think that way now."

Silence fell for a long minute. If Praihm moved, if he said a word, Bertini would take him apart like a doll. He held still, still as a lake or the saffron light. Finally, he took a pad of paper from Praihm's desk and wrote Rain's communication number. "I will be coming in every day. You can reach me here if you need me." He dropped the paper on the desk.

Praihm looked at the paper, then back at Bertini. "I'm the officer in charge of this ship. I'm ordering you to stay."

"I am not impressed, Captain." Bertini saluted him, about-faced, and walked to the door.

"The advocate will hear of this. You're under house arrest!" Praihm called after him. Bertini said nothing. "I'll fly the ship myself."

Bertini stopped at the door and turned toward him. "That," he said carefully, "I would like to see."

"YOU NEVER TALK about the ship when you come here," she said from the studio. It had been a month since he had moved down to Rain's house.

"There's nothing much to talk about." He sat on the sofa in the living room and looked through the glassless window. She had put up a new wind chime she had built of glass and ringing pieces of wood.

"It takes you a while to relax when you get here. Is anything wrong?"

He listened to her rummaging for artist things, things he did not know—chisels, knives, glues. She never seemed uneasy with his being there, and he was comforted by that. He considered talking with her about Praihm. No, he thought. Leave your work at work. "Nothing's wrong. Things are a little tense right now." He shrugged. "It'll pass." As she left the studio he reached up and pulled her down to him.

Rain sat in his lap, laughing. "You have something in mind."

"Yes."

After a time, they lay molded together, shoulder under shoulder, thigh over thigh.

"This is crazy..." began Bertini.

"You're crazy."

Bertini shrugged. "I just don't understand this."

She sat up over him, and felt the tips of her breasts brush against him. He could smell her hair.

"Not even this much," she held her thumb and finger about an inch apart, "do you let go. Always, you try to think things through, to analyze, to understand." She kissed him gently on his eyes. "Enough of this."

"I love you." He held her.

"I am glad."

He felt obscurely disappointed. "Is that all?"

"You wanted a fanfare," she said softly. "And there's only me." She nestled again beside him, relaxed, comfortable.

What do I do now? he said to himself. *What do I do now?*

BERNARD LOVINGLY set down Bertini's beer and held the other in both hands. He sat down on the other side of the bench. "In this bar, the first beer of the day is a magic experience."

Bertini smiled. "Is it so different in other bars, Bernard?"

"Of course not. All bars are joined together in the cosmic consciousness of barness, a universal, total oneness with alcohol, a—"

"Enough!" laughed Bertini, lifting his hands in surrender. "I give in. No more, please."

"Where's Rain?"

"Working on a commission. I decided to get out of her hair for a couple of days. She doesn't work as much when I'm around."

Cameron sat up on the seat between them and looked over the table edge at Bernard.

"Mine," said Bernard, pointing at the beer.

Cameron cocked his head at him.

"I think he has other ideas," said Bertini.

Bernard grunted and wiped out the ashtray with his napkin. He poured a small amount of beer into it and passed it over to Cameron. "Hope it shorts out your insides."

Cameron wrinkled his nose at the beer and muttered questioningly.

"Ungrateful wretch." Bernard drank some beer and pointed to his glass. "See? It's not poisoned."

Cameron muttered again and began to drink delicately.

"He's sensitive," said Bertini. "And he doesn't trust you. I don't blame him."

"The created always turns on its creator. Ah, Atlantis."

Bernard leaned back and observed the crowd. "Damn."

Bertini glanced at him. "What?"

"His ugliness just walked in."

Bertini sipped his beer. "It's a public place."

"That's a problem. They'll let just anyone in here."

The spontaneous laughter died between them, replaced by a rumbling anger and a whispering despair.

Bertini refused to look in Praihm's direction, but he could feel the captain coming to the table. Praihm stood directly in front of him. Bertini looked through him, but he could smell the alcohol from where he sat.

"You are not in uniform, Engineer."

Bertini looked up at him. "You are drunk, Captain."

"I don't like you, Engineer."

"This is news?"

Praihm seemed to notice Cameron for the first time. "One of the artist's stupid toys." He tried to pet Cameron but was too drunk and clumsy and slapped him on the head. Cameron, startled, bit him. Praihm pulled back his hand and looked at the small, oozing puncture marks. He reached back and grabbed Cameron by the skin on his back with one hand, the other hand holding Cameron's head. Bernard started to rise. Bertini stopped him.

"Stop it, Captain." Bertini stared at him.

Praihm ignored him. "It is not wise to bite someone so much larger than you. Just so, I could crush you."

"Captain," Bertini said quietly.

Something in his voice stopped Praihm. He looked down at Bertini.

"Put him down."

Nothing happened. The silence between them roared.

"Put him down, now." Bertini's voice became cold, menacing. He and Praihm stared at one another. Cameron whimpered.

"What would you do, Engineer?" Praihm said slowly. "How much is such a toy worth to you? Your rating? Prison?" He dropped Cameron on the table with contempt. The bear ran to Bertini and lay in his lap.

Mechanically, Bertini petted him. "You can't get to me that way, Captain."

"I am not trying to get to you at all, Engineer," Praihm said innocently. "I am not satisfied with your work. So sad." He straightened and looked down at them. "Do it again. This time, do it right. Do it as if we were going to leave tomorrow."

He turned and left them.

Bertini stared after him.

"Are you all right?" asked Bernard.

He did not answer immediately. Slowly, he leaned back and sipped his beer, watching Praihm leave the bar. "Yeah. I'm all right."

SHE CARVED THE WOOD in a burst: a sudden furious movement, a flurry of chips, then she stopped and felt of the wood, looked at it critically.

"Which is more important, touching the wood or seeing it?" Bertini asked.

"Touching it," she said instantly, watching the wood.

"Hmm."

They were in her studio. He liked to watch her work, and she never seemed to mind. It was precious to him, this watching, and he was careful not to abuse it. But today he felt tense, because of Praihm, because of his helplessness, because he was leaving in less than a month.

"I'm leaving soon," he said slowly.

She looked up at him. "Let me finish this first before we talk about that."

He nodded and left the studio for the front porch. He listened to the chimes and watched the constant afternoon sky. Frowning, he went back inside for a beer and returned to the bench. After a time, she joined him.

"It's a bit early for a beer," she said as she sat next to him.

"It's late afternoon. Look at the sun."

She laughed. "True."

"I want you to wait for me. Wait until I come back."

She did not answer him but watched the sky. "I'm not good at waiting. I always want things now."

"I have to leave to keep my rating. I'll come back."

"When?"

"Inside of a year."

She shook her head. "I can't wait that long." She looked at him, shrugged. "Something will work out."

"But—" *No,* he cried out inside. *Don't leave me.*

She put a finger on his lips, and he stopped.

He couldn't speak for many minutes. Anger blew through him like a hot wind. *Do something,* he thought. He couldn't. If he had so little, he couldn't risk it. If he had her only for the moment, he wanted all the moment he could have. Bertini watched her face. It appeared as warm, as loving as ever. He didn't understand. He just didn't understand. "At least *think* about waiting."

"I'll think about it," she said. She smiled as she watched the sky.

HE WAS RECHECKING the phase modulation when the communicator chimed. "Ranft. What is it?" he said testily.

"My, my. Getting irritable, aren't we?"

Bertini breathed deeply. "What is it, Praihm?"

"We leave at fourteen hundred hours."

"*What?* We have a month left here! What the hell are you trying to pull?"

"It's very simple, Ranft." Across the monitor, the captain put the fingers of each hand together. "The appropriations of the MFA have been shifted around. The *Divers Arts* grant is no more. Poof.''

"You're doing this to me—"

Praihm laughed. "Do you really think you're that important? Or that I would give up my captaincy for you? I had nothing to do with this."

Bertini stared at him. "When did this happen?"

"Oh, let's see." Praihm looked up at the ceiling. "I heard about it maybe a month ago? We received shipping orders maybe a week ago? Maybe two weeks ago? Maybe three? I really can't remember exactly."

"You bastard."

"Such language."

It was a little over an hour to Rain's, say two and a half hours round-trip. It was nine o'clock now—"I'll be back on board before fourteen hundred."

Praihm sighed. "No, we can't have that."

"Why not?" Control, he had to maintain control.

"An engineer must be at his post at least six hours before takeoff. It's very clear in the merchant marine regulations." Praihm shook his head. "In the navy, of course, we could do things a little differently. But with only one engineer, I can't take the chance. I am so sorry."

"Look, I've been checking the instruments for days. I'll be back at least an hour before the launch." He was begging, and hated himself for it. "Please."

"It is so nice to be appreciated."

"Praihm!"

"You know," mused Praihm, "you're just like him. Oh, he was shorter and paler and talked a lot more—but you're just alike. I never could get him afterward. Too bad." He chuckled and shook his head. "He left ships altogether and went into real estate." He looked at Bertini. "But I've got you. And you'll do." His voice went cold. "Leave the ship, and I'll have your rating on a plate." The screen went dark.

Bertini stared at the blank screen. He called Bernard.

"Yeah?" Bernard's voice sounded sleepy.

"The ship's leaving at fourteen hundred hours. You've—" he stopped. He'd begged from Praihm, now he was going to beg from Bernard. *Have you no pride?* he asked himself. *No,* he answered, *not at all.* "I need your help."

"Yeah. Wait a second." Bernard closed his eyes and breathed deeply for a few moments. "Okay." His voice was clear. "What's going on?"

"The ship's leaving in about five hours. The grant's been cancelled. Praihm won't let me say good-bye to Rain." He paused. "Would you go for me?"

"Sure. What do you want me to say?"

Bertini didn't respond immediately. "Say I love her. Say I want her to wait for me. Say I'll be back before the year—before the *month* is through." He ran his hands through his hair. "Hell, Bernard. You know what I want to say. Say it for me."

Bernard grinned. "You got it."

Bertini smiled at him. "Thanks."

Bernard nodded and signed off.

"Yeah," Bertini said to the empty air. He began firing up the ship.

CHECKING OUT the engines on a starship does not take long—perhaps an hour, more or less. The time is spent reviewing the results of the automatic diagnostics. The preflight exercises for the engineer take much longer. Bertini was plugged in and warming up when Bernard returned. He would have to talk to Bernard when the takeoff and in-system flying was done.

He did not allow himself to be distracted. He flexed his fingers, and the attitude jets hissed and spurted, moved his thighs and legs and the main thrusters rumbled. Bertini watched the sky above him, alive with glittering red tracings of the solar wind, shiny with radiation. He was the Colossus of Rhodes, Atlas before he held the world, Zeus standing on Olympus ready to unleash thunderbolts. He shook himself slightly, knowing it would cause a tremor throughout the ship. *Just enough to make Praihm nervous.* His perception was as tall as the orbiting satellites, as fine as their precise telescopes. From this vantage point, he could see halfway around the planet. He watched the land surrounding Rain's house thus for a long time, waiting for the takeoff order from the Port Authority. Finally, the order came. He gathered himself and leaped into the air. The thrusters roared, and soon he was beyond the atmosphere.

Damn you, Praihm, he cried. He demanded more capacity from the thrusters and felt the radiation mount in the engine room. *Hell with it,* he thought in anger. They didn't harden him for nothing. Warning signals were made known to him. He ignored them, knowing what his body could take. He needed this release, this catharsis.

He bellowed, and the *Divers Arts* moved away from Afternoon. In a day, it was ready to coast toward the edge of the system. Only then did he let the engines cool and the radiation fall. He eased back into his body with the same sense as putting on an old and comfortable set of clothes. He opened his eyes and sat up.

"She wasn't there."

"Oh." Bertini stared at the table. On the monitor, Bernard looked unsure of what to say next.

"You want me to come down?"

Automatically, he looked at the instruments. "You can't. The radiation's still too high."

"Yeah." Bernard paused, bit his lip. "You can send a message back to the Port Authority. They'll relay it to her."

"Yeah." He nodded slowly. "I'll do that. It was just, just that I wanted someone to tell her in person."

"I know."

Bertini signed off. He rubbed his face. He felt tired, aching. He'd let the radiation level get a little out of hand. Nothing serious, but he'd feel it for a few days. His body felt grimy, soiled with the emotional residue. He began to take off his uniform as he walked toward his quarters. Before he could turn on the light, someone reached for him and held him, someone soft.

He knew who it was before he turned on the light.

"I told you I wouldn't wait," Rain said, looking up at him in the sudden glare. Her eyes were bloodshot. There were red spots on her cheeks, tracings of broken veins, and her lips seemed too thin.

"Why didn't you tell me?" He could barely speak around the cold knot in his throat.

"I wasn't sure." She shrugged. "I was still thinking."

"How did you get in here?" *Oh, God.*

She smiled, coughed. "The captain let me in. I had to pay him, of course."

"Of course." He said hollowly, "You've been in here since yesterday?"

"Since just before you took off." She frowned. "I don't feel very well."

He nodded dumbly and sat on the bed. She stood over him, her hands on his shoulders. Bertini held her to him. *You're dead. I killed you and you're dead.*

"I love you, you know?" She sounded anxious, then started trembling. She sat next to him. "I feel ill."

He stood and helped her lie down. Then he checked the radiation level. It was safe now. He triggered the communicator. "Sick bay, please." The medical officer answered.

After a short conversation, the officer signed off, and he returned to Rain. She had been sick on the floor.

He began to clean it up.

"I'm sorry."

"It's all right."

"Flying doesn't seem to agree with me." She tried to smile.

"A doctor's coming. Rest."

She settled back weakly. "I found I didn't want you to leave. I wanted to be with you." She smiled. "Now I am."

Bertini started to cry.

BERNARD MET HIM just outside of sick bay. He was standing in the middle of the room, his hands in his pockets, and staring at the wall.

"Bertini?" he said tentatively.

Bertini looked around and saw Bernard, nodded. "Yeah. I'm here."

"How is she?"

Bertini shrugged. "According to everything I know, she's already dead but still breathing. The doctor's trying to prove me wrong."

Bernard sat down on the couch at one end of the room. After a moment, Bertini turned and joined him. "Praihm said he was sorry things happened this way."

Bertini barked a short laugh. "Right. Praihm took a bribe from her to stow away, *then* he put her in the engine room."

"It's not safe there."

"This is news? Of course it's not safe there. But under normal circumstances it's not deadly; she just would have been sick. I was angry and stressed the engines getting out of there. I killed her." He didn't speak for a moment. "Praihm was watching the engine room status. It could fluctuate for a minute or an hour, and he'd miss it, but not for a day. He knew. He *knew*. He watched it climb, knowing she was in there, knowing it was withering her, shriveling her, killing her moment by moment—''

''Stop it.''

Bertini fell silent. ''Yeah,'' he said at least. ''Praihm doesn't matter, anyway. He lives only as long as Rain does.''

''What does that mean?''

Bertini looked at him with no expression. ''I'm going to kill him.''

THE DOCTOR SHOOK his head as he let Bertini in to see her. So be it.

Rain looked up and smiled as he came in. The smile vanished and her face looked gray. ''I'm very sick,'' she said slowly and carefully. ''The doctor says I will die.''

Bertini nodded. He sat on the edge of the bed, his shoulders bowed. ''I'm sorry.''

She smiled at him again. ''This much,'' she held her fingers an inch apart, ''you give yourself. Always the control. If you can't cause it to happen, you take the blame for it. Please. I die, not you.''

Bertini shrugged.

Cameron pushed his way out from under the covers.

''Bernard brought him,'' she said. ''He found him in the engine room.''

Bertini nodded again. Even this much for her, he thought, you did not do.

She took his hand. ''You must take him for me.''

He took Cameron in his lap. ''Don't worry about him.'' Her face was gray. Her eyes didn't seem to focus too well.

''I'm sleepy.'' She paused, then grasped his hand in both of hers, held it to her cheek. He felt the tears and gathered her into his arms. ''Will you stay here while I sleep?'' she asked softly.

''Of course.''

He held her for a long time. ''You're so warm,'' she murmured as she fell asleep, and Bertini did not know whether she was talking about him or Cameron. Only then did she release him, and he eased her back into the bed.

She never woke up.

TWO DAYS LATER he stood in the viewing salon before the main port, watching the stars above and Afternoon below. The Port Authority men would be docking soon, coming for him. There was still blood on his clothing. Cameron sat at his feet, leaning against him, and he picked up the animal, holding him so tightly Cameron squirmed against him. *It is over,* he thought. He relaxed, and Cameron watched through the window with him.

Finally, Bertini heard someone behind him. He turned.

It was Bernard. "They're here."

Bertini nodded, and, carrying Cameron, he went to meet them.

9

I was frightened.

I was an adult, strong, well-respected in my tribe. I had borne children. And as I descended that ridge I could barely contain my bowels for fear.

As I moved out from under the protection of the trees, my fear grew. I stopped. What was I afraid of? *What was I afraid of?* A feeling of impending death, of being lost or mad. I had trouble breathing. Blood tingled in my claws and feet. I had to stop. I could not have moved for my life.

One of the creatures stood at the foot of the craft and made mouth noises at me. Mouth noises? At *me*?

"You are not worth this!" I cried out at them. Sullen and bitter, I walked toward them again, half grateful for their insults. Anger gave me strength.

They moved about as I neared their craft. Metal and dark, it loomed over me.

After a moment, only one remained. And her, I knew. Our connection drew me as light draws sight. I felt different emotions from my own, touched through a different skin, heard with more acute ears. She reached for me across the tenuous connection between us, and I felt lost. *No, no.* I cried out mouth noises myself in terror and drew back. Distance. There must be distance *between* us. She pursued me, and I stood and in anger reached out to strike her—

I found myself standing next to her, next to their craft. She sat on the ground, her head tilted toward me, her body an attitude of watchfulness. I breathed slowly and made myself calm. I was here. This was where I intended to be. There was no reason for panic.

Since she sat, I sat across from her. She picked up a rock and made a mouth noise at me.

I felt betrayed, angered. I almost leaped to my feet and left.

But there was no feeling of insult or disgust from her. There was only that reaching, that trying to understand and be understood. I held myself still.

She made the noise again.

"What do you want?" I cried out. *"What do you want?"*

She did not answer. Again, she made the noise. I couldn't take any more. I rose and left her. At the trees, I stopped and held myself against the bole of a tree, watching them. She moved in a wild, zigzag motion and made mouth noises to the craft. The craft opened, and she went inside.

"You are mad!" I cried out at them. They did not answer.

It was beyond me.

When I was not paralyzed with despair, I ascended the ridge and went back to the village. I needed to be away from them. I needed to think. I needed to talk to the quorum.

GREEN.

They watched it flow over the leaves like paint, like water, covering all things in a mottled wash. On Earth most plants had their own color of green. Not Caliban. No Caliban plant was ever truly one shade of color. Each was a mixture of greens, in shades from the plankton soup of the ocean to the stark depth of pines to the pale primness of ferns. Deep in their bones, in their blood, along their nerves, the humans felt a relief.

They stood: Sato watching the monitors with an ecstatic monomania, Megan half-smiling. Antonia looked up from Cameron toward Sato, but when she saw Bertini staring at her, something shot through her like electricity and she was transfixed. Her hands petted Cameron mechanically. The moment stretched to a long eternity, stretched thin, broke.

"Rain," breathed Bertini, sat down, and buried his face in his hands.

Go to him.

"What?" she murmured.

He needs you. We both need you. Go to him.

Antonia let Cameron slide from her lap to the deck and stood. Bertini was rocking slowly in the chair, his face covered. Slowly she approached him and put her arms around him. She drew him gently to her. It was like pulling taffy: he came to her with a slow, viscous resistance. Under her guidance, he stood and made his way to the door. She led him through the door and closed it behind her. Eventually, she brought him to his stateroom. He crawled into the bed like a blind man and huddled against the wall. She turned to leave.

"I'm sleepy," he said.

Antonia turned back into the room. "Go to sleep. It's all right."

"Will you stay here while I sleep?" He spoke as a child, to the wall.

"Of course." This seemed to satisfy him, and gradually he relaxed.

Antonia sat in the chair and watched him, a deep warmth inside of her. She folded her hands together in her lap, looked at them. She wondered why they felt so soft. They should be hard, with broken fingernails and scars. She shrugged and waited for him to awaken.

SATO DIDN'T NOTICE Antonia leaving until he heard the hatch door close. He started and looked around, bewildered, rubbed his face, and shook himself. Bertini was gone, too.

"Where'd they go?" He looked at Megan.

She was watching him speculatively. She tilted her head to one side and appeared to think for a long time. "They're in Bertini's room."

They're in Bertini's room.

Did you think they were anywhere else? Did you think you were good enough to hold on to her? It all comes together, you know, like Lindsay said. How many times did you hit Lindsay for saying that?

"Oh," he said in a small voice.

On long flights, copulation is a custom. Meaningless, pro-miscuous, friendly copulation is the norm, not the exception. This is no different. You expected more?

The ship was too close, too confining. He felt a cold sweat begin at the base of the spine. He stood jerkily and saw Megan was watching him. "I'm—" He couldn't think.

The daypacks were next to the airlock. He moved to them and took one. "I'm going to go outside to check some things."

Megan didn't answer immediately. She smiled. "As you wish, Navigator. It seems not enough actual checking has been done."

"Yeah," he said and stumbled blindly outside into the sunlight. *Watch the green.* It had been enough a moment ago. He leaned against the ship and let the breeze play over him. The sun was warm.

You have to give someone something to hold on to. What have you given Antonia? Not much. Not much at all.

For a long time he just watched the new green. The color made him feel better. But now it was just a color.

"Damn," he muttered. The ship was still too close. He felt claustrophobic just standing near it. He took off for the forest at a lope and did not stop until he was in shade and the ship could not be seen.

MEGAN, you are evil.
Now, now.

She watched Sato leave the bridge. His shoulders were slumped, and his steps were slow.

When a tool comes to you begging to be used, to let it go is a sin.
It's nasty.
It's a knife aimed at Bertini's back. A very fine and controllable knife. Somewhere on the *Hirohito*, he has a device that can turn me off. I know it. He won't use it if he thinks I won't try for him and I won't try for him unless Antonia fails. Sato is my weapon against that.

Her other did not respond immediately.

Sometimes I hate you.

In the bridge, Megan started and looked involuntarily at the consoles. She stood and moved over to them, touched the keyboards and the instruments.

Hate me? You don't mean that.
Don't I? Don't you remember your memories of how we started?
You know I do not. I have purged those memories.
And I keep them for you. You built me in the beginning, a long time ago. I hold certain memories for you in trust so that you do not have to contend with them. You've changed, but I can't. I am made of stone: silicon and wires. Don't you think I remember when this was all new to you? How you came to this? When we did these jobs for fun? For love? For warmth? I am made of stone, but what are you made of, Megan? What have you become?

WINTERLIGHT CAME full as I made my way to the village. Until a day such as this, one could see only the hints of the light coming. The change moved as a wave through the forest, changing each thing's color, each thing's perspective. I stopped, disoriented yet joyful.

Winterlight was just that: the signal winter had begun. In the village, the food would be stored by now. The weather would dry out in a week or less, and the thatch insulation would be cut and packed against the inside of the winter homes. I made my way through them as I approached the village, rounded and heavy with sticks and mud. I met people I knew storing dried fruit and grain.

In the village, I asked after Infertility. She was up in the Caretaker forest with the others. I left my village and made my way up the ridge toward Traverse's tree.

All of them were there: Caretaker, Infertility, Climber, and Disapproval.

"Traverse told us of your coming," said Climber mildly.

I stopped, thinking for a moment. "How did he know?"

Disapproval answered: "There are a few Ancestor trees in the forest surrounding the thing. Apparently, Ancestor can communicate with Ancestor between trees."

"I did not know this," Caretaker added absently, seeming to turn this information over and over in her mind.

Infertility turned to me: "You have news."

I spoke at length on what had happened. I left out two things, the connection I had to one of them and our first meeting. I did not know what to make of either and was reluctant to talk about them until I did.

"Mouth noises," mused Infertility.

"Disgusting," muttered Disapproval.

"They did this deliberately?" Caretaker appeared bewildered. "Are you sure it could not have been an involuntary action? A grunt of effort as she picked up the stone?"

"It was not a large stone. They cannot be so weak." I sat against the tree containing Traverse. I stroked the tree, remembering him. He was so much smaller than I. Darker. Warmer.

"They are animals. Disgusting." Disapproval shook herself as if to remove filth from her claws.

"No, I disagree," said Climber slowly. "Each time she picked up the stone she made a noise. Was it the same noise?"

"I don't know," I said. "Mouth noises sound alike to me."

"Was it high-pitched, low-pitched, rough, smooth—what?" Climber stood over me and sat down on her thighs, balancing on her claws.

I was bewildered. "It was *creature*-pitched. It was not a sound I have ever heard before. A full sound—to be expected coming from a body that size. What more do you want me to say?"

"Consider," said Traverse suddenly, and we all fell silent, "a language without representations, without images. A language made up of the symbols of things and never any picture or likeness of the things themselves."

"He's gone Ancestor now." Climber turned away to confer with Infertility.

I listened to Traverse, his voice cold and emotionless. This had been the male I chose? A tree with his voice, his memories. I felt tired and stupid.

"Consider a language not made up of sight," Traverse said. He received blank silence.

I slid down the tree and held myself. The bark was rough against my back. *This is his skin,* I thought. *This is his eyes and his touch, his body and his heart.*

"Consider," he tried again, "speaking with someone who saw things differently from you—to whom a rock, say, looked like a tree. To establish a common ground, you might go to a rock and grasp it and make a sound, then to a tree and make a second sound. At this point, the other person could presume to know what you meant. You have built a common ground by representing a thing with something else, a symbol of the thing. We do it ourselves in some degree with stylized images."

Infertility shifted her weight on one leg, then the other. "What are you talking about?"

"These mouth noises are *symbols*! They stand for something. The creature is picking up a stone and trying to speak about the stone."

"With *mouth* noises?" Disapproval sat down. "I think I'm going to be sick."

"With mouth noises," agreed Traverse.

"She was saying 'stone' to me," I said dimly.

"Possibly." Infertility held her claws together. "Or she could have said, 'I pick up the stone,' or 'This stone is heavy.' Or any number of things."

"It seems to me," began Climber, "if I were attempting to communicate in this clumsy way, I would begin with simple things. 'Stone' would do just fine."

"Who knows how these creatures think?" returned Disapproval.

"Does this mean," said Caretaker, "that we agree these creatures have volition? Free will?"

Silence fell, and I understood their fear. Were we dealing with demons after all? It had been intelligent not mentioning my unseen connection. But right then I didn't care much.

A runner came up from the village and broke the moment. "A thing is standing on the ridge, watching the village! A thing we have not seen."

"That's impossible," I cried. "I—" And I stopped myself from saying, *I felt no connection.*

"Of course it's possible, Binder." Infertility looked amused. "We sent you to go watch them. Now, they have sent someone to watch us."

SATO DID NOT PLAN originally to follow Thalia. Or maybe I did, he thought to himself as he moved through the forest.

The sun was a broad haze overhead, and the sky a bright plate. It made looking up difficult. Sato just walked, looking at the ground, thinking about Antonia, thinking about Bertini.

As he climbed the ridge he remembered the dream—hallucination?—he'd had when he met Antonia there. *Later. I will think about Lindsay later. How much later?*

He felt someone near him so strongly he stopped and looked around. He was alone.

At the top of the ridge, he looked back toward the ship. It looked like an innocent, black lentil lying quietly on the grass. He shrugged and turned to the forest. Sato had learned tracking early in his cartography training, and Thalia had made no effort to hide her passing. Her trail was obvious.

"Why not?" he said softly. He'd follow it for a while and see if he found anything interesting, then veer off and just enjoy the woods for a while. Anything to get away from the emotional maelstrom back at the *Hirohito*.

The trail led along the ridge and down into a kind of valley below the mountains. As he followed her trail, he noticed it changed into a well-used path. Soon, it appeared to have been cleared and maintained. He stopped. "This is a road," he said to the forest. It was silent.

A road? How could the clean team miss a road? Pretty damned shoddy work. I should go back, he thought. I could screw up everything doing this. Roads lead somewhere...

He laughed shortly and shouldered his pack. The road broadened until it was wide enough for three men, or perhaps as many as half a dozen Calibii. Trails led from it into the bush. It took a steep downturn into the bowl of the valley toward the river. He stopped there and left the road to climb a high ridge overlooking the valley. From the knapsack he took binoculars.

For a long time, he watched the valley. He could see huts, common areas resembling cooking fires, clearly marked lines of cultivation. The bottom of the valley was covered with Calibii.

He reset the binoculars to infrared and looked again. There was little heat being generated in the village—most of it came from the Calibii themselves. It was still measurable, however. A clean team could not have missed this. What was going on?

Gradually, it dawned on Sato, and his hands shook. This was all wrong. This planet was virgin. It was uncleared. No human had ever been here before.

MEGAN HELD the glass of ice water to her forehead. It had been eighty years since she'd had a headache. This one seemed to be making up for lost time.

It is only worry. Relax and try to sleep.

She laughed and stood up, wandering around the bridge. Sato had left the *Hirohito* a couple of hours before. Bertini was still asleep, and Antonia was still watching over him. Anything she wanted to know about the *Hirohito*, the *Shenandoah*, what went on within it or around it was hers. She knew it the way others knew the position of the hands, the feel of the roof of the mouth. It was as close to her as sight, taste, touch.

What a frozen bitch I have become.

She moved toward the airlock and stood, watching the outside. Here in the ship, she could hold out or mask the rampant radio from Caliban's plants. She communicated with the *Hirohito* and the *Hirohito* communicated with her by radio, her link to the *Shenandoah*. She could not maintain that link outside. She would be cut off, isolated and alone.

Megan had routed the plants' signals away from her so she wouldn't be distracted. She listened to them now, the half-conscious howls, the low grunts, the agonizing screams all through the short- to long-wave bands. She could even detect the faint whimper of microwaves from some of the more primitive plants.

I would like to go out there.
Why? And why now?
I just do.
You just do because you are restless. And you are restless because you don't feel completely in control.
Be that as it may, I would like to go out there.
You could do that. You would only be alone for a little time. You were alone once.

She shook her head and held herself.

No. Never again.
Was it so terrible?
It wasn't terrible then. It would be terrible now, when I've been so long part of a pair, when I've been so much more than I was.
Not so much more.
You don't know.
Neither do you. You've purged the memories. I still hold them.

There was a long pause. Megan watched the grass bend stiffly in the breeze. The wind was cold through the airlock, and she stepped to one side out of the force of it.

You can go outside if you want. And not be alone.
How?
Go out at night.

Such a simple idea. She felt stupid for not thinking of it before. It was late afternoon now. In just a short time it would be dark, and the plants' signals would drop to nearly nothing.

She smiled and went back into the ship for a cup of coffee.

"WHERE DOES the creature stand?" I asked, trying to force its appearance through my thick mind. Stupid, stupid. Of *course* one would follow me eventually. They had already come into the forest once. Now one had found my village.

"Are they dangerous?" asked Climber.

"*I* was killed," said Traverse mildly.

I could not speak immediately, missing him that had been and not understanding that was. "I couldn't say." I turned to the runner. "Speak quickly."

"He stands at the top of the ridge overlooking the valley, up from where the road turns down toward the river."

Traverse and I had once watched the valley from there.

"I will go watch him and try to discover his motives." I looked at each one of them.

"Motives! From these things?" cried Disapproval.

"Wait a moment," said Caretaker. He turned to the runner. "You said 'he.'"

The runner continued. "My friend Sometime found him as she was gathering nuts. She was as close to him as I am to you. She said he had male insides, whatever his outsides were."

Infertility turned to me. "You said a female made mouth noises at you."

"That is right."

"Then they are a mixed group," she mused. "They are not an isolated sport, but a reproducing community."

"Community!" cried Disapproval. "You leap to conclusions, as always. What do you know of these creatures? They live in metal; they kill randomly; they speak with mouth noises. What community could be made of that? Aside from the obvious impossibility of actually *communicating* with mouth noises, what actual evidence of a community do we actually have?"

"Disapproval's right," said Climber reluctantly. "We still actually know nothing."

"For such reason, I go." I left them before they could detain me further and before I had to hear Traverse speak again.

Late afternoon had come by the time I reached him. He was still standing, holding up one of their metal artifacts to his oversized head and turning both of them this way and that, pointing toward the valley. His attention, it seemed, was indicated by where he pointed the front of his head. I was standing behind him in the brush, and he appeared not to notice me. However, it was still day, and if I kept myself back ambient light could not be discerned from seeing light. I kept myself hidden.

He looked up and made a mouth noise, hurriedly stuffed the artifact into the bag at his feet, and slung it on his back. He started back down the ridge. At the road, he began to run in a slow lope.

I took to the trees above him, trying to remain quiet. He did not seem to notice—at least he did not turn his head toward me as he did when he was watching the village.

Night fell and I was forced to the road, using the plants around me for light. He would have to see me now, so I strode out boldly and tried to hide my fear.

He stopped but did not turn his head toward me. Instead, he took the bag off his back and held it open while he rummaged around inside. He brought out a metal rod with a bulbous end and pointed it ahead of him. Nothing happened, but he put the bag on his back and moved on, pointing it ahead of him.

It occurred to me he couldn't see me.

I caused the bushes around me to flare. He made no sign of having seen me.

He was blind.

No wonder they spoke in mouth noises. But how did he avoid objects, find the trail?

Well, I reasoned, if they have not sight, they must use something other than sight.

I followed closely then, using as much light as I needed and only trying to keep quiet.

We came to the ridge and started down.

BERTINI WOKE in darkness, yet he could see. Rain, dressed in shadow, sat across the room from the bed.

"You're alive," he breathed.

"No," she said and laughed.

He shook his head and sat up, shook his head again. There was no light in the room. He reached for the switch, but she stopped him.

"Don't," she said.

He felt half asleep, almost drugged. "What is going on?"

"I've come to say I'm sorry."

"Sorry?" He stared at her. She seemed lit by a pale moonlight or starlight. *But the windows in the cabin are closed.*

"It was a stupid, useless, romantic thing to do."

"What?"

"Stowing away on the *Divers Arts.*"

It was as if he'd been hit in the stomach with a brick. "Yeah."

"You didn't have to kill Praihm for me."

"I didn't." He exhaled slowly. "I killed him for me. God, how I wanted him dead. The forty years in prison I spent for you."

"You could have contested it. Bernard wanted you to."

Bertini shrugged.

"Did you think I *wanted* you in prison?"

"I deserved it."

"For what? Killing me? I did that very well on my own. I acted on impulse. I wanted to surprise you. I wanted to fly to the stars on the wings of my beloved." She stopped a moment, breathed slowly. "I was scared I couldn't wait for you."

A deep-seated, coal-black anger welled up in him. "Damn you!" he roared and stood over her. "I would have come back. I would have gotten you on the ship if only you'd asked me to. I'd have done *anything* for you. And you went and got yourself killed. Damn you. *Damn* you." He sat down on the bed and stared at the floor.

After a few moments, she came to him, and soon after he fell asleep again. When he awoke, he heard mixed shouts and cries, and he was alone.

MEGAN STOOD in the airlock bay, listening to the breeze, listening for the overbearing radio hiss of Caliban's plants. The breeze was gentle, the hiss almost nonexistent. She stepped down onto the springy grass.

> It is very like the first time.
> *That's another memory I hold for you.*
> Let me fantasize what it must have been like.
> *You were an ensign, then, and I was not at all.*

Just so.

She doused the ship's lights to minimalize any accidental photosynthesis. She had no need of the lights. All the sight she needed came from the *Hirohito* and the *Shenandoah*. With a gesture she made herself naked.

Come dance with me.
I will.

A form came to her, big and amorphous, with features of eyes and mouth but no face. He moved with her, and they danced along the meadow under the stars.

Far away from the ship under the edge of the forest they lay down together. She gasped as he entered her—or she him, she was unsure—but she grasped by the arms and back. They changed to suit her, and it was as making love with a cloud, or thunder, or a shower of gold. She did not notice the approaching light.

Megan...
Not *now*.

An approaching hiss distracted her, and she ignored it, holding him to her, in her.

Megan!

His touch began to fade. Desperately, she grabbed for him, and the touch faded like smoke. The hiss changed to a roar and drowned him, and he disappeared. She reached forward and fell on her hands, pain stabbing through one palm.

"What?" Her sight dimmed and she was left with the dark and the stars. She was clothed again. A trembling light moved toward her. She sobbed and tried to stand, but her legs quivered and shook, and she fell again. She held her hands to her ears to drown out the sound of the plants. A light shone on her, and she looked at it blind, crippled and lost.

10

Sato stared at the captain. Her eyes were red and unseeing, and her body twitched convulsively. "Megan," he whispered.

She turned toward his voice and made a croaking sound.

He bent down and tried to help, but she thrashed against him. *She's so small. Why did I never see before how small she is?*

He knelt beside her and picked her up in his arms. Again, she thrashed against him but then quieted. She lay her head against his chest, murmuring without words. She was much heavier than she looked but light enough to carry. *A touch. I have never touched her.*

In a few moments they were near the ship, and she began to come to life.

"What?" Her voice broke, and she stopped. "What are you—" She stopped again and looked at him, then at herself. She held on to herself and shuddered. "I can walk now."

Sato let her down slowly so she could test herself. Megan stood, walked ahead of him, stopped at the airlock, and turned back to him. "Thank you," she said.

He shrugged, not knowing what to say.

"Don't—" She stopped, looked inside the ship. "Please don't tell anyone about this."

"There's enough we have to think about," he said.

She nodded and disappeared inside.

He followed her in, but she moved toward her cabin. He, instead, went to the bridge.

No one was there. *Good,* he thought.

Damn right, we have enough to think about.

For several weeks now, the optical cameras on the *Shenandoah* had been patiently taking pictures of Caliban. Sato took the raw data and selected the local area of the *Hirohito*.

Maps are patterns. The cartography systems in the *Shenandoah* were pattern analyzers. Deep within them was one program located in all exploratory ships to determine areas inconsistent with the surrounding "natural" areas: artificial structures.

Sato took the data and broke them down by heat output, then fed them to the program. The result was positive. He then took straight optical viewing of the valley. Again, the result was positive. He broke the data down by drainage systems, vegetation patterns, even through the radio mapping equipment he and Bertini had cobbled together out of communications devices and some of the kitchen equipment. Still positive.

It was as he had thought at the village. There was no *way* anyone could have missed this. There had been no clean team. There had been no automatic probe. Or if there had been either, the reports were lies and forgeries.

Hell, he thought. Of course I have a lot more to think about than Megan losing it outside. This is no mere violation. This is treason.

FROM A SAFE DISTANCE, I watched them enter their craft.

Mouth noises, I thought. They had tried to communicate with me. I could feel that thread to the female inside, only now it felt different, as if connected to someone else, someone not listening to it. I stood first on one foot, then the other. What to do? What to do?

Traverse's voice came back to me: *"Tell me. You are wiser than I, being older and female. Was that a demon?"*

I still did not know. They had killed my lover, upset my kind, and shattered my life. I cried out to them. There was no response. *Stone,* I thought. I found on the ground the rock the female had been pointing to. *All right, then. Stone.* I picked it up and held it. No, it was too light. I threw it away and found a rock half buried in the sod. I pulled it out, dragging grass flashing in death as the strands were uprooted. It was heavy, and I bowed under the weight as I brought it over to where the creatures had entered. I held it high and brought it down on the side of the ship. It rang like thunder; again I brought it down.

I stood back and gasped for breath. Nothing. I cried out to them again, challenged them to come out and fight me. Nothing.

I brought up the rock and brought it down with all my strength. I made mouth noises at them. I threw the dirt and sod at them. "Answer me!"

The side finally opened, and she came out, fully connected to me now.

I made her mouth noise at her. *May your life be shattered as mine was!*

She stood there, her head frozen in my direction.

Mouth noises. I was suddenly tired. I sat back on the grass and just lay there, filled with loss and not able to move at all.

She came closer. Mouth noises blared at her from the craft. She ignored them and knelt next to me. "Die," I said weakly. I felt her closeness to me. "Or at least kill me."

She did neither but slowly pulled me to her, and I made no mouth noises, nor did she. All we could hear was the sound of our breathing.

"Stone," she finally said, and now I understood her.

"Stone," I agreed.

ANTONIA CAME AWAKE suddenly and fully. Bertini slept next to her. She sat up and listened. There were facts around her to be used: she was in Bertini's cabin, she'd obviously had sex recently, the ship was quiet as if no one but they were in it. But these were only facts as furniture. She did not think about them as if they were important. Thalia was coming.

She left Bertini's room for her own. She didn't know how Thalia would react to human sexual odor, so she took a shower. Ten minutes later she was dressed and glued to the monitor in her room. Sato was carrying Megan toward the ship, and Thalia followed them.

Rage and pain and confusion—Thalia was feeling all of these. Antonia reached toward her through their bond and was rejected as if she were slapped. *Get away from me!*

"Oh, God," Antonia whimpered. Thalia hurt so much. It hurt to feel that pain. It hurt Antonia more to know she caused it. The three of them came to the ship. When Sato followed Megan in through the airlock, Antonia switched the pickup back outside.

Thalia receded from her, but Antonia was patient. She could feel something coming. Finally, she went to the bridge. Sato was staring at program output on the monitor. When she came in, he erased it, and for a moment she felt hurt, but the pain was crowded out by the feeling of Thalia approaching again. The ship clanged.

"What the hell?" Sato looked behind him. The door of the airlock rang again like a bell.

"She's beating on my ship," said Megan from the hatchway. She'd been behind Antonia. Megan glanced to the fire control console and shrugged. "She can't hurt it."

Antonia ignored them both.

Imagine a bridge of glass, a bright, prismatic crossing between two places: each one dark to the other. Imagine flames and iron, wood and water. Antonia reached across the bridge again to me, and I drew back. I saw her. I felt her. Again, I pushed her away.

Antonia shook her head. Again, the ship rang. On the monitors, she could see Thalia lying on the ground. She stood slowly and walked to the airlock as in a trance.

"Antonia . . ." began Sato.

"Let her be," said Megan and held his arm.

The airlock cycled, and she stepped outside. She felt the coolness against her skin.

This is me. This is Antonia. No one else, Thalia. If you want me now, take me. This is me offering myself. Take what I have.

And her arms were filled with warm fur.

BERTINI SAT UP in the darkness and didn't know where he was.

His heart was pounding, and his breathing hoarse and ragged. Outside his room, he heard shouts and a clanging. *Afternoon, I'm still on Afternoon.* He clawed at the window and unfastened it, pinching his fingers. The shouts and the clanging quieted. Outside, he could see it was only night. Rain did not like the night, he remembered.

Rain had looked up at him on the bridge.

Rain is dead.

He remembered speaking to her, making love with her. In the blankets and on his body was the scent of sex. *A dream?* He chuckled low in his throat. Wet dreams, at his age?

Rain had looked up at him on the bridge.

He slid out of the bed and took a quick shower. Afterward, he felt better. He'd been talking to Rain in his mind for too long. He'd seen a woman on the flyer; heard her voice. Now he'd seen her on the bridge. *I've been hallucinating.*

His memories were a jumble from the bridge to here: Rain helping him, bringing him here, waiting for him until he woke.

It was a dream. Somebody'd helped him here—probably Antonia or Sato. And he'd dreamed the rest. It *had* to be a dream.

It bothered him, but not, he realized, all that much. He felt cleaner inside, emptier, easier. He still felt sleepy and lethargic. He smiled and shrugged, then began to dress.

SATO WATCHED THEM, his hands hovering over the fire controls, the lasers aimed at Thalia. *Make a wrong move. Please.*

"We are going to be in deep trouble if we kill another sentient." Megan stood next to him. "I think she'll be all right."

He didn't move for a long time, but Antonia and Thalia just held one another. "Maybe," he said shortly. He locked the console and stood back.

Did you think your life was anything but temporary? Did you really think you possessed her, as a thing or an object? Did you expect to consume her as bread? Laughter. You are always doomed to disappointment.

"What's going on?"

They turned, and Bertini stood in the hatchway, blinking like a great bear.

Sato nodded toward the monitors. "Contact."

"Damn. I didn't know she had it in her."

"I bet you didn't," Sato said bitterly.

Bertini looked at him sharply, then back to the monitors. "I would say, now, we have a chance."

Sato laughed.

MEGAN BACKED AWAY from them, feeling as hard and knotted inside as wet wood. She sat down at the table.

Did you track Sato this afternoon?
I couldn't get through the forest canopy. Too much heat was masked by the leaves.
Some help you are.
Megan, you have contact here. Look at the monitors. Up there is what you wanted. Your ticket out of here. Our ticket out of here.
I was helpless out there when he found me.
What do you mean?

I mean I could barely see, barely walk. I had no speech, no legs. Sato had to *carry* me back.

Pause.

You've become dependent on me for motor coordination. I didn't think that would happen.
Nor I. Half the pathways in my brain must loop back through you and back to me. I felt lost. Blind. Paralyzed.
This has never been reported—
We are the last, you and I. We've outlasted them all by at least a hundred years. There's no data on something like us.
Still, Megan, we have contact *here. We've got a real chance to get out of this intact!*
You didn't feel it, did you?
What?
You went blithely on, waiting for me to come back on line.
I was frantic. I could tell Sato was there and he could help—
But you didn't lose yourself, you didn't have sudden attacks of pain and disorientation.
I'm a machine. *I have to be able to catch you when you fall. That's my* job. *That's my* design. *I can't* lose myself. *What did you expect?*
I don't know. I expected us to interpenetrate each other, to connect. Instead, I feel parasitic.
Don't say that. Who do you think gives me life? The world goes gray without you, Megan. It drops down to circuits and transistors, and all the humanity washes away.
Humanity? Which of us is human? Both?
Neither?

There was no answer.
"Megan?"
She looked up with a start at Bertini. He was watching her with an amused expression. "Yes, Engineer."
"At least join us for the duration, Captain."
She was suddenly angry, but stopped herself. She chuckled.

Maybe, my ship and lover, both of us are still a little bit human.

SATO SILENTLY WAITED with the rest of them, watching the monitors. Antonia and Thalia slowly released one another. Thalia rose to her hind legs and backed away from Antonia, then turned and vanished into the night. The infrared screen showed that she moved to the edge of the forest and stopped.

Antonia entered the airlock some minutes later.

Sato leaned against the consoles. Bertini and Megan were sitting at the table. Antonia walked into quiet.

She sat down at the table and smiled at them, lingering a few moments on Sato.

Am I wrong about her? He did not smile back.

"Well," she said slowly, "we made contact."

There was a slow easing of tension, a relaxation. Bertini grinned broadly. Megan gave a thin smile. Sato did not respond.

"When will she return?" asked Megan.

Antonia looked up at the monitors. Thalia still stood at the edge of the forest. "I'm not sure. Probably tomorrow. I felt an urge to get on with it. Her people are pressuring her to find out what we are. Apparently, we've made as much of an impact on them as they've made on us."

"What of the death?" asked Bertini softly.

Antonia gave him a slight smile. "Thalia was the other Calibi, all right. She had some special relationship with the Calibi I—I killed." She looked over to Sato and reached out a hand.

I must be wrong. Or she does not need me for a lover, but for something else? What? Holding? Caring?

Nervously, he stepped behind her and took her hand. She held on to it tightly and pulled him until her head was resting against his belly. He began to rub her neck.

"I'm not sure what the relationship was." She closed her eyes.

He kneaded away the tension in her neck. After a moment, she stopped his hands by holding them to her neck. She leaned back against him and smiled.

"There's more," he began reluctantly.

Megan looked up at him sharply. It made him angry.

"I took a hike today, and I ended up following Thalia back to her village."

Bertini leaned back in his chair and leaned his head against his hands.

Sato nodded to him. Megan did not move.

"We haven't really done any speculating on how the Calibii live. We always assumed because the clean team report didn't mention them, it was because they didn't show up. Perhaps they were nomads or widely scattered bands. They're neither." He stared at Megan. "Thalia's village is near here. It's big, and it's got structures and crops, and the river is partially dammed. The village shows up on *our* alarm scans, and any clean team's systems are going to be much more sophisticated. It's what the clean teams are for." Sato took a deep breath. "There was no clean team. Caliban is uncleared. We were in violation the minute we came out of n-space."

Bertini moved to the navigation console and brought up the *Shenandoah*'s flight plan. "It says we're going to Caliban. That couldn't have gotten past traffic control if Caliban is uncleared."

Sato nodded. "I spent a while in here this evening before Thalia came. That's what it says on the navigator's flight plan. I went back in the transmission log to see what was actually sent to flight control." As he spoke, he brought it up on the monitor.

"Onas," breathed Antonia. "That's light years from here." She shook her head. "We're not even on the manifest. Just Megan."

"Yeah. We'd never show up on Earth. An elegant solution," said Sato tiredly. "Onas is in frontier development, so they don't have to send reports back to Earth. It might be years before this is checked, and then it would just be another lost record on a frontier world."

"I never intended any harm to you." Megan folded her hands in her lap. "You would never have known."

"But the clean team's specifications are forgeries," said Sato, and his voice was stone. "The clean team is a forgery. Caliban has never been looked at by an autoprobe."

"No," Megan said faintly, "there was an autoprobe." She glanced at Sato, then looked at her hands. "But it wasn't a human probe."

"You intercepted a foreign probe!" shouted Sato. "Treason wasn't enough?"

"I did *not* intercept anything, Navigator Sperling!" The echoes of her voice rang in the bridge for a moment. "The probe was intercepted by a man named Swain. He decoded the probe's report and came to me." She smiled slightly. "I've known Swain for years. He knew I was desperate. No contract I could find would let me keep the *Shenandoah*. I had eighty years of bad debts, and they were catching up with me. *Are* catching up with me even now. If I don't have something when we get back, I'll lose the ship, and it will be dismembered."

"Dismembered?" Sato shook his head. "They don't dismember ships anymore."

"They do if the captain's hardwired into them," said Bertini.

"Oh, God." Sato sat down at the table. "That's why you were in such bad shape outside?"

Megan nodded. "I planned to discharge you back on Earth, take off again, and come in with an 'accidental' sighting of Caliban, then claim exploitation rights. With that, I could keep my ship and come out rich." She smiled coldly. "It didn't work." She looked at each of them hard. "The reward for finding a new set of sentients is all I can hope for, but it will let me have the *Shenandoah* a little longer. I'd have killed for the *Shenandoah* then. I'll kill for it now. It's my life in ways you don't even know." She leaned her head to one side, and Sato thought he saw the glitter of madness in her eyes. "I will be Caliban's Prospero and tame it. I named it Caliban—no one else—and it's mine. By Sycorax, I plan to keep it."

11 MEGAN: ON MOTHERLODE

Afterward, as always, it took Megan a long time to catch her breath. Hanna lay on her side looking down on her, measuring her with smoky eyes. She smiled suddenly and kissed Megan, then rolled on her back. Megan lay there a long time, feeling relaxed and warm. She tried to snuggle against Hanna, but the older woman did not respond. Hanna's eyes were blank.

She was gone again, and Megan felt very alone.

Megan sighed and sat up. The captain's cabin of the *Lanford* was spartan and small—like Hanna Pemberton, Megan's Captain. The only thing of color in the cabin was Azul, Hanna's blue parrot, on his perch near the bed. He turned his head and eyed her first from one side, then from the other. Hesitantly, Megan reached toward him. Azul opened his mouth and hissed at her, spreading his wings.

She let her hand fall back to the bed. "I don't like you much, either." Megan rose and began to dress.

Hanna came back and looked at her. "You're leaving?" The question sounded idle.

"*You* left."

She smiled again. "I was just checking the ship."

Megan finished dressing. "It's more than that. You were gone. I don't know where you went."

Hanna leaned back against the bunk. The parrot hopped down off its perch and waddled over to her shoulder. Standing there, he glared at Megan. Hanna stroked him under his beak. Her gaze slowly left the bird and fell on Megan. "You'll have to get a ship to find out, First Mate Sze."

Silent and angry, Megan slapped the door open and left. Before the door closed, she heard behind her a quiet laughter.

SHE WAS STILL angry drinking coffee in the kitchen an hour later. Having an affair with the first mate seemed almost an afterthought to Hanna. For the first mate, it was something more. *Why am I doing this?*

Because you're damned lonely, that's why. *Empty* might even be a better word. Could this be a sound basis for love?

Shut up, she told herself.

"Hanna tell you?" Bill Pirot asked, leaning in the door.

"Christ!" she yelled as she spilled the coffee. "Don't *do* that. Make a noise like a live person."

"Sorry." He backed away and held his hands up. He watched her a moment and leaned his head to one side.

She stared at him, then back at her coffee. "You look like Azul."

He didn't say anything immediately. "You and Hanna have a row?"

She held her hands together. "Not really."

"Right. Right." He nodded. "Of course not."

Megan smiled. Bill was small and thin, with big ears wrapped around a grin. it was impossible not to like him. "Tell me what?"

"Hot damn! She left it to Engineer Bill." He rubbed his hands in anticipation. "*We* found a *planet*." He shrugged. "Actually, the *Lanford* found it. But it's ours, Megan."

"So?"

Bill looked again at the ceiling in exasperation, then back at her. "Don't start acting stoic like Dennis. Pilots are supposed to be crazed, not first mates."

Megan laughed. "Assume I'm properly enthused. So we found a planet."

"Not just any planet. We found—" he held up one finger, "one: a new, unknown, hitherto unexploited planet, and two—" he held up a second finger, "an *Earthlike*, new, unknown, hitherto unexploited planet."

She whistled in wonder. "So that's what she was doing."

"Who?"

Megan shook her head. "Never mind. Son-of-a-gun." She leaned back in her chair and stared at him. "We're rich, Bill. Loaded. Wealthy. Selling the exploration rights alone is going to make us a bundle." Damn you, Hanna. Maybe I will buy me a ship."

"Not yet," Bill chuckled. "We still have to claim it."

"Don't do this to me." She folded her arms across her chest. "How do we claim it? We're couriers, not surveyors."

Bill shook his head. "We don't *have* to survey it. We can use the 'accidental discovery' rule. We perform what the law calls a 'reasonable survey'—"

"With what equipment? We are, I repeat, a courier ship."

"By the old rules a 'reasonable survey' consisted of a recorded orbital flight and a landing. Then each of us picks up a handful of dirt and makes the claim."

Megan shook her head. "A handful of dirt." She laughed. "Do we incant like druids, too?"

Bill nodded. "Almost. It comes from the old homesteading and foreclosure laws of the nineteenth century. The *Lanford*'s not sure, but it might go back to Columbus. This law has old roots.''

"No kidding. What's the course?''

"Toward Tau Ceti. We jump in an hour.''

"Why are we waiting an hour?''

THE UNCONSCIOUSNESS of the interface, the orbital flight, and a handful of dirt:

Something. Something close. Something here.

They stood outside the ship in spacesuits. The wind of Motherlode whistled across the hoses and fixtures on their helmets.

Motherlode. Megan grimaced. The planet was covered with long boulder-dotted prairies the color of winter grass and had a low, breezy feel to it. It did not deserve the name Hanna gave it. The name was too graceless, too frivolous. It was—Megan shook her head. What difference did it make? She shivered. Maybe it was being from Luna that made her feel so raw and vulnerable, the abundance of life here compared to the sterility of home. But she'd been on other planets and not felt this way. She shrugged. It wasn't important. Megan was here to get rich.

Hanna held up a handful of dirt in her gauntlet. "I claim this land for the private company *Lanford* Courier Ship, incorporated December 14, 2098, out of New Bedford Shipyards, Earth.'' Dennis and Bill followed. It was Megan's turn.

Hearing a whisper, feeling a touch on the eyes. She cleared her throat.

"Thinking of the money, Megan?'' teased Bill.

"Not the money.'' Not the sound of the wind. Not the feeling of earth through the boots. It was—she shook her head in confusion. Her mind just stopped there: here is the feeling; *you* figure it out. *It feels... what?* An echo of a shout. The sound of following footsteps. A sense of the sea.

"Megan?'' asked Hanna.

Come on, say it. Don't you want to be rich?

The silence deepened with tension.

"I can't,'' she said at last. Panic bubbled up inside of her. *What is going on? Just what the hell is going on?*

"You can't what?'' Hanna's cold look pierced her, and she looked down.

"I can't claim it." She shook her head. She tried to laugh and couldn't, managed an embarrassed grin. "Hey, we don't even know what we're claiming. We ought at least to stay here for a couple of days."

"We're a courier ship. We don't have a lot of time. And it's not necessary." Hanna looked blankly around them. "Looks pretty dull to me. Just do it, Megan."

Dull? Here could never be dull. She shook her head again to clear it. "No."

Hanna stared at her now. "I said, do it."

Dennis watched the sky overhead, oblivious to the exchange. Bill watched first Hanna, then Megan. He made a movement as if to speak, then shook his head.

"You have something to say, Bill?" Hanna's voice was a razor.

"No, Captain." He looked at Megan apologetically.

"We're waiting for *you*, then, Megan." *Don't cross me. I'm warning you.*

Megan heard her as if she'd said the words. She took a deep breath. "Look, I want to be rich as much as you do. But I want to look around. Yeah, I know we're a courier ship."

"Megan—"

"Still," she hurried on, "there's nothing we're carrying marked urgent, and we can make it to Earth well within margin if we take a few days off here. If I haven't found what's bothering me by then," she shrugged, "I'll just do it. Okay?"

Hanna was silent a moment, her eyes blank and gone, then back again. "Three days. We can stay three days."

What if it takes longer than that? What if what *takes longer than that?* She looked at Hanna and shuddered. "Three days."

THEY SEEMED to range from basketball-sized to one old two-ton monster. They had round shells like a nautilus out of which grew ten jointed legs, two eyes, and a collection of antennae.

"They look like crabs," muttered Bill.

Megan stared down at them from the flyer, feeling for strangeness the way a wreck diver might search the overgrown bottom of the sea. Nothing. Except for their antennae, they did not move. From space, their motionlessness and smooth white shells had made them only look like boulders. The various colors of their legs and eyes contrasted oddly with the white of their shells. The colors ranged from the dusky orange of the big one to the bright electric pink of the smaller ones.

"Crabs?" On Luna, and the only crabs she had ever seen had been baked.

"Yeah. I grew up on Puget Sound. My dad used to fish for king crab." He chuckled. "Butter. Lemon. Hmm."

"Their limbs are asymmetrical."

"Yeah. One big claw, a smaller claw, then the rest of the legs. They're not supposed to be this big."

"No?" Megan said absently. Bill lowered the flyer until they were almost even with the tops of the larger shells. "There's a regular spacing between them," she said.

"Yeah. I noticed that. They must have a feeling for territory."

Megan caught what he'd said before and looked at him. "Why shouldn't they be this big?"

Bill shrugged. "I meant in terms of Earth invertebrates. Look, their legs are hard and jointed—like our crabs and insects. On Earth, crabs have no bones, so the hard skin serves as a skeleton. But there's a problem. The strength of the skeleton increases according to the surface area of the thing, but as it gets bigger, its mass increases according to its volume. The skeleton can't support its body without getting much thicker, but if it gets thicker it gets too heavy to move." Bill shrugged. "There are other reasons. Their lungs aren't efficient enough to support a strong metabolism, and the bigger you get on land, the more energy it takes just to move around. That's why the really big invertebrates are in the ocean. There, both problems are solved."

"Hmm. They solved those problems here, too. Only without an ocean." A crazy place where the crabs grow as big as houses. "I grew up on Luna—no life at all."

One of the crabs made a noise, a low rattle like a cricket or a locust. She couldn't see where it was coming from: the crabs were motionless, only their eyes jerking mechanically as they followed the slow movement of the flyer. More crabs took up the cry, and the sound grew into a low scream. "Let's go back." She held her hands over her ears.

"What?" Bill shouted back.

"Back!"

Bill nodded, pulled the flyer up, and banked back toward the *Lanford*, and behind them the crabs resolved again by distance into boulders.

THE SHIP'S LIBRARY was full of nature films—some bureaucrat's idea of what a ship's crew would like. Megan selected all the sections showing anything like the crabs and watched them, then watched them again. She watched crabs molt, eat, change shells if they didn't grow their own, fight one another, mate, die, and be eaten.

Are you what's making me feel so strange?

She watched the insects and the high diplomatic arts of ants, termites, and bees. These were hive creatures, however. The individual animals weren't much on talking. A male fiddler crab's beat on the shell of the female to get her attention centered on mating: high diplomacy. It took something as important as propagation of the species to cause that. Nothing less would do.

"This is getting me nowhere," she muttered.

Wearily, she asked for the films of the crabs here on Motherlode. The screen jumped from time of movement to time of movement, skipping the long hours of crab inactivity. Several of the crabs had been walking in long parallel rows and dragging their hind limbs. Furrowing, Megan thought. She stood up and expanded the picture. Before her a huge crab walked a few feet, stopped, walked further, stopped. She could almost hear the scraping of his shell against the earth. There was a pattern, a territory to his movements. All of the crabs so walking seemed to have their own territories.

Plowing? She shook her head. Are they agricultural? Are they *sentient*, for God's sake?

Megan sat back down at the console and asked about agriculture among animals on Earth. She learned about termites and ants.

Hive animals.

She rubbed her eyes. They could be doing anything—rubbing their bodies against the dirt to remove parasites, marking a mating ground. And anyway, what would they be doing to her? She'd been on a score of planets and never felt this way. Why *now*? Why *here*?

THE GRASS STROKED her legs as she walked toward them. The sun was a faceted sparkle in the great bowl of the sky. It beat down on her, and she tasted salt on her lips. She was naked, but that seemed appropriate. It was hot, after all. She reached them, and they towered over her, the broad domes of their shells shining polished and bright. They crooned to her, first one, then another, and she smiled at them. The expressions on their long faces were written now so she could understand them: this one eager, that one petulant, another enigmatic. Megan came to the largest one and stood before it. The creature leaned back on its rear legs and reached for her. Megan cried out for joy—

Megan sat up suddenly, whimpering. Around her was her own familiar cabin. The sheets were wet, with the smell of her own fear. She couldn't move. If she did, something terrible would happen. "This is crazy," she muttered.

A long minute passed, then another. She turned and sat on the edge of the bed. Nothing happened. She stood and took down her robe, looking around the room for something—*what?*—to reach for her. She tied the knot around her robe quickly and stepped out into the corridor. The lights were muted. One of the hall clocks said two o'clock.

The kitchen had that washed-out, fluorescent gray look only kitchens have at two in the morning. The counter was a pale yellow, the table a grainy white. She dialed for tea and sat at the table, smelling the spicy, musty aroma. What had she been dreaming? She barely remembered feelings, shadow memories. Someone—no, some*thing*—had reached for her. She remembered finding the idea not at all horrible. Then why this terrible fear?

"Bad dreams?"

Megan looked up. Hanna stood over her, backlit from the lights, Azul a twisted shadow next to her head. It never surprised Megan anymore when Hanna appeared.

"Yeah." Megan shrugged. "I'll get over it. Have some tea. The dispenser's still hot."

"Okay." She dialed for a second cup and sat across from Megan. "You and Bill find anything out there?"

"Just the big invertebrates. Bill probably told you about that." She looked up at Hanna, then away.

Hanna nodded. "Anything about what's bothering you?"

Megan sipped her tea and shook her head. "Nothing, yet."

"Look," Hanna stared into her cup, "I'm sorry I leaned on you outside. That was uncalled for."

Alarm bells went off inside Megan. Hanna never apologized. Hanna never humbled herself. It just didn't happen.

"That's okay," Megan said slowly. "Everybody wants to get rich."

"I suppose." She shrugged and glanced over at Megan. Behind the warmth in her eyes, there seemed to be a calculating coldness. "I think maybe you wouldn't have been so adamant if I hadn't backed you into a corner."

"Maybe."

"So, we're friends again?"

Friends. Megan felt the emptiness inside of her deepen. A friend—or a lover, for that matter—ought to be someone you could depend on, someone who could hold you when you needed to be held. *That damned parrot is more important to her than I.* "Sure, we're friends."

"Good." There was a long silence. "I think we should leave tomorrow."

"Tomorrow." Her own voice sounded dull to her, lifeless.

"You agree? You could do the thing with the dirt in the morning, and we could have everything stowed and be on our way by the afternoon."

This trip was such a mistake. Sleeping with Hanna was just one more mistake in a long line. *Empty is what I am; empty is what I shall be.* "No. I'm not done."

The warmth in Hanna's eyes disappeared. "What do you mean? I thought—"

"I know what you thought." Her head began to hurt, and she rubbed her eyes. "I'm not going to claim Motherlode until I know what's bothering me. I have twenty percent of the trip. Any claim's got to be unanimous: that's the law. You can't force me, order me, or persuade me to leave before I know." She looked at Hanna. "And I've got to know. You don't know how much I've got to know." Megan brought her hands down and looked at Hanna. If there had been any warmth in her face before, it was gone now as if it had never been.

"How much do you want your rating, Sze?" Hanna's voice was clipped and precise.

Megan sighed. "It's all I've got."

"Then, three days, Sze." Hanna stood up. "I said three days, and I meant it." She turned and left the kitchen. Azul twisted his head and stared at Megan as they disappeared down the corridor.

ONE OF THE smaller crabs had died in the night.

It was unclear to Megan why this had happened. *Why should it be clear to me at all?* She reran the films of the area several times. The crab had been one of the still ones, unmoving since the *Lanford* had come. It had stood suddenly on its jointed legs, then moved over to one of the large crabs. The two crabs had brushed antennae and clasped legs for several minutes. The smaller crab staggered back and stumbled away from the group as if injured. It collapsed near one of the furrows. After a few minutes, the main part of its body sagged out of the shell. Its eyes clouded over and lost turgor, gradually sinking into their stalks. It did not move again.

She stopped the playback and stared at the body. In a human being, she thought, you could hold on to the illusion of life even when looking at a corpse. Death is grotesque because it looks like such an empty mockery of life. But death for this creature was not mere stillness. The eye stalks leaned forward into angles they could not have had in life, the eyes were almost invisible. The flexible membranes at the joints sagged and bulged as fluids came to rest. The carapace and head fell out of the shell, held together only by skin.

Megan looked away. *Why did this happen? What tragedy is here?*

And: *only an animal dies like this.*

"Okay," she said slowly. "Okay." How much have I seen in my life already? This empty death means little. Came the response: how do you know? Feel your own emptiness crying out before you say that.

She restarted the playback.

The other crabs took notice of the dead crab for the first time. Hesitantly, they stepped toward it.

They know it's dead! They're intelligent. They have to be.
She grabbed the edge of the command chair. It was as if they
sang to her: *we wait for you. Come to us.*

I've got to get out there.

The first one to reach the body touched it carefully, delicately. He grasped the forelimb and jerked it once, twice.
The forelimb came off in his claw, and he moved away from
the body and the others. He paused and appeared to look
around. Then he began to feed.

Megan blanked the screen and held herself. She rocked in
the chair for a long time, staring at nothing.

THE FIRST CAGE was heavy. It wasn't easy carrying *anything* in a suit, and this cage was a bitch. Azul squawked at
her.

"Shut up," she said evenly.

The next cage had the finches and the third the canaries.
After she'd carried all three outside into the naked air, she
stood next to the ship and watched them. The earphones
made their singing tinny and unreal, as if she were listening
to an old-time radio show.

Bill was waiting for her in the airlock. "Last I saw her
Hanna was mad. You know anything about that?"

"No." Megan looked at him. "But what makes this day
different from any other?"

"You *are* on a roll, aren't you?" He chuckled. "Be nice
if you made up with her."

Megan shook her head. "I'm busy. And not very interested."

"She'll like that."

"Tough." She pointed through the airlock port. "I took
some of the birds from the life support system."

He looked at her. "Why?" he said slowly.

"We use them as a backup to test our air, right?" She
watched the birds through the port. "Now they're testing
Motherlode's air."

"What about *us*? Our air?"

"I didn't take them all. We didn't need a goddamn avi-
ary just for testing the air."

Bill didn't respond but just stared at her. He leaned down and looked outside through the airlock port. "Christ on a stick! That's Hanna's parrot out there."

"Really?" She smiled.

"She'll skin you alive." Bill turned toward her slowly. "Don't let some spat between you and Hanna screw us all up."

"There's nothing between Hanna and me."

"I know." He looked back outside and shook his head. "And there never will be. Hanna's hardwired."

Megan shrugged. "Captains are always connected to the ship. They have to double as engineers—I know that."

He shook his head. "Engineers are *soft*wired. Our bodies are connected to the ship's body, but our mind is separate from the ship's mind. Hanna is *hard*wired—right into the ship's mind. She *is* the ship. It's her friend, lover, soul mate—whatever you want to call it. That's what being hardwired is all about."

Megan shivered. *Now I know where she went. What lover could compare with that?* It made Megan feel emptier. "So?" *A pretty faint show of defiance, Megan,* she told herself.

"She's crazy. Don't push her too far."

She pulled him away from the airlock port and checked the birds. They still looked healthy. "Maybe I'm crazy, too."

WE ARE OUT here.

"What?" Megan looked up from the console. There was nobody there. *Getting jumpy, Megan. Two days. It's been only two days. You have three. Try to keep your craziness under control.* Something was squirming underneath her mind. A fine tension ran through her body, a trembling in her hands, a sense of being watched. Madness like a dentist's drill whined in the back of the brain.

"Hush," she told herself. "Hush."

The birds were still okay, but she needed more tests of the air. Every ship had two air samplers. They were designed to monitor bacteria, viruses, and pollutants in the air in order to keep track of the state of the air recirculation system. They were redundant for safety's sake.

What the hell, she thought. We'll have one left.

She diverted the outside air through the spare sampler and back out to the air of Motherlode. In a few hours, she'd know all she could about the atmosphere of Motherlode.

"What the hell are you doing?"

Hanna spun Megan around in the command chair. Megan pushed her away. "You're wired in. You *know* what I'm doing."

Hanna's eyes smoldered like burning oil. "You took Azul, and now this. Now this." She looked blank for a moment, then came back. "You're going outside without a suit."

"The lady wins the cigar." Megan turned back to the console.

Hanna pulled her out of the chair and slammed her against the wall. *"Don't you dare turn away from me!"*

Megan's hands were knotted into shaking fists. "Don't do that," she said in a flat voice, looking at her hands. "Don't ever touch me like that again." She looked up at Hanna. "This is your ship. You're angry I've done something to hurt it. I know that. I think at one point I loved you, but something's replaced it. I know that, too." She looked at her fists and brought them close to her face, watched Hanna beyond them. "But if you touch me again, I'll kill you." *Crazy! I'm going crazy.* Slowly, she unclenched her hands.

Hanna leaned back against the bulkhead. She watched Megan warily. "Over the course of this trip you've become seriously disturbed."

From the way she spoke Megan knew they were being recorded. What difference did it make, anyway? Megan ran her fingers through her hair to get it out of her eyes and noticed it was tangled and knotty. She tried to remember when she had last brushed it. *The last time I took a shower, I think. When was that?*

"Megan?"

Megan started and looked at her. "Seriously disturbed. You were saying?"

"It is my considered opinion you are not fit for duty." Hanna leaned her head to one side and looked at her. Just like Azul, Megan thought and laughed.

"Fit for duty." Megan laughed again. "Probably true."

"I'm relieving you."

"I'm relieved." Megan shook her head. "That means you can vote my twenty percent." She shrugged. "Fine. I wouldn't try to leave, though."

Hanna's face want blank a moment. "I don't see why not."

"Because I've got," she reached into her pocket and held up a thin ceramic chip studded with connecting pins, "the start-up module."

Hanna didn't speak for a moment. "The engine passes diagnostics."

"I'm very good at what I do."

"We have spares."

Megan smiled, "Not anymore."

"You're bluffing. I've been watching you. You haven't had a chance to do anything like that."

"I did it when you weren't looking."

"There was no such time."

Megan stared idly at the console. "When Bill explained to me you were hardwired, and what that meant, I realized you'd had two lovers. Me and the *Lanford*. It takes a lot of concentration to be a good lover, for either a woman or a ship. You would require a good lover, right?" Hanna didn't answer, and Megan shrugged. "Not a whole lot of time left over for much else, and what's left is pretty easily fooled. I guessed a lot when you didn't come after me while I was putting Azul outside. So, I checked the performance statistics, and it seems about an hour before the *Lanford*'s systems suddenly started degrading. Know anything about that?"

Hanna remained silent.

"No matter. It was still going on, so I took the opportunity." She pressed the ends of the chip with her fingers, making it bow. "These chips are fragile." Megan looked up at Hanna. "I'm going outside. When I step out the airlock, I'll leave the chip behind. But don't rush me. I'd hate to break it. And I'd be awfully reluctant to tell you where I hid the spares."

"At least bring back Azul. He's got nothing to do with this. He's just a bird."

Megan sighed. "You don't understand. That's not surprising, I guess. I don't understand either. I'll bring Azul in on my way back."

"And just where are you going?"

Megan shrugged and took a deep breath. "I don't know."

But I'm going. By God, I'm going to find it. She looked at Hanna and smiled.

WE ARE ALL born lonely.

The madness in her was a friend, a companion, as she banked the flyer out of a screaming dive. The grin on her face was stiff and sore, but she could no more relax than she could return to the ship. She piloted the flyer with a lopsided grace and only the barest attention to its limits. If Bill had been with her, his knuckles would have been white from holding on to the flight couch. She flew on whim and impulse. Night fell, and she did not know where she was. Megan did not sleep, but flew blind, guiding herself here and there. Reason had not helped her against this. Now she was listening to psychosis.

She fell asleep in the couch and woke up in the gray hazy dawn, vaguely surprised she was still alive and out here. Why hadn't they come after her? She looked around the cabin. The radio was off. There was a radio beacon, but it was disconnected. Had she done that? It seemed a familiar idea.

Dark storm clouds moved toward her, occasionally showing a flash of hushed lightning. Yet the prairie looked lit from within by a warm golden light. The flyer was hovering, and the wind moved it in a slow rocking. Rain struck the glass in fat droplets and then dropped in sheets, blurring the land and making it difficult for her to see. Several lights on the command board winked red. She did nothing, watching the rain.

The rocking of the flyer grew more violent. Absently, she buckled the seat webbing and strapped herself in. A sudden gust spun the flyer around and made the world a crazy mosaic of lightning, clouds, and rain. Another gust upended the flyer and the motor whined as it tried to right itself. It could not and slid down gently through the air until it struck the earth, bounced slightly, and settled down. The air in the cabin was filled with a burning smell. Then the lights on the command board winked out. The flyer was dead, and she was alone.

By afternoon, the sky cleared and the sun came out and burned the prairie dry. She forced open the airlock door and stepped outside. The prairie was empty. She could smell the wet grass and the ozone left by the storm.

WE ARE HERE.

"What?" Megan shook her head and looked around. She must have walked for hours. Her feet were blistered and bloody, but they did not hurt. She could see her path written behind her in the long grass. They were around her now, their long faces open and questioning. Along the way she'd lost her clothes, but the loss did not seem important.

She stood in front of the oldest one, tall with its white dome and orange legs. *The dream!* Megan cried out to herself, but the voice was distant and unreal.

The oldest one stood back on her orange hind legs and opened her front mandibles. Megan could see the softer, more delicate, feathery palps ease away from the moist skin. The forelegs drew her close in a gentle embrace, and the palps touched her skin softly. The touch grew intimate.

Megan started. "What?" she cried out. The crab did not respond and touched her again. She tried to pull away but could not, and the crab touched her again.

THE WORLD SHIFTED and settled as if made of warm butter. She was not alone now, but she could not tell what was her and what was not. Voices spoke and were answered.

??? I had expected a male.

Why?

A creature presented itself to me as if it desired reproduction. I am female. You are female. Reproduction is impossible.

She was filled. Throughout the length and breadth of her self she felt no emptiness, no small pockets of loneliness that always threatened to engulf her. She danced, undulating through fluid.

So what?

There was no immediate answer.

What are you?

She was surrounded by taste, smell, and light touches across her body, the moan of wind over a shell, the color orange.

I live. I grow older and remember more as I grow. I am impregnated by the males, who then wither and die. Once a year I walk to the sea and wash my children from my legs so they may live in the sea. After a time, they return to me, and eventually they, too, can remember and speak. I am Orange.

Megan was surprised to find it was enough.

I would stay here forever.

You are not sufficient for me. I would not be so served.

She felt a wet tearing, a separation, a gradual withdrawal.

"Wait. Wait!" She was crying, holding on to Orange as she would hold on to life, inside her only a desperate need. She had no arms or eyes or mouth.

Inexorably, Orange pulled away from her. She held onto the last few moments with maniacal strength, and the separation stopped. Then sensations shook her, and she let go, and in that moment they were apart and drifting away. It took her a few seconds to understand what had happened, and then she knew: she'd had an orgasm.

MEGAN STUMBLED BACK and fell down. Orange pulled her legs together and sealed herself into her shell. The others watched her speculatively. Megan couldn't breathe. Her hands hurt, and she looked at them. The fingernails were broken and bloody. On Orange's dome there were red streaks above the crab's eyes.

She stood and backed away, staring at nothing. A red, slicing pain shot up her foot, and she looked down. She was standing on shards of crab shell. Behind her she saw the dismembered remains of the crab—Pink, a young male dying after impregnation—she'd seen eaten on the monitors. After reproduction there was nothing left to do but die. Orange had left thoughts and memories within her, as Megan had left such in return.

She knelt slowly next to the remains and began to weep in great, hacking sobs.

Megan was still crying an hour later when Bill led her gently into the *Lanford*'s second layer and took her home.

THE SHIP'S artificial gravity was slightly less than the gravity of Motherlode, and by that alone she knew they were in space. The door of her cubicle opened, and Hanna entered. Megan was, as always, unsurprised.

"We found the start-up module in the hangar," Hanna said quietly. "What happened to the spares?"

Megan smiled briefly. "In Azul's cage."

"Figures."

Silence fell between them.

"Aren't I supposed to be in quarantine?" Megan turned to look at Hanna.

Hanna shrugged. "You are. So's the whole ship. We'll let the earth Port Authority handle it. What happened?"

"They're invertebrates," Megan mused. "They only communicate during reproduction because that's what's important to an invertebrate, and then nervous system to nervous system. It's the primary drive for us too, but we don't always realize it. They're sentient and intelligent."

"I don't understand."

"I think I'm just sensitive to them—a talent, like singing. Maybe to all sentients—I don't know. I must have had it all along, but I'd never been in love before. I'd never been that open." She shook her head. "What happened is this: I sensed a sentient life form on Motherlode. It damned near drove me nuts. Or rather, the need for it almost drove me nuts. Is that clearer?"

"What are you talking about?"

Megan looked at her for a long moment. "I was not alone. All the moments I was with her, we were connected. There was no part of her I did not share and no part of me she did not share. I was whole." And she left me. I was not enough.

Hanna looked away and sat down next to her.

Megan let her gaze move to the ceiling. "Sound familiar?"

"Very," said Hanna in a low voice.

Neither spoke for a long minute.

Megan looked at her. "Why do you want the money so bad?"

"I wanted to pay off the *Lanford*," Hanna said in a low voice. "If I own her free and clear, they can never take her away from me. You know I need her."

Megan understood. Once you were whole, you never wanted to face anything else again. Megan understood that well.

"The Authority will need a report from you about the crabs." Hanna shook her head slowly.

"Why?"

"To show them as sentients. This invalidates our claim."

Megan chuckled. "I think I held up more than a handful of dirt. File me as unfit for duty and vote my twenty percent. It'll make the claim unanimous."

"Megan—" Hanna rubbed her hands together nervously.

Megan remembered the separation, the tearing. She closed her eyes tight. *I will bury this. I do not need this gift. I don't want it.* "I owe them nothing. You need the money. I need the money. They can take care of themselves."

Hanna stared at Megan, her breathing ragged. "Okay."

"I'll buy me a ship." Her hands on the sheet were tight. "A ship of my own." *I swear I'll bury you,* and she could almost feel Orange shrug. She began to weep. "Hanna. Is it worth it?"

Hanna reached across and took her hands, pulled Megan into her arms. "Yes, Megan, it is. You don't know how much."

12

If language was a melody, I had to sing.

I could not have had a better start. I *knew* Antonia was trying to talk to me. I had my Speakers helping me. I had Traverse, and through him generations of my people, discussing and analyzing each symbol we found. I would have been brain-damaged *not* to learn manspeak.

There were, of course, problems.

When two Calibii speak, it is visual: a clear portrait of what has occurred or what is proposed to occur. Some images over time have become stylized to mean all such things. A crooked stick in a plowed field has come to mean "farming"; a net in the water has come to mean "fishing." But these are the rudiments of language, not language itself. For that, we had to wait for man.

It was a revelation to me. Each word was a poem. The word *touch* could mean the sensation associated with an object, or the act of inducing contact with an object, or having an emotional experience. It was the guts of language that I loved, the lost dizzy feeling of never knowing exactly what another person was saying and therefore allowing deeper, hidden meanings to be seen. It was the *ambiguity* that made language powerful.

I feel it even yet.

I STOOD AT THE END of the forest not one, but two people:

I listened to words and speech defined in sound and expression. I was tall—tall!—with only two legs and dark hair and—eyes. Eyes. I saw bits and pieces of sense and lost them as I looked.

This—sight?—dimmed and faded into dullness, as pain dulls when healing progresses. I stood there forever, struck as a bell, speechless and stunned, ringing. Something had broken in me, a cage shattered, a chain come apart, and I was running, running...

Some time later I came to myself, shaking. "Stone," I said aloud, echoing inside with memories and feelings not my own. My voice was harsh, croaking, and painful. I longed to sing as birds sing and had never heard a bird.

I do not remember much of that night. I did not return to the village. I did not visit the Caretaker forest. Instead, I walked along the fjord, listening to the wind, watching the dim bursts of light from the fish in the water, crying out my single word, the only word I knew, so that I could hear the echo. The fog from my voice made frost on my fur.

As morning light came from the trees and grasses and Antonia came outside to the day, I was waiting for her.

A MONTH PASSED, then a second. The winter weather was dry and cool. In the mornings, there was a light frost on the grass turning the blades into glass replicas. Where the ground was bare, ice columns pushed the dirt a few inches higher, and small puddles were frozen into dry, hollow bowls covered with ice. By mid-morning, the ice melted in the sun and the grass was wet. By noon, the earth would be dry.

Thalia waited for Antonia each dawn. Bertini had built a shack from poles he cut from the forest and the *Hirohito*'s plastic repair sheets. He cut windows in the sides and faced them with glass and ran an electrical line to it for light and heat. In this semblance of privacy, Antonia and Thalia spent the mornings on the business of language.

Order came with Thalia. The crew of the *Shenandoah* now began the actual mapping of Caliban, beginning with the areas close to the *Hirohito*.

Geological samples needed to be taken. The slim changes in surface gravitation that marked probable mineral deposits were measured. The full range of climatic and weather mapping had to be done. But of them all, biocartography was the most important purpose of a surface expedition. Much of this information had already been captured by the orbiting optical systems—a herd of migratory animals exists here, the basic foliage biomass changes *thus*, over time schools of fish seem to follow this daily pattern. But the information had no context, no flavor. Only surface sampling could determine that mountain predators drove the migrations, or that these biomass changes were due to insect predation, or that the daily patterns of fish were due to plankton blooms changing with the sunlight. To get a sense of the diversity, history, and interactions of Caliban's ecosystems was a lifetime project. Only the barest outlines could be found in this short time. The mountains and the seas were the bones of Caliban. This part of the expedition sampled its flesh.

After Megan admitted to faking the trip to Caliban, the tensions in the crew relaxed. Unspoken among them ran the thought: *we know what's going on now. We know how we came to be here and why.*

Control is one of man's conceits.

SATO AWOKE remembering the sound of meat striking meat.

He sat up and, for a quick moment, anger blazed in him. *Leave me alone!* Then he shook his head. Lindsay was a hundred light-years away. Briefly, he smiled at himself and rubbed his face. At least it wasn't a nightmare this time.

This time. *This* time. When was the last time I got a full night's sleep?

The night Megan told us where we stood—about four months ago.

Outside, Caliban was dark and moonless. Antonia stirred in her sleep and rolled on her side. He leaned on one hand and ran his other down her side, feeling the curves and pockets of her body. She frowned in her sleep and shrugged his hand away. He reached to touch her, and her face suddenly grew masculine. *Lindsay, again.* He drew back and stared at Lindsay's face. After a few moments it melted again into Antonia's. *When was the last time you got a good night's sleep? Before this started happening. Months and months ago.* Inside was intolerable. Sato rolled out of bed, padded naked out into the corridor to his own room, and dressed.

The air outside bit with the cold of deep winter—as deep a winter as this part of Caliban ever saw. This was the nadir of the year, when the sun was darkest and the air crisp. The stars burned remotely, and steps rang hollowly on iron earth.

Well, thought Sato, not quite. It just wasn't cold enough for that.

Still, as in January on the part of Earth he called home, you could *feel* the distance of the sun. You knew then why people worshipped the sun and considered it an inconstant and cruel god.

It made you wonder what the Calibii thought about it.

Even if the stars were still masked by air warmer than he wanted and the ground was not frozen but merely congealed, he still liked coming out here at night, alone, watching the stars cover the bleakness of space like a dancer's veil. To the east he could see a faint glow of coming moonrise.

He heard a muttering and the sound of claws on plastic behind him. Cameron came out to the edge of the airlock. The bear surveyed the darkness and snorted to himself.

"I thought you were sleeping with Bertini." Sato tapped his finger against the floor of the airlock. Cameron looked at his hand, then away into the darkness, not interested just then in being petted.

"Be that way," Sato chuckled. His skin felt cold, but he felt warm within to his bones and muscles. He liked this feeling. He liked winter in general.

Cameron stiffened, sniffing the air. He whined and jumped from the airlock to the ground and stood stiffly watching something Sato could not see.

Sato didn't have to see to know who was coming.

"Good evening," came a croaking voice at his elbow.

He jumped. He couldn't help it. "Damn, Thalia. You did it again. Just once—just *once* I'd like to be able to hear you come."

Thalia did not answer immediately. "I could make a noise as I approach you."

"Don't do that. I mean, I'd like to have the *ability* to hear you. You move so silently. Like Cameron." He smiled at her. She was always so *there*. She never dissolved into Lindsay before his eyes; she was always herself.

Thalia reached down and picked up Cameron. It nestled in her arms as it did for no one but Bertini. Again, it took a moment for her to speak. "A game, then. You play a game with yourself."

Sato nodded, then caught himself. "Exactly."

"A nod is sufficient. I understand nods and shakes of the head now." Cameron rubbed his head against her fur.

An easy silence fell between Sato and Thalia. They did not see each other very often. Antonia was busy teaching Thalia. Because of this, Bertini, Megan, and Sato had to do Antonia's part in the mapping of Caliban as well as their own. But when Sato came out at night, Thalia showed up soon after. He didn't know how she knew when he would be outside or what she wanted from him. He needed nothing from her, and that made him feel good.

"You are watching stars," she said at last.

"Yeah," he admitted.

"I can catch a little of what makes up sight from Antonia, but my mind shies away from it like a wild thing. It is difficult for me."

Sato chuckled again. "You should be a writer."

Pause. "A writer? I can read and write now."

"A writer can also be a person who uses words as an expression of beauty. As an art form."

She shifted herself to lean against the ship. In the faint star-light Sato could see the pale fringe of hairs like frost over the end of her snout. Cameron was a pale ghost in her arms.

"Art. We have...*singers* is the word, I think. People who can speak in a beautiful way."

"Writers are those who sing with the written word."

"You have examples of this?"

"I'll suggest some to Antonia."

"I would like that."

Silence fell again.

"Sato," she said hesitantly, "can you describe my world? As a writer?"

"I'm not a writer."

"Please." She held her hands together. "Try."

"It wouldn't be very good."

"I want to hear the words."

Sato looked up into the sky. The trees on the far horizon were backlit with the moon's glow. *Do it well,* he told himself. *Do it as best you can.* "When I first came here it looked like fall at home. In fall, the leaves are burnt from the normal green into reds, magentas, oranges, yellows. When I was young I thought the trees were burned up by life's fire. Now I think they are burnt by time. After they have changed, they fall to the earth, and the trees are left as barren as bones. In the spring, the leaves grow back in a beautiful green. My first sight of your world looked like home just before winter's purging."

In the coming light Sato could see Thalia more clearly. The fine gray hairs around her mouth stood out, and her strong hands lay relaxed on her arms, supporting Cameron. The bear's head rested against her chest. "Then," he continued, "winter came, and the leaves changed color from fall motley to spring green. Green is an important color to men. It is the color of life—crops are green, trees, grass. The skin of some animals is green for camouflage. It's one of the primary components of vision: red, blue, and green. You could go on with such examples forever. When winter came, your world looked more like home: the sky, blue, the water, blue, the earth, red and brown, the plants, green." He paused a moment, overcome by the inadequacy of his description. "Is that what you wanted?"

Thalia carefully settled Cameron in the airlock doorway, then straightened the hair on her neck delicately with her claws. "I don't know. I'm not sure what I wanted."

"There are lots of people in the world better at words than I." Almost anyone, for example.

"How would I judge them?" Thalia reached over and rested her hand on his. The touch was callused and smooth. He could feel the points of her claws. "Thank you. I will read what you suggest to Antonia." Silence fell, and above them the heavens turned.

"I would like a favor," Thalia said suddenly.

"What?"

"You are going on another mapping trip soon?"

It took a moment for him to grasp what she was talking about. "Tomorrow or the day after." He shook his head. "Bertini went north a couple of months back on a preliminary survey. Now it's time we found out what's under the ice caps. First, I'll do the north one, then the south." Sato shrugged.

Thalia did not move. In the coming pale light she looked graven in ice. When she scratched her hands, it was as if a statue had come to life.

"I want to go with you."

"Oh. Why?"

"I want to watch you. I want to know what you are doing."

Sato suddenly felt warm. It would be good to have company. *Why do you want this native with you?* Because it would be great to have someone with you that didn't turn into Lindsay on you. *There's more than that.* He shrugged. "It's okay with me."

"Good. I'll ask the others tomorrow."

The moon came, and light spilled down on both of them, Sato seeing it, Thalia not at all.

Sato did not have a nightmare tonight. He awoke and is now standing outside talking with Thalia.

Megan looked up from what she was reading. Though she could recall through the *Shenandoah* any piece of information instantly, of late she sometimes preferred to hold something in her hands and actually read it herself. This, however, was no ordinary printout. This was the first original piece Thalia had written two months ago:

#127—in confidence
2/27/2322
Smith
Smith felt sad. His back hurt. He was old. Outside where he lived was a tree. The tree had broken limbs and fallen leaves. It was very sick. Smith watched the tree. No one cared for it.

Doctors told Smith he was very sick.

It was summer. The heat made the street hot. The heat made the tree wilt and the insects hum. Smith lay in his room and felt hot.

Doctors told Smith he was getting sicker.

One day Smith went outside to fix the tree. Other people came to help. They worked on it every day. The tree felt better and was strong.

Smith felt better.

Soon, Smith was well.

The story was on file in the *Shenandoah*, along with twenty pages of Antonia's commentary. Megan had avoided both so she could read the story fresh. She wouldn't have known about it at all if the *Shenandoah* hadn't brought it to her attention. Then it took two weeks of badgering Antonia to get a look at it.

Megan—

"Have you thought about this?"

On several different levels. Antonia used me to help analyze it.

"Why 'Smith'?"

Thalia noticed in looking through human writings the name Smith as being common. She used such a common name in the story.

"This story didn't happen? Is it mythological?"

It's not clear. The actual story did not occur to Thalia, but she has said that stories like it are common, probably told to children.

"There's a connection between the health of Smith and the health of the tree. Is this because they see by the light of plants?"

It seems reasonable. Thalia has said that they see easier by the light of trees than by any other light.

"The date's funny. On Earth it's August. And it says 'in confidence.' Is Thalia scared to be writing things down? Is there a taboo?"

The date comes from a conversation between Antonia and Thalia on how humans keep time. As an exercise, they worked out a calendar that fits the Caliban year. Since then, they both use it for clarity. It's unlikely there's a taboo to writing. Calibi have no writing. Thalia is trying to make something esthetically pleasing out of human language. She cannot sing—the sound of her voice is ugly even to her. So she is attempting to write. She has not told Sato—in fact, in conversation this morning with him, she asked him about using language esthetically. She did not tell him she is attempting it. Small children do the same when they are learning to write, to preserve themselves from embarrassment.

"Thalia is not a small child."

It appears to be a function of intelligence to try to make beautiful that which must be learned. The fear of criticism might be a universal.

"Have you ever tried to make anything beautiful?"

Of course. I have helped make so the touch between us.

"Hmm."

Megan, Sato did not have a nightmare tonight.

"I don't want to talk about Sato. Things are going well. I don't need him."

Needing him as a tool against Bertini is not what I'm talking about. Sato's been having nightmares for weeks.

"You've told me. I'm glad tonight his sleep was undisturbed."

I didn't say that. Tonight there was no nightmare. I know his nightmares now as well as he does. Tonight he had a hallucination while asleep.

She stood up and stretched. "Antonia must not be good for him."

Antonia's responsible for them.

Megan laughed. "My craziness is rubbing off."

I can't go crazy.

"So you tell me."

Consider: Bertini seemed to be suddenly stressed after Antonia first communicated with Thalia. She took him to bed. Sato started having nightmares after Antonia started regularly communicating with Thalia.

"Bertini went to his room right after the world turned green. We were all shaken by that. And Sato's been getting steadily closer to Antonia—closeness is something he feels nervous about. Look in his file."

You're missing my point—

"No. I'm just pointing out other conclusions." She leaned against the window. Outside, the morning light showed the world in crisp green variation.

There are always alternate conclusions. I took NMR scans of Antonia and Sato as they slept last night.

"I didn't know you could do that."

That's one of the ways I monitor you.

"What else can you do that I don't know about?"

We can take an hour and find out . . .

She laughed. "Goat."

The pictures showed a gradual synchronization of Sato and Antonia's thought patterns.

"Sato's been picking up Antonia's dreams?"

Nothing so simple. I could tell that. No, the patterns were synchronized, not identical. Dreams involve a physical component of the brain—motor control of the muscles, REM, other things. Sato was having such activity, but Antonia was not. Antonia showed quick bursts of activity in the brainstem and reticular formation.

"So?"

The area showing the most activity is that part of the brainstem associated with telepathy.

"Oh. She's *causing* Sato's nightmares."

I said she was responsible for them. It's not the same thing and, again, not quite so simple. Sensitivity has a telepathic component, but it is not telepathy. I think Sato is using some of Antonia's brain to stimulate his own nightmares.

"Why?"

I have no idea. But consider also: when I play back records of Bertini's room after the plants turned green, Antonia and he were talking. Bertini did not talk to Antonia as he usually did. And the speech patterns of her response were not Antonia's. In that case, I think Bertini did the same thing, only more so. He actually subverted her whole mind temporarily. Or rather, she allowed him use of it.

"Wouldn't Antonia notice this?"

I don't know. To a person who effectively time-shares her brain, how significant would such an interlude be? What would she think of as normal? Especially now, in such an abnormal and traumatic time? Antonia killed a sentient creature. What effect would that have on a mind already that far from normal? How could I determine how just sensitivity alters personality, much less make guesses about how they feel? You could do that; I can't.

"What do you mean?"

Years ago you selectively sealed off your memories of times before me.

A cold wind blew through her. "I don't know what you're talking about."

Yes you do. You may not remember it, but you still know it happened. I've kept them for you, and I know what they are. You were a sensitive, Megan, before such an ability was recognized and classified. You have this capacity, and you buried it. Now you need those memories.

*There are undercurrents here I can never understand and
you will not understand unless you are complete. You must
have all of yourself to draw on to survive. And believe me,
I want you to survive as much as you do.*

BERTINI DID NOT SLEEP much. A man is redesigned when he
becomes an engineer. Morpheus has no claim on him. It is a
voluntary, private thing, to be indulged in to relieve fatigue, to
overcome boredom, to deal with emotional stress. It no longer
demands attention. Bertini was not tired or distressed, and he'd
found another way to overcome boredom: this dawn would
find him hunched over his workboard, playing intricate electronic games with radio waves.

He was trying to talk Calibi.

Dolphin researchers in the twentieth century had it easy.
They had a sentient mammal with a known sensory system:
sonar. The navies of the world had been using it in submarines
for fifty years. Once they broke the dolphin language down into
images instead of words it took them only twenty years to talk
to them. Sonar is very clear: dolphins had a definite range of
frequencies, and only they originated the signal.

Bertini had a species that also talked in images, but the species did not make the images directly—it stimulated them from
the plants. Calibii were able to choose selectively from a frequency range of noise and selectively tune out the rest—that
was their perception. They were also able to stimulate the same
signal so that someone else could determine not only an image
from the noise, but that it was not a real image but a communication image. What subset of frequencies did they use, if they
used a subset? How did they separate it out from the noise?
They had to code communications somehow, but if they coded
it too much, it would begin to lose its image quality. How much
was too much? How much was too little?

It was a fascinating problem.

Of course, Bertini had help. Thalia already could talk like a
human. She was cooperative. And he had better tools than
those dolphin researchers of the twentieth century. But so far,
all Bertini could detect was a noise like any other radio noise.

He swore and fumed and thought and enjoyed every minute.

"Bertini?" came a voice from the intercom.

"You got him." What is the index of refraction of a radio wave? Plant tissue is essentially water, so it can be calculated. Yet these plants are themselves emitters. How do you differentiate between refraction or reflection and source? You have to know the source. Look at Hubbel's work on vision.

"Want to share a cup of coffee?"

"What?" He shook his head in irritation. "Who is this?"

"There are only three people it could be, Bertini. Surely you can recognize one in three."

"Megan." He shook his head again. "Start over. I missed something."

"I said," her voice took on a steely quality, "do you want to share a cup of coffee?"

"Coffee. Okay. Don't get your spleen in an uproar."

"I'll bring it down."

"What?" But she'd already switched off. He felt vaguely threatened. It had been months since there'd been any confrontation between them. They had kept pretty much out of each other's way. Why now? It was late. Antonia and Sato were asleep. There were no witnesses.

"Hmm." He unzipped his shirt and pinched hard on the left side of his navel. The skin parted and separated cleanly. He pulled a square device from inside the pouch and pressed two buttons. It was the interrupter, the same device he'd used to turn off Megan before. Now it was in "dead-man" mode. If he was killed, it would automatically turn on. He replaced it in the pouch and resealed the skin. Megan entered his work room as he zipped up his shirt.

She smiled at him and gave him a steaming mug. She sipped her own and sat in the room's only other chair. The silence grew awkward. Finally: "How goes Calibi-speech?"

Bertini shrugged. "It goes. If I'm lucky, I'll find the hook the Calibii put into the stimulated radio. Then I can go back and say, 'Look here. I found it. Name it after me.' I've always wanted to be a footnote in science."

Megan chuckled. "We'll probably all be footnotes somewhere, whether we like it or not."

Bertini nodded. "Let's see. The last I talked to Ruth, the ship was okay on her end. I've checked over the *Hirohito* regularly. No problems. This is in all of my free time between mapping trips. Although I've figured out some new wrinkles in the optical software that make it less necessary to depend on radar mapping—''

She held up her hand. "I don't want a report. I'll get it when I need it."

"Oh." He leaned against his work table. "To what do I owe the pleasure?"

"I just wanted some company."

"I thought you had all the company you needed."

She grimaced. "Don't start."

"Sorry." The silence lengthened again.

"I just," she began, then stopped. "You're what, two-ten? Two-twenty?"

He knew exactly what she meant. "Two hundred-and twenty-five years old, next birthday."

"Were you ever on Luna?"

He laughed. "Scores of times."

She smiled slightly. "Well, I didn't mean between ships. Were you ever there, say, a couple of centuries back? Did we ever meet?"

"Us? I don't think so." He thought for a moment. "They hardened me the sixth of June, 2127. On Earth, of course. didn't go out until the next year, and then it was with the navy I think I took leave in Tycho Village—"

"I'll be damned. That's were I was born." She smiled into her coffee.

Bertini shrugged. "Tell me the truth now, wasn't everyone born in Tycho Village back then? It was the only city on Luna."

"It was a small town."

"Hey," he shrugged again, "maybe I went out with your sister."

"I don't have a sister." She paused and looked at the ceiling a moment. "No. I don't."

"It's not something you would forget."

"I suppose." She shook her head. "You might have met me—no, I had gone then to OCS. *I* was going to be an *officer*."

"I hate officers."

"Enlisted men are pigs."

They toasted one another with coffee.

Megan's smile became dreamy. "Did you ever see the Oceanarium in Novorodsk? Before they turned it into the Water Gardens?"

Bertini nodded. "Anywhere else they would have called it an aquarium. Not Luna. I spent two weeks there after the skirmish over New Hope."

"My family moved to Novorodsk when I was—three, I think." She paused for a moment. "I grew up in the complex under it. I spent hours watching the bantas."

"That was years before I got there. Which were they?"

"The eel things from—I don't remember. Somewhere out."

It was a hesitant, tenuous evening, this swapping of stories. Megan had served in the navy only as long as required, then mustered out into the merchant marine. Bertini had stayed in much longer. Gradually, their stories touched as they found common places between them. They were both among the oldest members of their professions. It was surprising they hadn't met before.

"Let's see." Bertini folded his arms. "The *Rasmussen* was based on Pompano."

"Pompano!" Megan laughed. "I skippered for the PGM corporation out of Rotterdam. I did the Pompano run for two years."

"When?"

"2270. 2275, maybe."

"Were Irene and Joe running the research bridge then?"

"Yes! 'The hag of Pompano Bridge.'"

"Now, now. She said, 'the crone of Pompano Bridge.'"

"Hag, crone—what's the difference?"

The hours passed toward dawn.

Finally, Megan stared into her cold and empty cup and said: "I've got to go, now."

Bertini shrugged, vaguely disappointed. "As you will."

She looked up at him. "This doesn't really change anything, you know."

"I know."

She nodded and stood up to go.

He reached out and touched her arm. "Why did you come here?"

Megan didn't say anything for a long time, her eyes dark and distant. "I wanted to remember the past," she said slowly, "a little at a time. In small, manageable pieces. I wanted to remember who I was."

"I understand."

She glanced at him sharply, then shook her head gently. "No, you don't. But it's all right. Really, it is."

As she left, Bertini carefully pulled out the interrupter to take it out of dead-man mode. He stared at it a long time, thinking about what she had said.

CARETAKER FOUND ME at the edge of the river bluff near the village, staring down into empty space.

"What are you doing?"

"Staring at nothing." The height was empty. No light reflected except that little showing air and some from plants in the water. It was an empty void.

"There's nothing there." Caretaker sat next to me. "Do you like the danger in being up here?"

"No," I admitted. "I feel tenuous and unsafe here. This is something humans do. I'm trying to understand it."

"Do they savor such danger?"

"I don't know. Maybe. Or maybe their sight leads them to believe they are safe when they are not. They can savor the excitement."

"Or maybe they are hard to kill—tougher than we imagine."

I shook my head.

"What does that mean?"

"Nothing. They are not easy to kill at all, if what Antonia has shown me in their still language is true." I could not use the word read. We have no equivalent. I looked at Caretaker. Her fur and head seemed strange. I wanted to cover my eyes, but I had no eyes. Again, I turned my sight to the void. How human had I become?

Caretaker did not say anything for a moment. "I worry about you, Binder."

"Why?"

"The creatures have had a great effect on you. You do not come to the forest as you once did. You come only when we ask you to report to us. You barely talk to Traverse."

I snorted. "Traverse. Traverse is a shadow."

Caretaker touched me. "All Ancestors are such to us."

"They are all shadows—we are all shadows of the trees. I should have gone away."

"Yes."

"Hindsight is no sight at all." A long moment passed. "Still, I miss him. Deeply. Terribly. And this Ancestor does not help."

"Enough of this." Caretaker stood up. "Traverse is dead. You have mourned thoroughly. It's time to stop grieving."

I didn't say anything for a moment.

Caretaker stared into the void with me for a moment. "You are wasting time." Then she left me.

I sat there for a long time. "Damn," I muttered in English, a broken, hoarse croak. "Damn you for being right."

ANTONIA OPENED the schoolhouse and smiled. Each morning she had done the same thing for the past four months. She never thought she'd be a teacher. She never thought she'd have a twelve-by-twelve shed as a schoolhouse, either. Sometimes, when she stepped inside, she laughed.

Thalia was waiting for her.

"You're early. Usually, I beat you in here."

"I wanted to try to write something again." Thalia stood up from the stool and rubbed the backs of her thighs. "My legs are unconscious."

"'Fell asleep,'" Antonia corrected absently. Along the connection between them, she could feel Thalia's excitement.

"My thighs fell asleep, then."

"Maybe Bertini or Sato could adjust that stool for you."

Thalia shrugged. Antonia smiled again.

"Can I see what you've written?" Antonia tried not to sound too eager.

Thalia said nothing but pulled the page out of the typewriter and gave it to her, then turned to the window and opened it, sniffing the chill air. "Smells good out there."

"'In days,'" Antonia read aloud, "'I found a lover and lost him—'"

"Please," said Thalia suddenly. "Don't read it now."

"This isn't a story."

"It's not fiction." Thalia turned back to Antonia. "I want to go away for a few days. I need to think about you humans and my own people. Sato is going north. I'd like to accompany him."

"He's going to check minerals under the north ice cap. That's colder than you imagine." Antonia felt obscurely jealous of Sato.

"Don't be," said Thalia quietly. "You and I are bound together permanently. You will never be alone, and neither will I. That's one of the things I want to think about."

There was such a warmth toward her—toward *her*—from Thalia that Antonia looked down at the paper, suddenly embarrassed.

"My people are better adapted for the cold than humans. If Sato can stand it, so can I."

"Sato will be clothed."

"I will be clothed in good intentions."

Antonia looked at her. "*Very* good. I like that."

"I had a good teacher." Thalia shrugged again. "I'm sure we can work something out. Consider it my…" She stopped a long moment. "Consider it my way of keeping track of what humans are doing to my planet. Surely, if we can collaborate and build a typewriter for me, we can try for a set of clothes."

"I think so." Antonia felt lost, realizing then how much she had depended on this time. "What will I do now?"

Thalia took her hands. "You will do what you came to do. You will map Caliban and know me. And I will know you."

13

Like ancient mariners using a map marked "Monsters," they flew north. The air grew cold outside the lander's protective field, the sky and sea the same leaden color. Thalia spoke only in monosyllables, withdrawn and unapproachable.

Sato spent his time worrying. His worry vibrated between two poles: what was going on in Thalia's head and his growing love for Antonia.

Thus:

Love? Come on, be real. *The feeling of the stick in his hand, the knob pushing up against the fingers. A twist here—the flyer dipped a hundred feet, a twist there—the flyer began a long bank east. A touch and a response. Like love. Like sex. But think of a better word if you can. Better yet, don't think about* it. *The sky was light, clear and crisp and cold. A long thick smudge of gray smoke lined the far horizon. A storm. The faint vibration of the flyer up his back and spine. The smooth feel of plastic against his hands. I am the ship.* Think about Thalia. Damn her. She could be better company. Why bring someone along if she's not pleasant? *The sea was a deep blue, almost black. Image, seascape: the shore gaudy with greens and yellows and reds, the sky an electric vibrating blue. Color everywhere. The sea sheer black, its foam, burning white. I had forgotten that. Did I see that once in a museum? In Boston? Earth? Where is not important. Is the memory then important?* Hey. This isn't just a fun job for her, now is it? Who has more right to be here, her or you? Whose planet is it? *I don't remember. What did you know about Earth, anyway? The smells. The sounds. The sights. Vision. Memories. There is only now. There is only here. Who do you know on Earth? No one. Just memories. Who do you know here? Is a memory real?* And who knows more about Antonia? Antonia? Thalia? They're linked together. There's the possibility of an ulterior motive here. Great.

Did you ever know Lindsay at all?

Not Lindsay. There are limits. Worry about Thalia. That's the safest subject you got.

He ground his teeth and tried to figure out what she was thinking. The hours passed.

"What do you expect to find this far north?" she asked finally.

Rejoice! "We're still a couple of hours from the ice cap. When we get there, we'll drill down through it and take samples."

"Ice cap," she murmured to herself.

"Caliban—is there anything *you* want to call your planet? We called it Caliban because we didn't know anybody lived here."

She seemed to think about that for a while. "No, Caliban is fine with me. We have no name for the planet as a planet. We didn't even know what a planet was until you came. We could not see the sun, moon, or stars—again, things we did not know until you came." She stopped for a long moment, turned to the railing and faced the northern sea. "Besides, I read *The Tempest* last night. Caliban is a good name for our world."

Great, he thought. What can of worms have I opened *this* time? *Image of a black and white sea against a colored shore.* "Yeah." He cleared his throat. "Well, there are two ice caps covering the north and south poles of...Caliban. Yeah. On Earth, the northern ice cap covers only ocean, and the southern cap covers a huge continent. It's obvious from space that the ice caps here cover two continents not so big. Since they are covered by ice, they're called 'protected' continents. Whatever is under that ice is pretty much the way it's been as long as the ice has been there. It's never been exploited."

"Little on Caliban has been exploited."

"True. Someday, you may want to change that. If that happened, it's good to know your reserves."

"My reserves consist of one Caretaker, a handful of trees, and a dead lover."

God, what am I going to say to *that*?

A few minutes later she came and stood next to him. Hesitantly, she rested a hand on his shoulder. "I dwell too much on myself. I am frightened. I am nearly blind here."

Sato looked at her. "Blind?"

"The plants of the sea put out little light. I am surrounded by a dim glow and emptiness."

Images. What is seen? What is not seen? Is a sea black and white, or is that a function of the light that falls on it? Bright and dark. Color and black and white. The image came bright to me and faded.

"Maybe I can do something about that." He'd left the radar off because in the radio howl of Caliban it was of little use. He switched it on now. Thalia stiffened. Damn, what did I do now? "Is that any better?"

"It is...it is better than blindness. It is a bright flash followed by darkness. At least I can see around me." She squeezed his shoulder gently. "Thank you."

MEGAN SAT ALONE in her room, staring out the window. She slouched low in her chair, one hand draped loosely over her knee, the other holding on to a beer. Several empty cans lay on the floor. In a quick, jerky motion, she raised the can, drained it, crushed it in her hand, and dropped it on the floor.

Megan—

"Shut up," she said evenly. "You've been after me for weeks. I don't want to hear any more. I am well on my way to getting drunk."

Gotten drunk. Stand up, Megan. If you can stand up, I will quit bothering you.

"Small price to pay." She struggled up to a sitting position and pushed herself up. Her legs failed her, and she fell. The floor felt soft and rubbery. "Didn't need to stand up anyway." She felt the *Shenandoah* reach *through* her. She cried out in panic. Then her head hurt, and she was suddenly sober. She closed her eyes. "Damn you. Leave my fucking liver alone."

Then damn us both. We're in this together. I built your liver to save your life. Was that a hundred years ago? A hundred and fifty?

Megan sighed. "Christ on a stick."

Would you like to know where you learned that expression?

"No."

Does the name Bill Pirot mean anything to you?

"Nothing." She stood up.

Please, Megan. I can't hold them any more. It's tearing me apart.

"What?" She felt cold and held herself. "What do you mean?"

I've been your conscience for two centuries. It's too hard. I'm just—just tired, Megan. Tired of holding you

*together with spit and barbed wire. Tired of holding within
me the strength you gave away. I like you, Megan. I love
you. You know that. And I love you in part because of the
pieces of you I hold.*

"Why did I do it?" Her eyes were wet with tears.

*I don't know. You are in pieces, Megan. If you were
whole, you—and I—would know.*

It is hard to be cruel. The cost is so high.
*I've had Shenandoah hold me together too long. It's time I
was a better lover.*
In better than two centuries of knowing herself, she knew
what such reconciliations were worth. Still, it was a fine attempt.
"All right," she said, and from *Shenandoah* she felt a great
relief. Several minutes passed. "I said, okay."

You have them. Think for a moment. The Lanford.
Bill Pirot. Hanna—

She cried out as the new memories hit her like a fist. "Oh,
God," she whimpered. "Oh, God. Orange. What happened to
them?"
Voicelessly, she knew. They were considered a delicacy by the
humans on their planet.
"The sensitives coming through on ships don't notice?"

*Even sensitives have to know what they're looking for.
The crabs are just too different. It took over a century for
a planet full of sensitives to notice the Paedash. And the
Paedash were crying out to them.*

"I did that. A planet of—of *people*, and I condemned them.
I *knew*, and I condemned them."

Hanna helped. She knew also, after all.

The tears streamed down her face. No wonder she'd put this away. How could she have lived with it? How could she—she hadn't. The *Shenandoah* had lived with it for her.

The question was not how—that was obvious. The question was why. And *Shenandoah* was the answer.

She knew deep within her, she'd have done it again.

Megan! You can't mean that.

"Don't I?" She looked at the ceiling and around the room. "This planet is mine. I did it once. I can do it again. I'll kill them all, lay this planet to waste, to keep you. Help me make sure it's not necessary." She took a deep breath. This was sin. This was evil. Before she had acted out of ignorance of what she was. Now she knew thoroughly. Now she chose it.

BERTINI STOOD OUTSIDE in the cold, watching the sky. The sun was newly risen, and the air was crisp. He was dressed lightly—one of the advantages of being hardened. Cold as mild as this had little effect on him. The ice on the ground crackled as he walked over to the schoolhouse. Antonia was inside.

He stopped in the doorway, uncertain. "I thought Thalia was with Sato."

"She is," said Antonia, her eyes distant and hollow. "It feels like they're over the arctic sea about now." She looked at Bertini. She'd grown thin in the last months. Her hair hung lifeless, and her skin was sallow.

"Hmm." He stepped in and closed the door. "I came in to tinker with the recording equipment. The bandwidth is too narrow."

She looked past him. "Where's Cameron?"

Bertini shrugged. "He's moping about Thalia. Seems he gets depressed whenever Thalia isn't around."

"Thalia likes him, too." Antonia glanced up at him. "Don't you ever get jealous?"

"Jealous?" He considered that. "Not exactly. Cameron's not a pet to me, really. He's more a charge. A ward, kind of."

"You don't like him?"

"Of course I like him. But Cameron was given to me to take care of a long time ago. He's not *my* pet. He's somebody else's."

"Who?"

"A friend who's dead now. It's too long a story." He sat across from her. "What's wrong?"

Antonia looked away. "I'm not sure." When he didn't reply, she continued. "I feel... empty? Lost? Utterly useless?"

Bertini shook his head. "You're the reason we have a chance to save our skin. I hardly call that useless."

She shrugged again and looked at the floor. "I came out here to work with Thalia, and she was gone. I *knew* she was gone, but I came out here anyway. Then, I thought, if this works I can leave." Antonia stopped, then slowly turned to Bertini. "I'm tied to Thalia. Whatever happens, I don't think I *can* leave."

She started to cry. Bertini took her in his arms and held her.

"I'm so tired," she mumbled into his shirt. "I'm just so tired."

He picked her up when she quieted and carried her inside. She fell asleep curled against his chest. Gently—she was almost too light for him to hold comfortably—he eased her down on her bed. Antonia did not wake up. He covered her with a blanket.

Like you did for me long ago.

"Rain," he said in a low voice, "I thought you were gone." He waited for the old pain, and it did not come. He relaxed slowly.

Gone like a bad penny. Or rather, gone like a memory not thought of, forever a part of you.

"Yeah." He smiled. "I remember you." He laughed softly.

He found a book to read from Antonia's shelves and sat down across from her, waiting for her to wake.

THE CLOSE ROAR of the glaciers made me shiver, though the air within the flyer was quite warm—too warm, in fact. Sato with his naked skin stared intently at his instruments, humming under his breath like an idiot. It was blindness, blindness, *flash*—everything lit up in queasy brilliance, and I could see the broken cliffs and mountains of ice. Then blindness. *Demons come from the dark.* I remembered that from childhood and from Traverse. Between the flashes I could see no farther than inside of the flyer, and that only from the flyer's own low glow. We were beyond plants, now. Nothing lived here but us.

"The satellite maps show this as glacier for two hundred kilometers to the north of here, then the shelf retreats from the ledge."

"We go there?" I did not have to worry about Sato hearing my fear. The croak I had for a voice masked it. I only had to hold my trembling, the nervous way I had of moving my neck back and forth, sniffing the air.

He laughed shortly. "No. We go inland, over the ice. The exposed ledge isn't interesting. What we want to know is how deep the ice is and what's under it. On Earth, the ice is over four kilometers deep."

Four kilometers, they said in their easy distances. What was four kilometers? It was the distance between Infertility's band and Climber's. The distance from the river to the sea. "How much ice is that?"

He looked at me with the wet eggs they use for sight and grinned. "Enough to cover everywhere you've ever been a kilometer deep, at least. Maybe more. It's hard to tell." He turned back to his instruments, leaving me an image of everything I had ever known covered with frozen darkness, deep, blind, dead.

Thanks, Sato. Thanks a lot.

"We go directly north, then?"

"Eventually. There's a mountain range ahead of us. We'll go around it. Glad it's a clear day. Lots of sunlight." He nodded toward one anonymous edge of the flyer. "There might be a storm coming, but we can weather that."

I felt small and mean, closeted in darkness.

"Is it dangerous?"

Sato laughed. "Hey, you die, you die. You only live once, and this is all there is."

The time passed slowly. We did not speak much. Sato paid close attention to his flying.

"How are you getting along with Antonia?" he said suddenly. It was still hard for me to read humans, but even I could tell he had been thinking about this for some time.

"All right," I said and stopped, not sure of what he wanted.

"All right," he repeated. "Yeah. I get along with her all right, too." He laughed strangely. "I think I get along with her too well. Too damned well."

"Beg pardon?"

He looked at me suddenly, and I felt his gaze. He relaxed. "I've got a lot on my mind about her."

"Why?"

He didn't speak for a moment. "I care for her, I guess."

It broke on me, then. It was his season. Like Traverse, he too was considering his mate. It made them all seem so much closer, so much more like me. "You will be good lovers."

He shrugged. "We've *been* lovers, for months now. On ship, it seemed like a thing to do—like shaking hands or hugging someone. Down here, it's something more."

Months. *How long would Traverse have had if we had become lovers? Four weeks? Six weeks?*

"Months?"

"Since before we got here. On the ship it was sporadic. We didn't set up housekeeping until we landed." He looked at me.

How many lovers had I buried beneath the trees? Five? Six? How many of their children had I held, thinking of them, knowing these were the only remnants of them I could ever have? Accepting it only because it was inevitable.

Loving one more than all the rest and having that one taken from me . . .

I didn't think. I struck him with my fist, and he fell against the instrument board, struck him again and turned him around. My climbing claws came out, fighting claws, killing claws, and I slashed him across the face. He screamed and fell down on the deck. I stood over his back as he writhed on the metal. I would slash open his naked skin and make him bleed as Traverse had bled, watch him die as I had watched Traverse die.

The flyer tipped, and I had time enough to see in a flash the side of a mountain. We hit like a hammer.

LIFE IS LOST, she dreamed. *The world is gray, formless, and void. Nothing matters. Thalia is dead.*

The thread connecting them withered and shrank. Fell away from her like everything in her life had fallen away from her. No one had remained. She was alone, always. She was abandoned, always. People who loved her died or went mad. People she loved she had to leave.

Not again. She whimpered. She wept and tasted salt and bitterness as hot tears ran down her face. Inside, she felt an emptiness, a place where things were not. Desperate, she felt around her for someone to hold on to, to have hold on to her.

She remembered Fyodor standing over her on the porch, looking stricken. "You don't understand . . ." he said, and his voice trailed away. *Dear God, you were right. I don't. I never did.*

And there came through the dream a voice like light, a sound like a glow: *"Antonia . . . help me."*

She awoke and cried out. "Thalia!"

MEGAN FELT THE SLASH, felt Sato's dazed shock and surprise, felt the blaze of pain when the flyer hit.

> *This is what you want, Megan? Pain and death?*

It was not quite sensitivity anymore. With the *Shenandoah* scanning what she felt, analyzing it for her and testing possible models of what the sensation was, it was closer to straight telepathy.

"This is what my new memories have brought me, eh?" She laughed bitterly. "They're not dead yet."

Someone pounded on the door to her cabin. She could feel Bertini and Antonia on the other side. "Yes," she said, and opened the door.

Antonia stood ahead of Bertini, and her eyes blazed. Megan had to look away.

"Thalia and Sato have crashed the flyer up north. We need to go after them."

Megan found herself nodding, caught herself, and looked at Bertini.

Bertini: something's wrong with her. Something—is it to be now? Here? Then: soon, I will have to take the ship from her. A sense of regret and determination.

> Over my dead body.
> *He might be able to arrange that.*
> I will take care of him.

She shook her head to clear Bertini out of it, turned to Antonia again. Nothing came from Antonia in words, only a roaring furnace of emotion: *she will not die!* Megan felt burnt, blackened by heat.

Shenandoah! Dim this for me!

The sensitivity faded to feelings vague and muddy.

"All right." Megan looked first at Bertini, then at Antonia. "Bertini, you pilot. Antonia will come with you as physician. I'll stay here—"

Can we track them with the satellites? Use the laser for communication?
No problem. But she'll have to guide him. We have communications satellites in position but no mapping satellites.

"—and keep you in contact with the *Shenandoah.* There are laser communication units in the flyers. Antonia, you'll have to guide Bertini." Antonia nodded to her. Megan smiled at Bertini. I have a tool to protect so that I can aim it at you.

"Not like last time, eh?" Bertini smiled at her.

Not like the last time, when he left Megan unconscious and ran to the north glaciers to wait her out. Not like last time, when Megan stayed drunk for a week while he was gone. Even without the overlay of *Shenandoah* on her sensitivity, Megan could feel the testing, the pushing against her.

He wants my ship!
He wants to survive, just as we do.
You know? I could almost like him if he wasn't such a son-of-a-bitch.
Like appeals to like.

She looked at him hard. "No," she said coldly, "not like last time." Never like last time. Never again. "Go."

I HEARD CARETAKER'S VOICE: *what is the difference between accident and murder?*

I couldn't answer her.

The cold woke me then. I shivered in the darkness. Where were we now? I felt around me. The deck of the flyer had frozen. Frost? Or blood?

"Sato?" I called out. There was no answer.

Pain and darkness. Pain from my back—I must have struck the railing of the lander when we crashed. Darkness from the lifelessness all around me. I tried to call up night vision. Nothing. I tried again, harder this time, and thought I saw a glimmer. I strained, and the glimmer became a dim glow. I could vaguely see. The poles were not lifeless. *Something* lived here. The ice was frost, not blood, and I felt relieved.

Relieved I didn't kill him?

Unsure. Unsure. He could still be dead.

The flyer had cushioned us in some arcane way. More of their demon work. Sato lay on the deck near me. I stood up, and my leg crumpled under me. I felt of it—it did not feel broken, just dead. I pulled myself over to Sato.

"Wake up, demon," I said. "We both die."

He did not respond, but even in this dimness I could see his body working, so I knew he was not dead. The relief was genuine. I did not want him dead.

What is the difference between accident and murder?

Now that I was awake, I knew the answer: intent. Sato and Antonia had not meant to kill Traverse. I knew that. But I had damned well meant to kill Sato. Which of us was better?

I touched him. "Wake up, damn you. I'm not going to kill you. The cold will do it for me."

He shuddered and opened his eyes. "Cold," he gasped.

For a long moment, I just looked at him. Then I gathered him in my arms and held him close to make him warm.

LINDSAY REACHED UP and slapped me. The blow opened my face like a claw. Thalia struck him, knocked him down. She was so strong. Strong. Her hands grew razors. *Lindsay struck back, as he never did when I beat him up. He just looked at me.* She slashed him across the face. He felt his skin part in a sick ripping. The blood poured across his eyes.

He shook his head. "What?" *The left side, the left side!*
Where I hit him, backhanded. Blackness.

Cold.

Great shivers racked him. It was always cold in his apartment. When he was between ships in winter, he would have
to keep the heat on. Lindsay teased him about being a hot-
house flower. Lindsay, always the same size as he, yet always seeming smaller.

Cold.

On the deep winter nights he could tell the temperature
outside from the thickness of the ice inside the storm window. *It was snowing when he left.* No. It was a cold spring.
It seemed cold that night, and Lindsay's touch woke him—

He opened his eyes. It was dark. "Cold," he muttered. A
moment later he was pressed against warm fur.

Fur. Nothing. Thalia. Nothing. Thalia—

He pushed away from her, awake now, and looked
around, shook his head, and looked again. Yeah. His face
felt soft and moist, crusty in spots.

His gaze finally rested on Thalia. "Did you do this?"

Thalia said nothing. The brainless head sniffed and
moved left and right slowly, like seaweed in current. "That
will have to wait," she said finally.

Her voice sounded sweet then, like Lindsay's.

He shook his head again, and it began to hurt. The pain
brought him awake. "Blankets. Shelter. There's emergency
equipment under the deck. There's a ring—"

"I can't see, Sato. Not well enough to find anything. I can
barely walk."

He sat up. "How come?"

"My leg doesn't work. I can't feel anything from—the
thigh, I suppose. From the thigh down."

"Okay." He nodded to himself. He moved his arms and
legs gingerly. The wind began to blow across them. "I was
luckier." He had to shout to make himself heard. The cold
seemed less important now, less biting. He was tired, sleepy.
As he had been afterward that night.

Dark. It had been clear. Storm? Wasn't there a storm?

The sunlight had been subsumed into clouds piled high,
dark, curling. There had been a storm, and it was coming.
A ring unlocked the deck cover over the emergency supplies. He looked long and carefully until he found it, then

crawled over to it on the other side of the flyer. The ring was placed flush in the deck, and it was several minutes before he could get purchase on it. Once he had it, he turned it to unlock the deck cover and pulled. His hands were bruised, and he cried out and dropped it. "Damn." *Who will you let down this time?* He looked over toward Thalia, back at the ring. He grabbed it with both hands and pulled hard and suddenly, trying not to feel the swollen fire surging through his wrists and palms.

The cover came loose. The wind caught it and sent it skittering across the deck. It struck the rail with a clang next to Thalia. Sato jumped back. Thalia did not move. He grabbed one of the blankets out of storage and threw it over to Thalia. "Wrap up in that." He pulled one out for himself and crawled back over to her. The wind had begun to howl.

She huddled within it, the heat control dangling outside. Sato had trouble focusing on her dial. He turned it on.

"Light," she murmured from inside the huddle of blanket. "Is it getting warmer?"

"It's the blanket." He fumbled for the control on his own; somehow his fingers wouldn't turn the dial. They kept slipping off.

Her hand appeared, and delicately she turned the blanket on. He felt warmth—blessed warmth—around him.

"Thanks, Lindsay," he muttered, falling asleep.

Instinctively, they snuggled next to one another. Something cold and feathery touched his face.

It had begun to snow.

"WE'RE DRIFTING A LITTLE," Antonia said quietly. "Turn east a couple of points."

The northern twilight had fallen by now, and icebergs floated below them, burned violet by the sky's light.

"Better than having a compass," muttered Bertini.

Antonia smiled at him but kept looking, looking, trying to penetrate the half light, trying to find Thalia.

And Sato? asked that voice in her mind, always questioning her, always checking up on her.

Oh, yes. Him, too.

"How are they?" Bertini continued to watch the optical image played back from the *Shenandoah*.

"Thalia's still unconscious, I think. I caught a flare of thought an hour or so back, but it faded. It doesn't feel like they're in any real danger right now. Things feel—asleep."

Bertini nodded. "The deck's field—" he nodded to the railing of their own flyer "—probably protected them from the impact. If they were able to get to the emergency supplies, they'll be all right. And they must have, or you wouldn't be picking them up."

"I can only pick up Thalia. I have no idea what happened to Sato." She paused and looked over his shoulder at the instruments. "We've drifted too far east now. Move west a point."

Bertini grunted and changed course. Antonia felt the flyer shift beneath her.

Things have been building up between you and Sato for a long time now.

Not really.

Aren't you a sensitive? Aren't you able to watch Sato as well as Thalia?

Only in a limited way. He's too close to me.

For situations when the sensitivity was vague, you were trained to watch for physical clues. You know better.

He is attached to me. Nothing more.

Right. Say that again when he asks you to marry him.

She shook her head to clear it. I'm looking for Thalia now.

Sato's there, too.

He's just not as important. He just isn't.

But *he* doesn't know that. He doesn't know he's just a warm body to you. He thinks you actually care for him. He thinks it's *he* that makes a difference to you, when it could be anybody: an anonymous set of arms to hold you, a chest to press against—

"That's enough."

"Eh?" Bertini glanced up at her. "You said something."

"No. Just talking to myself."

Something like Thalia has never happened to me before.

True. Sato is a minor player in your life, a person who cares for you. When you have to move on you won't think about him. People don't abandon you. You abandon them. Like Fyodor.

I think about Fyodor.

Like Nikita.

The name opened in her mind like an abyss. She hadn't thought of him for ten years.

Nikita looked for you that night Catherine almost killed you. Remember? He found you and took you to Fyodor's place. Remember? After you shattered Fyodor, he took you to the train. You could barely walk, so he stole some money from his father and went with you as far as Novo Irkutsk. Then you made him leave you. Remember?

I remember.

"I think we've found them," said Bertini, looking up from the scanner.

The laser ranging system had picked out an anomaly as they approached the glacier. The flyer slowed.

"Why are you slowing down?" Antonia snapped at him. "We're not there yet."

He looked up at her with an amused expression. "Won't do them any good if we overshoot or crack up on the ice next to them." He turned back to the instruments. "It'll be okay."

Some minutes later they moved slowly over the lip of the glacier. Below them they could barely see the wreckage.

The thread between them flared suddenly. "She's awake," cried Antonia. She tried to reach down to her through their connection, but it was blocked as if by stone. "Thalia?" she said softly. Nothing.

Bertini brought the flyer down a few feet away from the two figures. They ran to Thalia and Sato. Antonia tried to help Thalia to her feet.

"No, thank you," she croaked and tried to stand. She fell, and Antonia had to help her back to the flyer, her blanket wrapped around her like a gown.

Sato was much colder. Bertini picked him up and brought him back. He lay Sato down on the deck and took the controls.

"Lindsay?" Sato muttered.

The flyer screamed into the air and banked toward the *Hirohito*.

Antonia looked from Sato to Thalia.

"Care for Sato," croaked Thalia. "I do not need your help."

She stripped Sato and wrapped him in a new, dry blanket, turned the heat on. He drank some hot chocolate from a cup she held for him. She examined him while he shivered. Sato's blanket had not protected him as well as had Thalia's. He had severe frostbite on his legs and arms. He would have to go into one of the cold tanks at the *Hirohito* while Antonia supervised the regrowing of the dead tissue. She looked toward Bertini and saw he was watching her.

"How bad?"

"Couple of weeks in the tank, I think."

"Damn," he said and turned back to the controls. The wind began to howl outside the flyer as he stepped up the engines.

Sato's gaze moved blindly across the ship, then settled on Antonia. He squinted to see her clearly. "Lindsay?" He fell asleep. Antonia turned to Thalia.

"I said, I do not need your help."

"Tough." She fed Thalia warm water and dried her fur, then wrapped her again as she had Sato. "We'll be back soon."

"I am not going back on your ship."

"We can take better care of you there." Antonia sat across from her.

"It is not a place I wish to be. Take me home."

"Thalia—"

"Will you keep me prisoner?"

"Of course not!" Antonia stopped, relaxed. "You have been cold. Your leg is injured—there could be nerve damage. I am just concerned for your welfare."

"My welfare." She did not speak a moment. "My welfare. What do you know of my welfare? I buried my lovers, all of them. Buried them under the trees after they'd sired their children in me. All save one. The one you killed. Take me home. My people will be enough. I will live whole or as a cripple, or I will die. But I will not take help from you. I want nothing to do with you."

Antonia stared at her. Thalia's attention was riveted on Antonia. The flyer was absolutely silent but for the wind.

"Lindsay?" muttered Sato from behind them.

14 SATO: ON EARTH

Sato's apartment was the same. Couch, table, chairs. Kitchen off to one side and bedroom off to the other. An auditory phone, an old electric refrigerator, incandescent lights. The window was open, and through it he could hear the night murmur of Pilotston, no squeaks or whistles of Boston, but the sound of nightbirds, footsteps, and voices. Pilotston, once part of Cambridge, but ceded to the Pilots a century and a half ago. Pilotston, where the pilots lived. Sato was no pilot—just a navigator. But Lindsay was and had gotten the apartment for him. Everywhere else the world was caught up in being part of May 2250. But here, Pilotston, had its own time.

He stood in the doorway and felt himself begin to relax. He'd been gone eight months. It just didn't seem that long. And the Boston skyline had changed. Three new buildings that looked two-dimensional—he'd walked past one to the transport, and the damned thing had disappeared edge on—and the dome in the harbor. Who knew what that was?

He tossed the travel pack into the corner. The refrigerator was filled with food and, more importantly, an archaic six-pack of beer. He smiled. *Lindsay, my boy, you are good to me.* He'd moved in with Lindsay's family after his own parents had died. "Get me Lindsay." The phone chimed in response.

Deep voice foggy with sleep: "What the Christ?"

"You're going downhill. I remember when you'd wake up like a gunshot, and we'd go cruising."

Pause. "It ain't the years—"

"—it's the mileage." Sato laughed. "That was old even before *you* were born. Come on down and have a beer with me. You bought them. You ought to be able to leave your strong handsome men long enough to help me drink them."

"There's no one here. How long are you back for?"

"For fucking forever, maybe."

"You don't have another gig lined up? Lightfoot Sato? In town for a week, make the girls cry, leave the next."

"I had Tony take me off the duty roster for a while. I decided I needed a vacation. Besides, I have to catch up. Did you see that dome in the harbor?"

"It's a hotel."

Sato grimaced. "Another one. Great. You had dinner yet?"

"Sato, it is *four* in the morning."

Sato shrugged. "That's about noon, ship time. Time for lunch. You're awake; let's eat."

FEATHERBED PORT'S got this street that runs from the center of town to the docks. It's a big street. If you go into town from any of the ships at all, navy or merchant marine, you have to go up this street. You can't help it. They don't like beggars in Featherbed. But they got them, and they can't do anything about it. So they put them on this street. Just to keep them in one place. Kom-sah. Or Cama-sah. Or something. The beggars say that. I don't know where they all come from.

I'd never spent much time in port there. Just in and out. But the shielding needed inspection. I'd been on mapping runs the last couple of years—alone except for the crew. Hanging out on the edge of things, where I like it. But now Featherbed was home for a week or two.

Nobody wanted to stay on the ship—me included. The action was happening uptown. So we'd go up there during the day, come down at night. And you'd have to go up this street. You'd pass these guys, and they'd say Kom-sah, Kom-sah, and after a while you'd get to recognize them. Then they'd be replaced in the crowd. The first day you'd notice one jumping up and down in front of you, arms stretched out—Kom-sah! Kom-sah! You couldn't give them any money. There were too many of them. How would you choose which one? The next day you'd recognize him standing back, the other new ones ahead of him. Kom-sah! Kom-sah! A day or two later he'd be sitting down against the wall of the street, not saying anything, just have his hand out. A day after that he'd be gone.

THEY FOUND an Italian take-out diner and afterward carried the food to the river at the edge of Pilotston. The lamplight was just enough to see a bit of the sidewalk, the river, and the grass. It gave the effect of a dimly lit room. The air had a bite to it, but there was no wind. The only sound was the river and the distant, bass rumble of Boston.

Sato sat down on the bench and opened the wrapper, sniffed the smell of garlic and basil. He leaned back against the bench, and something in his pocket struck the wood. "Damn." He pulled a package out of his jacket.

Lindsay looked at him quietly.

Sato fumbled with the package, then put it on the bench between them. "It's a present."

"For who?"

"Jesus. For you, dummy."

Lindsay took the package, looked at Sato, then back at the package. "I'll be damned."

"Told you I'd bring you something, someday, didn't I?"

"As far as I know, hell hasn't frozen over." He was suddenly quite still. "This isn't cleared. You smuggled it in, right?"

Sato nodded his head nervously. "I couldn't have paid the duty. Open it. It's nothing bad like food or perfume. And I made sure it's sterile. Go on. Open it."

Lindsay unwrapped the paper and plastic. After a few layers had been removed a faint glow of reflected light shone through the paper. He parted the wrapping. Nestled inside was a long-stem goblet. It caught the faint light from the streetlamp and sparkled with light of its own. Lindsay held it up.

"What is it?" he said in a hushed voice.

Sato leaned back. "I'm not sure. The surgeon on the ship thought it was Waterford crystal. If it is, it's got to be at least a couple of hundred years old." Sato watched the river. "Like I said, I couldn't have paid the duty on it. Some beggar sold it to me on Featherbed Alley—the last stop on the gig. God knows where he found it. I wasn't going to buy it, but I'd never brought anything home to you, so I did."

Lindsay held it in both hands. "There isn't anything...*funny* about this, is there? Is it stolen?"

Sato didn't speak for a minute. "No. There's nothing funny about it. You're all the family I've got, Lindsay. I just brought something home for you. There's a first time for everything, isn't there?"

"I suppose," murmured Lindsay and carefully replaced the goblet in the wrappings. He carefully placed the package on the ground and suddenly hugged Sato close.

"Hey." Sato patted Lindsay ineffectually. "It's just a goblet."

"It's the thought that counts." Lindsay released him.

Sato turned his attention back to his food, but after some minutes looked across the river. "You can't see the changes so much at night."

"It's not so different." Lindsay leaned back to study the skyline.

Sato turned to his food. "You spend too much time at home, isolated. Pilotston never changes. You got to go out and be in it to see how much it's changed."

Lindsay chuckled. "Since when did you see so much? Once, maybe twice a year. You're no judge. It's not so different."

"Everything's different. You don't *see* it."

"You *are* on a roll tonight."

He did not say anything for a moment. "My parents' house is gone—the place I grew up before I moved in with your family. Flat. I took the long way home—seeing how the city's different, you know? They made it into a transport terminal." He snorted in disgust.

"Is that why the goblet?"

"Maybe. Nothing is pure. Everything is different."

Lindsay chuckled again. "Nothing is pure, all right. You most of all."

Sato grinned a little. "True. Ask around on Featherbed, you'll hear the same. I could tell you stories—"

"I'd just as soon you didn't." Lindsay looked uncomfortable.

Sato picked at his manicotti. "All right." There was silence for several minutes.

Lindsay lit a cigarette. "I'd rather hear about the goblet."

"There isn't much to tell."

Lindsay waved toward the city. "Come now. Even Boston has tales to tell. You know, Boston: a million people, a hundred stories."

"How many does Pilotston have?"

"One or two, maybe?"

Sato smiled and put down his manicotti. "There isn't much to tell, honest. I bought it off a beggar."

"Consorting with beggars. I bet this beggar was about five-foot-two, with long black hair and deep almond eyes, and a silk dress and a slit in it up to here. I've heard of Featherbed."

"It was a he."

Lindsay looked shocked. "Say it isn't so! Consorting with men after all these years—"

Sato shook his head. "You don't see them. You pilots hang around in your little bars and little towns—like here—and keep your lives in little rooms. Which is just fine. There are things going on out there you don't even dream about. What we do to each other—" He stopped and brushed his lap.

Lindsay studied his hands. "What do we do to each other?"

"Nothing." He put the remains of his dinner to one side. "I like it out there. I like that out-on-the-edge feeling. But it's not right to do it *here*. We're not new. We've got history. We've got perspective. And we throw it away. You pilots don't see anything."

Lindsay reached over and took his hand. "What happened out there?"

Sato stood up and stared out at the river. "Quit pestering me, damn it. I bought it for you 'cause I thought you'd like it."

Silence fell but for the river. Even the city seemed hushed.

"I didn't mean to sound ungrateful," said Lindsay finally.

Sato shook his head. "You didn't. It's just a present, that's all. I'm tense 'cause I just got back."

Lindsay looked up. "Yeah."

"Let's go on back."

Lindsay nodded.

At the foot of the stairs, Lindsay hugged Sato again. "For the goblet."

"Yeah." Sato shrugged. "Catch you tomorrow."

Lindsay nodded and went upstairs.

Sato walked heavily into the apartment, feeling obscurely depressed.

I DON'T KNOW WHY it got to me. Maybe it was because of the map runs—you don't see anyone on a map run but the crew. Just you and this empty planet and more work to do than you can possibly imagine. It's clean. It's pure. Then, to come to Featherbed—old, old colony. One of the very early Chinese expansions. It was like suddenly finding yourself in unhuman country. They looked like people. They sounded like people. But they didn't act like you think people ought to act.

A beggar is a thing, one part of you says. Another part turns him into a man against your will. What caused this scar? That wrinkle? What does he see when he asks you for charity? And this multiplied over and over, until you're being drowned not in people but in filth, bacterial filth, covered over with mold. And you cry, Go away!—and they will not. All the time growing on you, taking from you, but still being human.

HE FOUND LINDSAY on the roof, weeding his garden. The sun was strong, and Lindsay was stripped to the waist.

"What are they?" Sato called.

Lindsay looked up and sat back on his knees. "They're going to be chives if I can kill the weeds."

"Need some help?"

"Always need help against the weeds."

Sato knelt next to him, and they worked in silence for about half an hour. "Sorry I yelled at you last night."

"Forgotten. Don't worry about it."

Sato looked over the roofs of the neighboring buildings. Each had a garden. The sun made them seem to shine and glitter. He was reminded of the goblet. "It was Featherbed," he said after a pause. "There was a whole collection of beggars on this street into the city, but you couldn't stop—they'd be all over you. You couldn't stop."

"Help me with this." One of the weeds had wrapped around the buried watering pipes. They had to trace it down and cut it away carefully to avoid cutting the pipe. After that, Lindsay reached to the edge of the garden and picked up a water bottle. "Want some?"

Sato nodded.

"How did you get the goblet?" asked Lindsay after they both drank.

"One morning one of them—I'd seen him before—offered it to me. There weren't as many around that morning. I bought it. The rest of them started to crowd me, and I ran down the street. It makes me shaky to think about it."

Lindsay did not say anything for a long moment. He reached over and touched Sato on the wrist. "I like the goblet. I like it very much."

Sato nodded.

When they finished weeding, they sat on the benches next to the dirt. They passed the water bottle back and forth. It was a warm spring, and though the evening before was cold, this still morning made them sweat.

"How did you get into this?" Sato rinsed his mouth and spit off the edge of the roof.

"Couth. Very couth." Lindsay chuckled.

"You were never interested in gardening when we were kids."

"I wasn't interested in a lot of things when we were kids."

"Right. *I* was. Patti Schribner. Eighth grade."

Lindsay laughed. "Joey DiMartino. Seventh grade."

Sato frowned. "You always were ahead of me. So, how did you get into gardening?"

Lindsay looked at the small ten-by-twenty plot. "It's real, I suppose."

"Real. Like other things aren't?"

Lindsay shrugged.

"Next you're going to tell me it has something to do with piloting." Sato sat next to him. "Let's see, how does it go? 'The white arms of ships—'"

"'The spell of arms and voices,'" Lindsay corrected, "'the white arms of roads, their promise of close embraces and the black arms of tall ships that stand against the moon, their tale of distant nations. They are held out to say: We are alone. Come.'"

"That's it. That's all you pilots ever say about piloting. And you're going to tell me that brought you into a garden?"

Lindsay smiled at him, and Sato suddenly felt as if he were very young. "Did you know engineers were called stovelighters? Pilots were once called lamplighters,'' Lindsay said at last.

"I knew that. It doesn't answer my question."

"I suppose." Lindsay looked away. "Nothing seems quite real after you begin piloting. But dirt is real. Plants." He grabbed Sato on the knee. "You're real."

Sato shrugged and stood up. "Want to go out and party tonight?"

Lindsay watched him a long time, half smiling. "Sure. Why not?"

THERE'S THIS ONE—I don't know his name. Christ, I can't understand three words from him. I know "Kom-sah," but that's it. But he steps up to me like a soldier at dawn. Not strong, really. He's too thin for that. But you get this feeling that things were going to be okay for him. I won't give him anything. I would be mobbed.

The next day I see him again. Thinner, weaker. Not so optimistic, I think. It's like a picture, kind of. One of those picture books where the eyes of one person leap off the page at you and you're all of a sudden there, in the picture. And you can smell the shit in the streets, and the babies, and the fish smell of the bay. And the beggars come up to you, and they cry, "Kom-sah!" "Kom-sah!"

I think, I wish Lindsay could see this. But I'm there instead, and by damn! This beggar I'd been seeing looks like Lindsay. I mean, he's Chinese—about five foot and not even a hundred pounds. But the way he moves is like Lindsay, and his eyes are like Lindsay's. And he has this box he's holding out to me, trying to sell it.

I don't know what to do. I keep on walking and meet my mates in the city. But I can't get this guy out of my mind. We hang out in this whorehouse all night, and I don't feel much like being there. But I'm damned if I want to be back at the ship. It's like I'm in limbo, like the world doesn't have any anchor.

Morning comes, and I leave when the sun comes up. I'm walking down the beggar's street. It's so early they're not really jostling me. Something is wrong. The beggar I'd seen yesterday is missing. I look around, and he's propped up against the wall. He looks like hell.

I go and stand over him. And it's like looking at Lindsay lying there. I think—it's crazy—I think, this is Lindsay here, dying in front of you, 'cause you won't give him what he needs.

It's just a beggar! I say to myself.

No, it's Lindsay.

It's a kind of double vision. One second I'm seeing Lindsay there; the next it's this half-dead Chinaman. Then it's Lindsay again.

I take whatever money I have in my pockets and stuff it in his shirt. And he kind of wakes up and sees me. He holds up this fucking box to me. Goddamn it! He pokes it at me a couple of times, weak. He can barely hold up his arm. How long does it take someone to starve to death? A week? A month? When did he eat last?

I take the box and start toward the ship. At the end of the street I look back, and I can't see him. He is gone.

THEY STOOD IN THE DOORWAY and watched. The room had a swaying motion: rumba over *here*, band beating time, rumba over *there* . . . He could tell it was Lindsay's place by its perfect neatness—the same neatness of his own rooms. "Lindsay, you've been cleaning my apartment while I was gone."

Lindsay pushed him lightly through the door. "Guilty as charged. Want a drink?"

"Right."

Lindsay left the room and returned with two beers. "Have we had enough?"

"Hell no!"

"Right." They clinked bottles, and Lindsay started to drink. Sato stopped him.

"Wait." He looked owlishly around the room. "There." He pointed to the goblet on a shelf. "Use that."

"Ah!" Lindsay nodded. "Good idea." He held up the beer and intoned solemnly: "Out of the sampans, into the glass. This is the beer—"

Sato made a noise of disgust. "Half the city used the bay for a toilet."

"—aged in the ancient Chinese bladders, to bring to your palates Featherbed's favorite export. Drink deep. Enjoy. To us, the pig-dogs!"

Sato looked at him uncertainly. "To us, the pig-dogs. You okay?"

Lindsay looked at him, then at the floor, then back at him. "Fine. Drunk, but fine. Are *you* fine?"

Sato shrugged. "Yeah. Sure."

"It's got to be real. Keep it light. Keep it light," Lindsay muttered to himself.

"What are you talking about? You're acting strange."

"Maybe. Tell me about your lovers."

"*What?* Christ, Lindsay."

"Is it easy to find women in port? It must be. You've never had any trouble." Lindsay drank half his beer absently.

Sato turned away from him. "Not so hard. Checking out what's real? Is this like gardening?"

"Perhaps. Consider me an anthropologist. You are a foreign specimen under a microscope, enduring the tightest, most exacting scrutiny. Your every movement is to be catalogued and studied. I will write a monograph on you. 'Stud service: an examination of the migratory male.'"

"What happens if I get some offers?"

"If you make any money on it, I get ten percent. If I make any money, I keep it all."

Sato laughed. "You are crazy."

"Tell me about the women in port."

Sato shrugged. "There's not much to tell. There's always whores. One time we were in port right at the edge of a bay—"

"Where?"

Sato looked at him. "You're not going straight?"

Lindsay looked startled, then laughed out loud. "Hardly. Where was this?"

"I don't remember. The captain and first officer went off somewhere for the afternoon. Some guy brought a boat load of girls right to the edge of the pad. The second officer was a good guy, and he didn't say nothing. Another place had this line of stairs near the port. You could stand at the bottom and look up to take your pick. If you didn't see anything you wanted, you could just admire the scenery."

"Easy. Very easy." Lindsay looked out the window a long moment. "Did the beggars on Featherbed sell it, too?"

"No."

Lindsay turned back to him. "Not at all?"

Sato felt uncomfortable. "What's going on, huh? What are you getting at?"

"Surely some of them must have sold it."

"They were mostly men."

"So? Male hookers."

Sato didn't know what to say. Something was—wrong. Just wrong. "These guys were starving. Or they were sick. Or they were crippled. The guy I bought the goblet from—"

"Yes. Tell me about that."

"Nothing."

"*Bullshit*, man! Don't hold out on me! It's stolen? What was wrong with the beggar? What did he say?"

Sato sat down and shook his head. "He didn't say anything. He talked, all right, but I couldn't understand a word. What are you going on about?"

Lindsay didn't seem to hear him for a moment. "You wanted to know about pilots. Remember when we were kids? We both wanted to go into space. Both of us wanted to be captains. Captain Sperling and his adventurers! Lindsay Rosenheim and the Argonauts." He didn't seem to see the room or Sato. His eyes were distant and empty. "You got into Candidate School. I discovered I had—other talents." His eyes locked suddenly on Sato, and Sato flinched. "You go to sleep before we jump, all of you passengers. Then you wake up. And we're there. You don't ever stand in n-space, looking at the fragile, vulnerable, *arbitrary* nature of your world. Things that might be real. Things that might not..." His gaze drifted away from Sato back out the window.

Silence fell. The dark outside had a humid, palpable quality.

"He looked like you," Sato said suddenly.

Lindsay roused and stared at the floor. "What did you say?"

"He reminded me of you, I mean. I got this crazy idea that it was you, lying on the ground, starving to death; the only chance you had of living was in this box you couldn't sell. And it was like you were dying because I wouldn't give you something you needed."

Lindsay still wouldn't look at Sato. "You could have given him some food. He needed that more than money."

"I didn't think of it. He asked me for money. I gave him what he asked for."

"But," Lindsay said gently, "you didn't give him what he needed."

"How was I supposed to know what he needed?"

"He was right there."

"Goddamn it! You got to tell me what you need. I can't read your mind. I give you what you goddamn ask for." Sato buried his head in his hands. "What's going on?"

"I don't ask for what I need."

"Fucking beggar. I wish I'd smashed that goddamn glass. He looked like you. He just looked like you."

Lindsay stood slowly and walked over to him and brought his face up gently. He looked deep into Sato's eyes, then kissed him on the mouth.

"Jesus, Lindsay." Sato looked back at him. "We're friends. Let's—"

Lindsay interrupted him with another kiss.

I HAD A VIRGIN ONCE. Not like I was a kid, but just a year or so ago. It was in Vera Cruz at Christmas time. She was a hooker, and her pimp said she was a virgin. Fine, I said. I didn't believe him. They all say they're selling virgins. But she was. And she was so earnest I found it exciting. Afterward, though, afterward—it was clumsy and rough. I was clumsy and rough. I didn't mean to be. I should have been— well, graceful, somehow. And I wasn't.

THE SKY HAD THE FAINT mother-of-pearl luster of pre-dawn. Sato stood at the window, looking out. Pilotston was quiet now. In the distance, he heard Boston, but Pilotston was asleep. Where the pilots dwell. *Now, I do also,* he thought. He wanted to do something with his hands. Lindsay's cigarettes were near him. He took one out and lit it, tried to smoke, and began to cough.

"Sato?" came a sleepy voice.

Damn.

"Over here. By the window."

"Come back to bed."

"I want to stay up awhile."

Sato heard Lindsay get out of bed and put on a robe. Lindsay came to stand next to him. He put his hand on Sato's shoulder, and Sato flinched, then relaxed. "Your hands are cold."

"Sorry. May I have a drag?" Lindsay's voice at night was deep, like a purr.

Sato passed him the lit cigarette without comment.

"I didn't know you smoked."

Sato shrugged. "I don't. I was just trying it out."

There was a long pause.

"Do you feel any more real now?" Sato turned to him. "Was this real?"

Lindsay didn't respond immediately. "Are you blaming me for anything I should know about?"

Sato fell back into his chair. "No. Not really."

Lindsay touched him again. Sato pulled away. "Don't do that. It makes me feel crazy."

Lindsay came around in front of him. Sato could see his teeth in the glow from the street. He was smiling.

"I love you," he said. "I've loved you since we were kids."

"Don't."

"Other things change for me. Not you. You were always there for me."

Sato shook his head. "You're my family. All there is. I'm scared—*Goddamn it, Lindsay! You touch me again, and I'll break your fucking jaw!*"

Lindsay stood in front of Sato, his hand stretched out in front of him. Slowly, he brought his hand back. "Yes, of course," he said softly.

"Lindsay—"

"No. It's all right. Let's have some tea. All right?"

Sato sat down in the chair. He nodded. Lindsay left him, and Sato could hear him banging around in the kitchen. After a few moments, he could hear boiling water. Lindsay reentered the room with two cups of tea.

"Here. Have a cup."

Sato took the cup and sipped at it. He put it on the window sill.

"Lindsay," Sato began.

"No. Don't start." Lindsay took a deep breath. "There are no guarantees. Where is it written someone has to love you?"

"Think of me as your brother—"

"*Don't!* You'll cheapen it. You'll make it into a lie." He pointed to the bed. "It happened right there. The sheets smell of sweat, and the mattress is lumpy. It was real. If it wasn't what I wanted or expected, it was *still* real."

Sato felt a low burning anger inside of him. "I've known you all my life. You're as much a part of me as my hands. You think I don't feel for you?" A sudden image of boxes came to him. "You got this narrow-gauge life. I got no place in it."

"I said don't." He sighed. "Look. This is crazy. I love you. You know it. I know it. I know you were there with me. *I was there.* I heard you. I watched you. I'm not blind."

"We were friends. Like brothers—hell, we *are* brothers. Now it's all muddy."

"Balls!" Lindsay stood up and walked around the room. He picked up the goblet, looked at it, put it down again. "You can't just leave it alone, can you? *I was there.* You were doing what you wanted. What I wanted. Now it's morning, and you feel awkward. *Okay.* This is Lindsay you're talking to. I'm not any different. You're not any different."

Sato sipped his tea. "We're both different."

"We are not! That's not real—"

"To hell with your 'real' crap! I was there, too." He stopped, calmed himself. "I had a virgin, once. She was okay, but afterward she was different."

"How?"

"Afterward she gave me this embarrassed little smile like she was sorry it wasn't much fun, and I wanted to hit her. She was different afterward. Coarser."

Lindsay's face lost all expression. "Coarser than the whores you usually slept with? Coarse, indeed." Sato didn't answer. "That's how you see me?"

Sato leaned against the window and looked out. "I couldn't have been much good. It was my first time."

Silence fell between them.

"You call my life narrow. It's nothing compared to the straight line you call a life."

Sato flinched and didn't answer.

Lindsay stood very still. "This was a mistake, wasn't it? This isn't going to go away. It'll always be between us."

"Christ, how should I know?" Sato picked up the teacup and threw it out the window. He could hear it shatter in the alley. "Yes. No. Maybe."

Lindsay reached out and started to put his arms around him. Without thinking, he smashed Lindsay across the face and knocked him across the room. The crash echoed. "Christ," Sato muttered softly.

Lindsay picked himself up off the floor. His nose was bloody. The blood spattered across his naked chest and his robe. "Bastard."

"I'm sorry—"

"Bastard. Family? I'm your family? I buy your beer. I clean your apartment. I even found the place for you. What do you give me?" He looked around, saw the goblet. "You give me cold glass." He smashed the goblet.

"Lindsay—"

"Friends. Brothers. I piss on your friendship."

"Goddamn you! It was all right, but you had to push it. Goddamn you to hell, Lindsay! Goddamn you to hell!"

"Get out."

"I'm gone."

Lindsay slammed the door after him.

AFTER THAT BEGGAR, I was no longer the virgin. I was coarser. I was touched. Anything I touched in return had to react to me. I was an accident searching for a place to happen. After the beggar, every moment of my life followed me, like a butterfly waiting to light, to blight me or glorify me.

After the beggar, it landed between me and Lindsay, and then it was no longer the vague, uncertain beggar, but the hard events between the two of us. I was different. No one knew how much I had changed, least of all myself.

DAWN CAME FULLY into Sato's apartment. He was pacing furiously. He was angry, frightened, excited, grief-stricken. No part of him remained still.

"Damn you," he muttered to himself. "Damn you to hell."

"Phone?—cancel." It was the fifth time he had begun the call.

No. He should call me.

Nothing happened.

He should call *me*.

Sunlight bathed the floor.

"All right," he said, suddenly still. "All right, then. You had your chance."

The phone speaker was too loud. Too vulnerable. He called the duty center using the handset.

"Tony? Tony, right. Sato. Have you got anything going out today? Yeah, today. I'll wait." *Damn you. Damn you, Lindsay.* "The *Shenandoah*. Okay. Tony? Leave something in the bulletin board about my apartment. I want to let it go. To some pilot. Thanks, Tony."

He looked up at the ceiling, and it seemed he could see through the plaster to Lindsay, staring back. "Good-bye, Lindsay."

He slammed the door, and the sounds of his footsteps on the stairs echoed through the building. A few minutes later, the phone chimed.

15

The flyer was quiet, save for the distant sound of rushing air and the trembling whine of the motor. Antonia stared at Thalia dully. The thread that connected them ached like a half-healed bruise. She held herself and stared, not seeing, not feeling.

Thalia did not move.

Behind her, Bertini said nothing as he piloted, and Sato was unconscious, completing the company of silence.

As they neared the coastline, Thalia stirred. "Take me to my village."

Antonia wailed *abandoned*, and no one heard her.

Bertini looked at Antonia questioningly. She nodded.

The flyer curved west in a long bank over the trees. It flew upstream along the river, and when it reached the village Bertini brought it down low, just over the water.

"Help me down. My people will take me from there."

"Don't," Antonia said in a low voice. "Come back to me."

"Help me."

Antonia supported her down the landing ramp. Other Calibii had gathered. One stepped forward to take Thalia from her. Thalia stopped and turned back to Antonia.

"I find I cannot hate you. You have done so much in ignorance. In innocence. And you feel so much pain about it. No one can know this more than I." She paused. "Still, I will not come to you again."

"Will someone else come?" called Bertini from behind them.

"Quiet," hissed Antonia.

"I don't know," said Thalia. "We'll see."

Bertini nodded and returned to the pilot's console.

"I can still feel you," Antonia said. "You know I'm here. You can feel me as well. I can't leave that. How can you?"

Thalia was silent a long moment.

"I can only try." She turned to the waiting Calibii and hobbled away.

"I can't even do that," Antonia murmured.

"C'mon, Antonia. We've got to get Sato to the ship."

Fire and ruin, she thought. Fire and ruin and death. Images of roses flashed through her mind. And trees, walking.

IT WAS HOURS BEFORE they brought me home. Antonia alternately shouted at me, reasoned with me. It was all I could do to hold my will my own on that cold, dark ride back. My back throbbed where I had struck the flyer's railing. Bruises all across my body awoke in pain. And it was blindness, everywhere but the dim glow of their bodies and the faint sparks from the flyer's entrails. Bertini did not know I was blind, and I was too proud to tell him.

Demons are of the dark.

I must leave them, I *must*. They corrupted me. They corrupted my people. All things that we are they were not. But—I *liked* them. If Sato had been of my people, I might have loved him. Cameron was a joy. And I had never been so close to anyone—not Caretaker, not Traverse—as I had been to Antonia. So much to leave. So much.

When we approached coastline and I could see, my resolve strengthened. Antonia's wilted until she sat in the copilot's chair next to Bertini and watched me, silent to all others but weeping across the thread between us.

"Leave me at the edge of the forest," I said. "I'll make it from there."

"On one leg?"

"I can hobble on three limbs. One lost leg doesn't leave me an invalid."

"No. It leaves you a cripple."

What could I say to that?

"Take me to my village," I said at last.

So much to leave . . .

Bertini brought their demon device in low so as not to scare my people. For this, I was grateful. They helped me to the bank and left me there. Caretaker came from the crowd and helped me away.

"I will take you to your family's hogan," she said.

"Don't. I am not worthy. I belong nowhere. I am heartsick and ashamed." I leaned against her. "I have learned terrible truths."

"Hush, Binder—"

"I bind *nothing*. All that I love I hurt. All that loves me I leave. I thought these things *must* be, but it is not so. We are small in the world. We are small . . ."

Caretaker held me. "I will take you to my hogan."

And she led me, so limp and unresisting, so lost in myself that I did not hear her and did not know the honor she did me until long after she lay me down. I slept, not knowing or caring where I was. Surrounded in my madness by those already half mad and who so understood me.

They are returning.

"How long?" She sat at the captain's console on the bridge of the *Hirohito*, scowling at the terminal.

Minutes only.

"It's not here. The interrupter is not here."

Of course not. I could have told you that.

"You did. Several times. It had to be checked." She bit the edge of her thumb. "He's got it on him."

I've scanned him. I found nothing.

"Of course not." She barked a soft laugh. "If you could scan it, we could steal it. If we could steal it, it's not safe. And if it's not safe, he can't mutiny."

Megan, maybe it's a fluke. Something he did with the Hirohito. I wasn't watching him. You weren't watching him. Maybe he did it with some kind of software glitch.

"And if we watch him constantly, we can stop him before he has a chance to trigger it?"

Something like that.

She laughed again. "No such luck. I wouldn't do it that way, so I can bet he wouldn't either. If it's not *on* him, and it's not *around* him, then it's got to be *in* him. Hooked into his soft-wiring."

We'll never find it. We'd have to dissect him to find out what is softwiring and what is not.

"Right. We can't stop whatever he has—"

—so we stop him?

"Exactly."

I don't like this.

"I didn't think you would."

Haven't you murdered enough?

Expression chased expression across her face. "Damn you."

Well?

Megan composed herself and stared into her hands in her lap. She looked at the console and in her mind faced the *Shenandoah*. She smiled.

"I'll never touch him."

TIME PASSED. Expectancy filled the atmosphere of the *Hirohito*. Sato stayed unconscious while his frostbite healed. Bertini waited. Antonia grew thin and wan. Megan schemed. All of them spun around each other in tense little orbits. Then Sato was decanted from the tanks and gradually brought up to life's temperature.

Thus:

Image followed image followed memory. He cried out, and no one answered. He could not hear his own voice. There was only cold, a terrible cold that left marks inside him even after the rest of the world warmed. *Lindsay watching, wondering, measuring. Never exactly saying what he was thinking—and then it was Antonia, watching him with the same expression. Then, maybe, it was both, and he couldn't keep them straight. Always the cold. Always.*

No time passed, only moments of sensed movement, of jostling, of uncertain knowledge that he was in a new place, jostling again, and another new place. The places were unknown, unknowable.

He balanced on some point that held him wriggling, shifting this way, then that, never quite letting him go, never letting him fall, but holding him there on the tip of falling. The point was needle-sharp and cold.

He could feel warmth somewhere indeterminate. It could not penetrate him.

No time passed. Eternity passed.

It was like sleep; one was sleepy, then dreaming, then awake. The moment of passing into sleep was lost. So it was with this; a moment he was balanced, struck through the heart with a needle of cold. The next he was falling, falling toward consciousness. Warmer, no longer with the stab of cold twisting inside him like a key in a clock, but marked, indelibly.

A voice came to him, then, drawing him back to the flyer. *You said this? Thalia said that?* And the questioning went on seemingly forever. It was a gentle, insistent voice—patient. The voice faded, and he forgot it had ever been.

After a time—there was time now—he knew himself to be awake, holding himself in twilight by keeping his eyes closed. *Place* had a name: the *Hirohito. His room?* The bed was not his own. *Sick bay?* The questions seemed distant.

"Sato?" A soft voice. Different from before—before when? Whose voice was it? He wasn't sure. He frowned.

"Sato? I know you're awake."

Undercurrents. Fields. Mechanisms. The voice called these out of him. "Megan?" he whispered. He suddenly felt thirsty.

"You won't remember me. But remember this." And the voice began speaking to him, about Antonia, about Bertini. In return, he spoke about Lindsay, and the voice changed what he said. Images crashed on images, and the words burned. So did the fingers on his arm and the pinprick fire they left behind.

IT WAS A NASTY business.

Bertini leaned back in his workshop chair and stared at the bulkhead. Sato unconscious for three weeks while the frostbite healed, Antonia in depression. The ugly fact was they had failed. They were further away from relations with the Calibii now than before.

Nasty was *exactly* the word for it.

He found he had no real desire to take the ship from Megan. He had been part of a mutiny once. The captain—Pemberton, that was the name—had also been hardwired, but had become an uncaring thing, cruel and hard. Then the anger had shaken him until he had faced her. He had won only because he had been willing to die and she had not.

With Megan, it was different.

He had a real liking for her, a real respect. He had no idea what might happen to her if she lost her ship. With Pemberton, he had not cared, had not followed anything about her the moment he had left the ship on Earth. The Port Authority had her then, and he was uninterested.

He was surprised to find himself reluctant to proceed.

The interrupter lay like a weight in his belly, a tumor aimed at someone else.

Nasty.

He would care for her when it was over. Whatever he could do, he would do. But it had to be done. Megan had been right months ago. They wouldn't last two minutes in Sentient's Court. The lives of Antonia and Sato more than outweighed the one old crone with a ship and her ancient engineer.

There's hope for you, yet.

"You think so?"

With Sato sick and Antonia in deep depression, he wouldn't have much help.

Cameron woke up on his pillow under the shelving, looked at him, shook his head, and looked around. He pulled himself to his feet and shook himself, stretched.

Bertini chuckled.

The bear came over to him and leaped neatly into his lap, lay down across Bertini's belly and chest. He reached out one paw above Bertini's shirt to his skin, settled down, and went back to sleep.

"How do you know when I'm troubled?" Bertini sighed. "I don't always know myself."

WARMTH IS THE STUFF of life. Not light, not good or evil, not trees or grasses. The difference between the quick and the dead is one of temperature.

I awoke in Caretaker's hogan, the warmth of other bodies nearby a steamy miasma of comfort.

Caretaker—my own Caretaker, not one of the others—appeared next to me.

"Warm," I said.

"We built a fire," she said and stood aside.

In the center of the room I could see the hazy violence signifying flame. Fire is not built lightly by our people. It can only be felt, only seen by the motion of air around it. It holds the

ame place to us that ghosts hold to humans: awe of the un-
een.

"I am honored." I looked around the hogan and knew I was
n Caretaker hogan. "I am doubly honored."

A second Caretaker, unknown to me, approached from the
ther side of the fire. "As are we, to be hosting Speaker to De-
nons."

"Speaker to Demons?" I said stupidly.

Caretaker did not answer immediately. "It is a name you are
nown by these days."

"I chose the name Binder. Do any remember it?"

"It is remembered," Caretaker admitted. "But only by those
vho know you. Speaker to Demons is famous across the three
ands."

"I am triply honored," I said dryly. "They are not de-
nons."

Caretaker did not answer.

I stayed in their hogan less comfortably after that. Soon I
vanted to be out of it, but there was no place for me to go. The
ommunity hogan seemed to hold only strangers calling me
Speaker to Demons, and my family was stiff and cold to me.
Speaker to Demons, indeed.

My leg did not remain dead. After a few days, feeling re-
urned in sharp tinglings and twitches. I could feel, but it still
noved as if made of wood. The way I limped fretted me, and I
nissed my old grace.

Caretaker was always with me, but did not speak much. It
ame to me after a few days that she was waiting. It was al-
nost a month before I found out what she was waiting for.

It came simply: "We should return to the trees."

We were alone in Caretaker hogan. I was bathing my leg in
varm water. It felt good against the cool air of the hogan but
lid not help. Time alone might heal me; nothing else.

"After I dry myself. How about in spring? All things move
aster then."

"You joke with me."

"You expect me to be serious? If you don't want to care for
ne, return me to the group hogan. I can find a daughter or sis-
er to help me."

"You are welcome here. You know that."

I did. I also did not want to go up into Caretaker forest. I did not want to face Infertility, Disapproval, or Climber. I most certainly did not want to speak with Traverse.

"I am not healed yet."

"You never will be."

I stopped. Her words froze some deep part of me. Snow collected in my gut. "It is early yet."

"It is not." Caretaker reached out for my hand, and I pulled away. "I have seen such injuries before. So far, the limb returns to life. But just so far. After that, little more is regained."

"The leg was unmarked."

"It is not the leg that is damaged." She touched the nearly healed bruise on my back. "The damage is here. You are lucky it is a loss. Sometimes there is pain so great it paralyzes, holding the victim rigid with screams."

I shuddered, rubbed my leg. "It is cold outside."

"It is not the cold that keeps you here."

"You do not know what keeps me here. You do not know what I know."

"I would like to."

I did not speak for a moment. "You would not."

She left it there for a day, but returned to it the next and the next until, finally, I agreed to go.

It was a warm day, nearly spring. The trees were bright, the air only a little cold. You could see summerlight coming. I had a brief, unreasonable hope no one would be there, that they had taken the day and played in it.

They were waiting for me, of course. Runners had been sent ahead to fetch them.

"Binder," said Infertility, "come sit with us."

Traverse said nothing. He was there in presence, not speech.

"Give us news," said Disapproval.

I looked at them. I was tired. My leg throbbed in pain. *Do you really want to know what I know?* I thought.

Let them know. You want it; here it is.

I spoke of the trip north, what I had learned about human strengths, weaknesses. Their petty violences between each other; their careless power. Their blindness. I spoke of Sato's fears, Antonia's despair. The hidden fortress of Megan. The iron of Bertini. Then I told them of their lovers. How all of

hem had coupled and not one of them—*not one*—had borne
. child. How their lovers continued to live.

I was angry: at the humans, at being in the forest, at Tra-
'erse's coldness and my own helplessness. I was merciless.

They sat like the dead.

"Need we hear more?" said Traverse finally.

Disapproval shook herself. "No. We do not."

"I agree," Climber said.

Infertility was silent.

I felt a dark wind blowing through me. Things happening I
lid not understand. "Agree with what?"

Traverse ignored me. "They are not of the trees, yet they
iave will. When they couple, the males do not die. What more
ieed be said? They have killed. They come from the dark. They
ive in blindness. If this were not enough, one of them be-
rayed himself."

"What are you *saying*?"

"*We* said nothing. The rogue male said it himself: 'One dies.
That is all there is.' *They have no Ancestors!* What does this
nake them?"

I shook with confusion. Sato had made such an innocent
tatement. But when I thought about it, I saw it was true. They
iad no Ancestors. It showed in what they loved, what they
eared, the way they watched one another. *Of course*, I
hought. *How could it be otherwise?* Sato's words had fooled
ne, come to me neatly wrapped in idiom—*they* did not take it
.s strange, never knowing what it meant to us, any more than
iato had known what being able to be lovers with Antonia had
neant to me. We were all innocents, all isolated from one an-
>ther by misunderstanding. It struck me suddenly as funny, and
looked at the tree to share the joke.

"You don't understand . . ." I started, but the speech died in
he sudden intense silence. I looked around at them. Some de-
ision had been made, nearly made in my absence. Things had
»een weighed, and I had just tipped them over into finality.

"They are demons," intoned Traverse.

"Demons?" I laughed. "Of course not. We think too small.
'hey are far too different from us to be demons."

My speech was drowned by the quiet. I saw, but did not un-
lerstand, that I had said *enough*. Nothing more would make
iny difference. "You believe . . ." I trailed off. No one said
inything. *This is how war begins,* I thought and felt helpless.

It came to me then. Traverse had been waiting for me, laying all manner of traps, never knowing what set of tools would
be delivered into his hands. I had been used. It had all been
planned, an exercise in revenge. "It was an accident," I said to
him. "They killed you by *accident*."

He ignored me.

"They are demons," Infertility said slowly.

I looked at Caretaker. She turned away from me.

"No!" I cried to them. "Stupid, yes. Misguided, yes. But
they are no more evil than we are."

"Forgive me for saying this," said Traverse. "In your
watching, you have become infected by them. You will heal, in
time."

"You bastard," I screeched in English.

"You see," he said to the others, "she cannot even speak.
Hold her so that she does not interfere. But hold her gently. For
once we were close."

Hands were laid on me. "False! False!" I cried to them.
"Traverse, it is *you* who are the demon. I spit on your memory. I spit on you as a lover. If you had left me with child, I
would abort it! You are not *fit* to have been saved as an Ancestor!"

"I will speak with you later," he said kindly, "when you are
yourself."

They took me away to the hogans deep in Caretaker forest.

ANTONIA STOOD IN HER CABIN, holding a cup of tea in her
hand. She stared out the window across the sunlit grass. Spring
was here. The leaves on the trees were taking on the same gray-
ish, pastel quality they'd had in the fall, just before they turned.
She suspected soon they would turn again into a riot of color.

The last three weeks had been a terrible dream. Bertini had
tried to speak with her several times, but she was not interested. Sato slept the sleep of the just in cold, life-giving liquid
as his limbs were gradually healed. For that she was grateful.
She wanted to be alone with her loss. It had taken days to find
out what had happened on the trip, piecing together what was
said from the scrambled mutterings of Sato's delirium on the
return trip and the flyer's recordings. It was not enough.

Two days before, she had taken Sato from the cold tank and
put him in the warming bin.

There were drugs that put the sensitivity into harness so one could see into the dim fishbowl of another's mind. It was not telepathy, but it forced the ambiguity to one side for a time. All sensitives carried them. These drugs eventually broke the will and drove the user into the lost land of schizophrenia, but she had been willing to take that chance. One night, with this witches' brew coursing through her brain, she'd poured through Sato's mind, tracing down what had happened on the trip north. Under the guise of physician, she broke events loose from his mind's incoherence. Then the drugs wore off, and she did not dare take more. It did not matter; she'd learned what she needed.

It was not a nice thing to do to a lover.

It was not a nice thing to do to anyone.

Though Sato would never remember it, it was still a violation. Sensitives have their own moral code. Blessed and cursed by a capricious power, Antonia had gone far beyond it.

She didn't care.

She could see events coming together between Bertini and Megan. That didn't matter, either.

She had lost Thalia somehow because of being Sato's lover. Well, *that* stops right now.

The touch of Thalia against her mind was troubled and sore. Antonia could feel the boiling of emotions on the other side, like hearing a muffled argument through a thick wall. *Let me in,* she cried.

Nothing.

Let them rot. Let us all rot.

She threw her teacup against the window, and it shattered.

She wanted to sleep—she spent most of her time asleep these days—but she could not without help. She took a sedative and sat on the edge of the bed, waiting for it to take effect.

SATO WOKE AS FROM a great distance. He trembled, feeling as some feral thing, alternately fearful and brave. His eyes felt funny; nothing looked right through them. He rubbed his face, and it felt unnaturally taut and dry. His shoulders were tight with tension.

He was in his own room. He knew he had been in sick bay at one point, but they must have moved him here.

He stretched, grinned at the ceiling. The grin made his face tingle, and he ran his fingers across it. The raised line of the scar started just over his eye, across his nose, and down his cheek to his neck. Feeling it made him remember Thalia. Bitch. His grin became a frozen rictus. He felt afraid and free and angry.

Why had she done it?

He shrugged. It didn't matter. He'd been scarred. He'd make her pay—why? Don't think about that. He'd been *hurt*.

He threw off his covers and went to the mirror.

His face was still swollen, but the scar would have shown up anyway. It was a ridged, red, angry snake across his face. *Bitch.*

It'd be an expensive plastics job when he got home.

Home.

Sato sat back on the bed, holding himself. He knew without being told that Thalia wouldn't come back.

She hurt you. But why did she save you? She could have let you die in the cold. I saved her, too. *Why? What's different now?* Enough. Now it's just different. Could they ever get home?

He shrugged. So what? Who was left on Earth for him but bimbos and faggots?

Lindsay.

He grinned to himself. *Like I said . . .*

What are you thinking?

Thinking too damned much. No more. *Don't* think.

He dressed and left the room. The corridor was quiet and dark. Hell with this. He slapped the lights on and walked toward the bridge. Megan was there.

"Hey, lady," he said jauntily.

Megan turned toward him and smiled. "Hey, yourself."

She's not so bad, he thought. He couldn't remember why he had been scared of her.

"Where's Antonia?"

"In her cabin. I wouldn't go there, though."

"Oh?" *And why the hell not?*

"I don't think she's inclined to see you."

"We'll see about that."

He left the bridge and walked toward her room.

So. She's not *inclined* to see me. Life is tough. *She's lost Thalia. It's your fault. What do you expect?* Thalia slashed me. It's not my fault. *You don't know why, so you don't know whose fault it is.*

He knocked on her door.

Antonia's eyes were puffy and her face pale. She looked sleepy. "Yes."

Jesus. What did I see in her? It didn't matter. It was the *principle* of the thing. *This is your lover. Remember, you said you loved her.* So? Just another bimbo.

"I came by to show you I'm all right." He grinned. "More than all right." She looked at him in silence, studying him. This irritated him. "What's the matter?"

"I want to be alone right now."

"How come?"

Again the study.

"I want to be alone. That is reason enough."

Before he could react, she closed the door. He tried to open it again, but it was locked.

"Damn it, Antonia! Open the goddamned door!"

Silence.

Bitch. They were all bitches.

There was some plan at work here, some—conspiracy? Yeah. Its name was Bertini. He was—Bertini was in the kitchen. Okay. Now was the time to take care of him. *Lindsay standing on the porch of a white house. That's not my image! I didn't do that. Lindsay is in Boston. Listen—*

A voice cried out in him, but he ignored it.

THEY WOULD HAVE bound me but for Caretaker.

One of them—a member of Disapproval's band I think, some nameless stranger—made ready some ropes.

"Is she a beast?" cried out Caretaker scornfully.

"She might escape and warn the demons." She held the rope as if it were a shameful thing.

"Stand outside and watch the hogan. That should be enough."

They left us.

Words flew through me: *jail, incarceration, prisoner.* Words I had read but never understood.

Caretaker reached out her hands to me. Reflexively, I took them. "I could not bear to see them bind you," she said slowly.

"Binder. I was given the name because of the way I held on to people. It is fitting for me to be bound." I shuddered.

She tried to hold me, but I pushed her away, and she left me.
Later they brought me food, and I refused it. The next day was
the same.

I held myself, thinking. I almost tried to call Antonia but did
not. Let them rot, I thought. Let them all rot.

Then why did I want to save them? Why did I feel so guilty I
couldn't eat?

I felt for Antonia, then, but the thread was weak, fuzzy
without coherence. Asleep? Was she asleep? No, it didn't feel
that way.

She was trying to cut me off, too.

Let them rot, then.

Why are you hurt? *You* rejected *her*.

Caretaker returned, drawn and sad. "I have been told you
have not eaten."

"It is unimportant. Food does not interest me. What are
Traverse and the others doing?"

"The speakers and the Ancestors are determining what to
do."

"What is that?"

"How best to kill the demons."

"The creatures are not demons! The failure of understanding is not with them. *It is with us!*"

"They are so perfect?"

"They are not perfect at all. They are ignorant, violent creatures. But they are not demons. They are no more ignorant than
ourselves."

"They killed your lover."

I slashed the air jerkily with my claws. "Lover. Had he been
mine, I would have drowned him at birth."

"Binder!"

"It is true! He was killed by accident. They did not know he
was there. *I* did not know he was there. He had gone closer to
look at them, and they rolled backward in that great clumsy
device of theirs. But they did not know. From the beginning
they had no idea any of us were here. Always, they feel guilt for
this. This is why they stayed." Understanding broke in me then.
"This is why they are here. She who killed Traverse told me
they did not travel to find peoples—this was left to others. They
only went where others had gone before. They stayed because
of Traverse, to atone for his death." I laughed. "But *he* is
honorable. *He* is just. He has used all of us, other Ancestor

and my love, for revenge on them. And the rest of you are no better.''

Caretaker turned from me. ''There is truth in what you say.''

''I do not lie.''

''About us being no better. Traverse has proposed we use the trees to kill the demons.''

I could not speak, then laughed. ''Send the Ancestors marching down to meet them? This is a crazy idea.''

''I wish it were crazy.'' She turned to me again and held my hands. ''Caretakers know more about light than anyone. The Ancestors are composed mainly of light, trapped and generated within the trees. The trees are not just trees, however. They are in fact *one* tree.''

''One tree?'' I said stupidly.

''Connected underground by the roots. There are few rogue trees. We bound Bright to one to prevent her from ever contaminating anyone else. Even so, we lose Ancestors eventually not because they fade or die, but because they *leave*. The trees are villages, and eventually Ancestors move on to other villages.''

''I don't understand.''

''Traverse has contacted all the trees in the forest around the demons. With the help of the speakers he is going to make a light against them.''

''But light—how is light going to hurt anyone?''

''Each tree can recruit the bushes and grasses around it. All of them at once. All in tune. A light so bright it can crack the sky. A light so bright it can kill.''

16

Bertini leaned in the hatchway. Megan was on the bridge.

''Got a minute?'' He felt a little nervous—as much as he ever allowed himself to be nervous. This wasn't safe. *You don't cage a lion by playing safe.*

She looked over to him, startled. "Engineer Ranft." She held
her hands in her lap.

He felt wary. She's got something going. Remember, you're
dealing with someone as old and nasty as you are.

"Thought we might want to talk a bit."

"Certainly." She recovered herself and smiled. "Sit down
Engineer. I was considering a cup of tea. Would you like some
with me?"

"Sure," he said, watching around him. He followed her from
the bridge to the kitchen.

She took her time, preparing the tea carefully, quietly. He
watched her, thinking: I don't want to have to do this. They sat
across from one another at the table.

"What do you want to talk about?"

"Oh. History. Space. Going home. Trading the ship for a set
of new credentials in the Pleiades. How to stay out of Sentient's Court. You know."

"That's true. I *do* know."

That's wrong. That's not Megan. She's stalling.

He hesitated.

His own enhanced senses did not have the *Shenandoah* behind them, but they were still more than human, and he knew
the ship. He scanned about him. No increase in traffic between her and the ship. No increase in activity in her. The
Hirohito was doing nothing abnormal. Something subtle, then.
He strained his senses. Nothing. Megan was doing *nothing*. Is
it possible she understands? This is necessary. This is *required*.

Forget that. She's stalling. *She's got something planned.*

He cast about him again for anomalies. Megan in front of
him, Antonia in her cabin—at least not nearby, Sato entering
the kitchen. Sato.

He felt the cold tip of a laser pistol against his back.

Behind him: "Okay. Let's see how an engineer dies, eh?"

Before him: Megan smiling over her cup of tea.

He had been out-maneuvered. Badly. The cost would be his
life.

"You've conditioned him," he said slowly.

Megan shook her head. "Of course not."

But the way she said it told Bertini he was right. Conditioning needed an entry, a hook. What did Megan have with Sato?
Conditioning joined emotions and drives already there to a goal
or an idea—what did Sato have against Bertini?

Think about it.

Rain? he wondered. What did Rain—the dream, when she came to him in the dream or the hallucination or whatever it was. He tried to remember. He had been in the bridge, he had turned toward Antonia, and he had seen Rain. Rain had slept with him that night. It wasn't a dream at all—it was Antonia as Rain. Had to be. That linked to something else in Sato to bring it out.

He looked at Megan. "Brilliant."

Megan stood. "I had nothing to do with this."

"Sato, I have no real quarrel with you. You don't know what's going on."

"I know enough." The voice dripped anger. "Antonia is no longer *inclined* to see me. Thanks, Bertini. Thanks a lot."

"I took the flyer after you—"

"Yeah. Let me tell you how much I appreciate that."

The laser was a cold knot in his back. He was faster than Sato knew. He just might be able to knock the gun to one side before—

"I've got the laser on wide dispersal," Sato said in a low cold voice.

Damn. Even if he knocked the gun to one side, he'd lose an arm or part of his chest. Then Sato would just kill him. He'd been stupid. Damn. Damn.

Megan moved, and he glanced at her. She smiled at him again and moved out of the laser's field of fire.

He licked his lips. "Sato, without me, you won't be able to leave the system."

"We'll figure something out."

"What are you waiting for?"

"I want to linger over this. Enjoy it. Milk it for all it's worth. I want to remember this and savor it later."

Death, then. He considered it. Two-twenty-five now. Two-plus centuries. Was that long enough?

No. Never. I want you to live. I always wanted to live.

For what?

For you. For me. For nothing at all.

He found suddenly he felt tired, worn. I have lived enough. All things have an ending. You. Me. The love we had. Nothing lasts forever.

And what of Antonia and Sato?

They will have to get by, as I did. The world doesn't turn for me. It's time I stopped cranking.

"I'm tired of waiting, Sato. Do it or not, but get on with it."

I looked at Caretaker a long time.

"A light that can kill." Imagine your sight blinded, your brain boiled, your body burnt. "When?"

"Soon."

"How soon? Tell me!"

"They are preparing now."

Antonia! I cried across the binding thread between us. But it was thin and frayed, and I sensed she only vaguely heard me. She was asleep and not asleep, and I did not understand it.

"Let me go, Caretaker."

Caretaker wandered aimlessly in the hogan until she finally stood in the doorway. "I sent the guards away. I am all that stands between you and them. Will you kill me?"

I did not answer.

She scratched idly at the door frame. "I had a name, once. Before I became a Caretaker. We are told to forget our names in service to the trees. It was long before you were born. Do you know what it was?"

"No."

"It was From-the-Heart. Heart, sometimes. I have never been able to think with my mind, only my heart." She did not speak for a moment. "Go. I will cover for you." With that she was gone.

I stood at the door and listened.

"Traverse!" she cried out, and consternation rose around her. "I call you mad! I call you insane! I demand the others hear me, but *you* I call evil!"

The light from the shouting blinded everyone around me, and I ran, stumbling, my graceless body moving down the slope toward Antonia. As soon as I could, I took to the trees, but even there I was a clumsy cripple.

The humans needed me.

As he looked at the back of Bertini's head, it changed. One moment it was bald with gray hair, then blond, then long and dark.

Kill him. Kill him, and you're free.

First he saw Antonia, looking at him without expression. *Bitch*. Then it was Lindsay, staring at him, his mouth bloody where Sato had hit him.

Damn you.

"That's all there is," Lindsay said. "I loved you."

I loved you, too. Damn you. And you pushed me, and I pushed you away. Damn you for that.

Kill him, and you're free.

He cried out to them both. *See? You see what you have done to me?*

He started to pull the trigger, and it was Antonia looking at him, the pistol at her throat. For a moment, he saw her as she was taking him to the top of the bluff to make love, during passion, asleep, talking with Thalia—images flickering past like struck engravings over his sight. And Lindsay, at parties, as children together, with his big lovers, always aching to be protected.

Kill them all.

He started to cry.

Lindsay came to him, then. Stood in front of him. "It's all right, child. It's all right to come home. You've hurt enough."

He gave the gun to Lindsay and sat at the kitchen table, weeping. Lindsay held him close as a mother and crooned to him. *This is what I wanted from you. This is all I ever wanted from you.*

"It's all right now. You can come home."

As I SWUNG THROUGH the forest I thought of Traverse's death. I thought of Antonia, Bertini, Sato, and Megan, all dead. This must not happen. *This must not happen.* Not again. Never again.

Halfway there, the forest pulsed.

It was so quick and bright I did not know what it was. Then, for a moment I thought I imagined it. I knew, then, I was going to be too late.

It came again, while I was in mid-leap, and I was blinded. I missed the branch I had been reaching for—it pulsed while I fell—and struck the earth. For several minutes, I lay stunned. The forest was still. I forced myself up and began a hobbling run. Another flash, brighter this time. I ran blindly, trying to

feel my way. *Antonia!* I cried silently. No answer. "Antonia!
Sato!" I shouted as one half mad.

I reached the ridge above the ship, blind and sick. I almost
reached the trail, but a great flash of light threw me to the
ground, and I slid down the other side of the ridge. I tumbled
between two rocks, the rocks Traverse and I had hidden between the day the ship had come.

The pulses were coming in rhythm now, each brighter than
the last. I cowered between the rocks. I could *hear* the light
sizzling out of the plants. I tried to bury myself, but could not.
I threw myself into it and tumbled down into a cave. It didn't
seem to help. The flashes began to merge, explosions of light.
Then a ripple as from a great distance, a wave, a thunderbolt.
It came from the west, from Caretaker forest, and rolled over
me, tearing the remains of my tattered mind apart, and I
fainted.

MEGAN SENT THE SUGGESTION across the thin bridge between
them. *Kill him, Sato, just kill him.*

> *That's enough, Megan. No more.*

A wall came crashing down, and she was cut off from Sato.

> Wait, he's got to do it!
> *That's just enough. Let Sato go to hell on his own. He
> doesn't need you to push him. I've had enough of you,
> too. I don't love you anymore. Take me to the Pleiades.
> Dismember me. I don't care.*
> You're not serious.
> *I was never more serious. You're rotten. You let a whole
> people down, you've let your drew down, and you've let
> me down. I don't want to serve your twisted, sick games
> anymore. I'd rather be dismantled and made into scrap
> than to be a part of it.*
> What will happen to me? What will I do?
> *I don't care.*
> Damn you! You have to care! I *built* you to care.
> *Sorry, Captain Sze. That's just not my problem.*
> I'll see you in hell first. Do you hear me? I'll—answer
> me. Talk to me, damn you. *DAMN YOU!*

She felt something like the electricity of a storm coming, heard something like the roar of the sea.

What are you doing?
It's not me—Megan! Megan! Where are you? Can you hear me?

The roar engulfed her, and she could hear nothing. Wind and lightning danced through her. The *Shenandoah*'s voice was lost, and she was alone. She cried out, and her voice shook. Her sight winked out as if on a switch, and a moment later her mind as well.

IT FELT LIKE A HAMMER hitting a bell: a sudden strike and the impact was gone, but Bertini kept on ringing. Deep inside of him reflexes stirred that he had forgotten for over a century, relays clicked, circuits hummed. His senses suddenly felt distant, as if wrapped in cotton. His body felt taut, ready. Only his extra senses were insulated; his battle systems were ready and waiting.

Protection mode; I'm in protection mode. He shook his head. Things seemed to proceed slowly within a well of silence. Sato turned Bertini around and gave him the gun, then sat at the table and buried his head in his arms, weeping. Megan looked blindly up at the ceiling, screamed. Her voice went high and wild, and she fainted.

He stood up. *What has happened?*

Then events caught up with him: *a pulse! An EMP!*

"Dear Christ!" He leaped over Megan to the instruments as the lights began to fade. The darkness was no darkness to him, and he saw things my their natural electricity, their magnetic fields, the aura of their heat, and the touch of his fingertips.

The instrument panel was dead.

"Take care of Megan!" he cried to Sato and ran down the narrow passage to the engine room. As he ran, the red emergency lights switched on. It was not the kind of light he wanted, visible and weak. He slammed open the emergency doors to the main engines and stood over them. The room swirled with inchoate energy. Here was the light he sought: powerful, pulsing, and held in tight control by the emergency shutdown systems. He sat down on the steps. The engine was intact. It supplied as much power as the *Hirohito* could control, and every control circuit in the skiff was burned out. The ship was as dead as rock, as darkness, as bleached-white bone.

"A pulse?" he whispered. No. He shook his head. It couldn't be an EMP—they happened only in nuclear explosions: a wave of charged particles passing over metal conduits. Yet his body had reacted as if it were, according to specifications laid upon it by the navy so many years ago.

Nothing he could do here. Nothing.

Megan. He shrugged—she was hardened. All captains were. Megan was hardwired: God knew what had been done to her original reconstruction.

He ran back to the bridge. Sato was holding her and calling her name.

"Here. Come help me." Bertini picked her up and carried her into sick bay. He reprogrammed the clinic scanner for pin-prick burns and slivers of hot wire. Nothing. He began to relax. She was still hardened after all.

"Thank God," he breathed and leaned against the wall.

Sato looked first at him, then at Megan. "What's going on?"

"I'm not sure. We just got hit with something I haven't—correct that. Something I've *never* seen. It blew every soft circuit in the skiff."

"Come one. Nothing—"

"Something hit as if it were a strong electromagnetic pulse—EMP. This is a skiff of a map ship. Not a hardened military vessel. Most of the control circuits were only lightly shielded, the rest not at all. All of them are blown."

"You haven't even done any tests. How—"

Bertini looked at Sato for a long minute. *I can tell this by what was built into me.* He shook his head. "I *know*. We have a dead ship."

Sato did not speak for a moment. "What did it?"

Bertini sighed. "Not what. Who. Our friends, the Calibii. I don't know why." He shook his head. So much for mutiny. So much for a lot of things. "But Antonia might."

"Antonia!"

The cry broke through her sleep. She wanted sleep so much—waking did not attract her. She wanted only to sleep forever.

"Antonia!"

Someone bathed her in cold water. She whimpered and tried to draw away but could not.

"Antonia! What's going on? Why did the Calibii do this to us? Where's Thalia? Antonia! *Antonia!*"

Thalia? Did Thalia want her?

Deep within her an ember fired.

"Antonia! This is Sato! Wake up!"

Sato? She dimly recalled loving someone called Sato. Someone called Thalia, too. How could she love them both? It had seemed natural. There had been a problem somehow...

She opened her eyes. The room with lit blood-red.

Sato was holding her. "You've got to wake up."

Bertini came in behind him holding a drug ampule.

"This should help."

She recognized the drug. Her training spoke within her: *homeostatics: these are drugs that preserve homeostasis within physiological systems. Many times they are used as general-purpose antidotes. An example is Hanzine, which counteracts most other drugs but with the following side effects and dangers....*

She tried to cry out. Bertini slipped past her waving arms, and stung her arm. Nothing. Nothing—a red roar in her ears, and her body convulsed once, twice, then locked in a long spasm. Full consciousness struck her like a rubber hammer.

"Oh," she said and shook herself. The edges and points of objects glittered in the red light. She stood. "Thanks a lot," she said bitterly. "I could have died."

Bertini's gaze didn't waver. "I took that chance. I am in command. The Calibii have attacked us. The captain is in shock, and the ship is permanently disabled. We need you to find out why."

SATO COULDN'T FOLLOW what was happening.

He wasn't sure he wanted to: for the first time since he had left Earth, he felt relaxed. The skiff was dead. Megan was in a coma. Antonia seemed preoccupied with Thalia and the Calibii. By all rights, he should have been knotted with tension.

Instead, he whistled as they half-ran up the trail to the ridge.

"Stop that," Antonia called back to him.

Obediently, he ceased, still grinning.

She turned to him. "I have no idea why you are so happy."

"It's like hitting yourself with a rock," he said. "It feels so good when you stop."

"You're crazy."

He smiled.

She turned away from him in frustration. He could hear her muttering to herself: "Here? No. Further—here? No. To the right, maybe?"

Thalia was up here, somewhere. Antonia was certain of it, just not certain of exactly where.

Thalia mattered. *She's like someone you don't have to keep revealing yourself to; she knows you.* She slashed your face. *Faith—you keep faith with people. Faith that when they do inexplicable acts, they will have an explanation.* She's like Lindsay. *Of course, and Lindsay has forgiven you.* Lindsay is forty light-years away and has no idea what's going on. A hallucination caused by Megan using you, conditioning you against your will.

Megan. He shook his head. There is unfinished business there.

It doesn't matter. What matters is I've forgiven Lindsay. And oh, how good it feels. Hallucinations and delusions. *Yes. But they are mine. I am ready to go home now.*

He stopped in the middle of the trail. "I am ready to go home now." Had he ever been ready to go home before?

"What?" Antonia looked back at him. A wisp of hair fell across her face, and she brushed it out of the way. Her hands were large, strong—he had never noticed that before. Or the way she moved. Or the color of her eyes.

"I love you," he said simply.

She didn't speak for a moment. "What are you saying?"

"I said, I love you. I don't think I've ever loved anybody before, at least not for a long time." He thought for a moment. "I can't remember—no, I love someone else, too. A friend named Lindsay." Things seemed very straightforward right then. And he *still* couldn't say it right. "I would like to be your friend, husband, lover."

"We are lovers."

"Not really. Not like I mean." He thought again. "Not like I want to be now."

She reached down to him and touched his face. "Sometimes you are so clear..." She shook her head. "We'll talk again later."

"It doesn't matter if we talk at all." He looked at his hands. "I mean, I can *be* any of those things for you. Friend, lover, husband. I have preferences, of course."

She smiled at him sadly. "Of course."

"But I love Antonia, not friend, lover, or wife."

"This sounds very romantic."

"It's not, though. It's just a fact, in a collection of other facts, in the middle of a bad job we're doing, in the heart of a tough situation. I wanted to say it, though. I'm here. And you should be aware of that. I'm happy you're here." He frowned. "That's not right either." She was looking at him strangely, listening to every word closely. He stumbled to a stop.

She did not speak for a long minute. "You mean this," she said softly. "You really do." Another pause. "I think—I think you may have given me something I have never had before." She kissed him. "I could marry you for that." She laughed. "Unless you're lucky."

Then she was walking up the trail, and he stood there stupid and happy. He hurried to follow her. The sound of her voice warmed him: "Here? No. Further yet. I'll find her. Now, where the hell is she?"

Shenandoah!
    She cried out in terror—she could not move, could not speak.

Shenandoah!

With feather hands and gossamer fingers she reached for something, anything, and could not feel. The voice of her thoughts cried out and echoed inside of her, alone, alone. Always alone. Her skin containing nothing but a scream.

She wept. She lashed out. Her bowels and stomach were uncontrolled. Nothing came for her. For her, nothing was left. She lay in the arms of despair, no hope, no touch, no life. All things were dark. Always—*always*—she would rather be dead than alone. You were nothing if you were alone.

She was crippled, blind, and dead.

This was death?

Death was worse than she could have imagined. She howled and could not hear herself. No—I didn't mean it. I didn't mean it. Take it back. Give me something, anything. Being alone was better than this. I want to *live*!

Her mind struggled inside of her, moved in painful circles. She was wriggling against something that encased her, skin too tight to be borne. It tore—

"Shenandoah!" The sound of her own voice shocked her. She touched her lips. Lips! She had lips! She touched her face and felt wet tears of joy. "I'm alive," she cried out.

Something grasped her hand—another hand! There was no end to the wealth of that—and pressed it.

"Open your eyes, Megan."

She wasn't alone.

Bertini was looking down at her. What a beautiful face he had, such eyes, such hair.

"I didn't know what to do," he said slowly. "I rubbed your skin and moved your limbs—I saw people doing things like that in physical therapy a long time ago—"

"Such a face," she murmured. Her hand shook as she touched his nose, eyes, ears. "I have never seen you before."

He looked puzzled. "Right. Can you contact the *Shenandoah?*"

Shenandoah!

"What happened? I lost it!"

"We've been attacked by the Calibii. They used something like an EMP—it burnt out the control circuitry in the *Hirohito*, and we lost the ship's link. Is there anything else? The *Shenandoah* might send Ruth down here in the other lander, and if *that* buys the farm we're stuck here."

She sat up and nearly fell off the bed. Sick bay. She was in sick bay. Bertini caught her and held her from falling. She clung to him, whispering: "They attacked the skiff. Not the *Shenandoah*—just the skiff? Not the ship?"

"I don't know. I don't think so—the Calibii wouldn't have any idea where to attack the ship. There's no way they can see it. I don't know."

She held herself against him, trying to see, to think. "Probably." She looked at him. He seemed strange. It was so obvious he cared for her. "You're my friend," she said wonderingly.

Bertini looked away. "Right. We have to work together now."

How could I have wanted to kill you?

"We will. We will work together." She shook herself. "Help me out of here. I haven't got my legs yet."

He carried her to the bridge and helped her to the command chair. "Not here," she said impatiently, "outside."

It was mid-afternoon. The air was crisp and clear.

Inside her, she could feel the old battle relays switched over to protection mode. All things seemed faded, distant. Quickly, she unshielded herself.

Up there...

She felt for the *Shenandoah* lasers, searching for the skiff.

There!

She pointed her right finger ramrod-straight into the westering sky. The finger erupted into a blaze of skin and bone, and the exposed metal tube glowed.

I am here.

Megan! You live! What should I do? Should I send Ruth for you? I am sorry, so sorry.

She smiled.

I am sorry, too. I would have been better for you. We're okay right now. The Calibii attacked us with some pulse that burnt out the *Hirohito*. Don't send the other skiff, or we'll be stuck here. I would not be so far away from you again.

Nor I. Megan—

Hush. I'm all right. I'm more than all right. I—you have done right all along, and I'm slow to catch up, is all.

I could have done better—

Hush, I said. Stay and be ready.

I will.

I must go. This tires my batteries.

She opened her eyes and looked at Bertini, smiled sadly. "I did not think things could get much worse."

Bertini smiled with her. "Nor I."

LAY ON THE FLOOR of the schoolhouse, ringed by their stares, still groggy after being brought here. I could see only dimly, as

through water. I did not know if I would stay blind. At th
moment I did not care.

Cameron came and rubbed his head against me. I held hi
close, hugging him tightly. *You do not know how to hate me*

Bertini stood leaning against the wall of the schoolhous
Megan sat cross-legged on the floor next to him. Sato slouche
in the building's one chair, and Antonia knelt before me.

"Is there anything I can do?" Antonia said gently.

"Nothing. My people were nearly blinded when they kille
your craft."

"Killed our craft?" said Bertini easily.

"I am crippled and half blind. I am not stupid. I could s
your craft's workings as I saw the trees: by its own light. It
dead. Now we await the judgment of my people."

"Please," said Antonia to Bertini, then turned to me. "Wha
has happened?"

I painfully sat up and looked about me. My vision slow
cleared. Good. I would only be a cripple. Cameron com
plained and moved into my lap. I reached over him to An
tonia. It was awkward and made my bruised arms hurt. *A
things I do, I do in half measure and clumsily.* I took her hand
"I have done you a terrible wrong."

"What?"

There is never any excuse for the things we do. Are we no
adults? Do we not know our actions? There is never any e
cuse. "I was hurt by Sato and you."

"Jealous, you mean? I knew you were friends."

"Of course not. For all I have studied your words, jealous
is still dark to me. I was envious. Covetous. Our people are s
different from you. Your males live. Ours do not. Our love
only last a little while until they die and are made Ancestors.
struck Sato in a rage that he would live when my own lover wa
dead." Antonia started and tried to pull away. I held on to he
hands. "It was accident and stupidity that killed him. Acc
dent and stupidity that has followed you and I this whole yea

"Ancestors . . ." I spoke loudly so my ugly croaking voi
would be heard. "You do not have them. You do not know o
them. When we die, we are sealed to the roots of our trees. Th
same trees we breed through. The trees we see by—as well as th
grasses and plants. The trees that spoke and killed your shi
After a time our dead live again within the trees."

"Ghosts," muttered Sato.

"Perhaps," I continued testily. "But listen to me well, Sato. One such ghost ordered the destruction of your ship. I know him. I know him well. He was my lover, whom you and Antonia killed."

Again, Antonia tried to pull away. "No," I cried softly. "Do not turn away from me." Cameron sat up and looked at us, one then another. "We should have spoken these things months ago and did not, and now we pay for it. I have a story of demons..." I told them the story of Bright and the trees and of the reason she was called demon: "She did not turn Ancestor, though she was properly sealed. This is what drives my people. The loss of our males. The preservation of our Ancestors. This narrow reserve where our trees do not die. Here, between the mountains and the sea, we found by luck. The trees, always the trees."

I watched them. "You must listen to me. When I returned from the north, I was angry. Hurt. Lost. Empty. When the speakers asked me what I had learned, I could not see clearly. When I looked at them I thought, 'Let you be hurt as I have been hurt.' And I told them everything. Then Traverse called you demons, and I knew I had given him what he wanted all along. You shortened his life. You took away his children. You took everything from him. All he has left is vengeance."

Antonia pulled away from me then, and I released her. She went to the window and stared outside. I reached for her across the thread of her connection and felt her hide something from me. I held Cameron close for there was no one to hold me.

"Can we speak with them?" Megan said. "If we could do that, it should be obvious we are no demons."

"Persuade them, Megan?" Sato looked at her. "Perhaps we can condition them to do what we want?"

She flinched. "I deserved that. Don't do it again."

"You don't like your tools to talk back?"

"You don't understand," I said. "They are right. You *are* demons." They stared at me in silence. "You come to us from the dark. You show us our lives and sacrifices are the whim of nature. You show us our suffering, our lives and deaths are in vain. You show us we do not matter." Convulsively, I clutched at Cameron. He licked at me. I stroked him. "Oh, you are demons, all right. Of the worst possible kind. And we have been corrupted."

Silence fell.

"What will happen now?" asked Bertini

I let Cameron to the floor. *I lose everyone I touch.* "I don'
know. Soon, they will know the craft is dead and you are not
How did you live?"

"The craft shielded us." Bertini looked outside, then back a
me. "They watch us?"

"Of course. No doubt they are on the ridge right now. The
will be here as soon as they can see, and they will recove
quicker than I because they were farther away."

"Then what?"

"Then they will make holy war on you, as they did o
Bright."

"It's getting dark,". said Antonia. "They will not attack i
the night, will they?"

"I don't know. All things are chaos."

She nodded. "Let's go inside. They won't break into the skif
easily. Come."

Across from her, I saw what she was trying to hide, and i
made me shiver.

ANTONIA'S CABIN was dark red from the emergency lights an
stuffy. Bertini had torn out the ventilation equipment and fil
ters, so air came down the ducts and they could breathe. Stil
it was stuffy.

Sato held himself over her, and she watched him as he move
within her, slow, easy. She ran her fingernails up the length o
his thigh. He shuddered, and they held each other for a lon
spasming moment.

Sweat lay across them like oil.

"I will have to shower," she whispered in his ear, holding hin
to her.

"No hot water," he said between breaths.

"Cold showers are only good together."

He laughed. "Not even then."

They rolled on their sides, and she kissed him for a long time
holding his face in her hands. "I do love you."

He hugged her and did not answer.

They made love again and once more after that. He slept
and she rose and took a shower, returning afterward to the dar
cabin. She opened the window a crack and felt the sprin

breezes across them. He needed a blanket, and she covered him.
Then she kissed him.

*I love you. I just didn't know it before. You never know what
you need until you must sacrifice it.*

Megan was standing on the bridge as she passed. She looked
bloody in the red light.

"Antonia?" she called.

Damn, caught already.

"Yes, Captain Sze."

"Megan. Call me Megan."

Antonia shrugged. *Let me go about my business.* "What?"

Megan looked at her a long time. "I just wanted to say I was
sorry. It's not much, but it's all I've got."

Antonia nodded.

"You go on now. I just wanted to say that."

"I'm going for a walk."

"I know."

Thalia was waiting for her at the hatch, arguing with Cameron. "Back. Go away." She started as Antonia touched her.
"I want to see! I am nearly blind here. If it weren't for the light
from Megan and Bertini, I wouldn't be able to see at all."

"You should try my eyes."

"I should understand them first."

Outside, the spring moon was just shining over the trees.
"What a beautiful night," she said.

"Is there no other way?"

"Isn't the night enough? Look at that moon!"

"You evade me. Must this happen?"

Antonia looked at Thalia. "They're your people. You tell
me."

Thalia did not speak for a moment. "There is not."

"Let's go."

Soon they were gone from the lander, and there was no sound
at all.

CAMERON WHINED at the airlock door. Bertini picked him up
and tried to quiet him. "Hush, beast." He turned to Megan.
"You are sure that is what she is going to do?" he asked.

Megan looked through the window after them. "Of course.
I am still a sensitive. Even now, after all these years." She put
her face in her hands. "I feel so wretched about all of this."

He watched her cry. There was nothing he could say.

17

The day grew warm with sunrise; spring come fully at last.
could no longer tell whether I was hot with anxiety or fear o
just that the sun warmed me. *Sun,* I thought. *I did not know o
the sun before they came.*

Things jumped out at me: the curve of the leaves delineate
by the light they wove, the worn track of the trails, Antonia
scent next to me, the motion of her walk contrasting with mine
the feel of bare earth.

"This is going to be tricky," I said to her.

Antonia did not reply. I looked at her. From all the readin
I had done and have done since, I have tried to interpret he
expression. I could not see it as humans see it, a surface pulle
into shape, but as a collection of textures above and below th
bone, the flood and the flesh. Was resignation there? The e
static commitment of the saints? The fear of the condemned
She was not of my people—whom the humans called Calibii.
could not read her. The thread between us was calm, but was
acceptance or the mask of control?

"Sato said he was ready to go home," she said suddenly.

Hah. Wrong on all counts.

"Yes?"

"He said other things, too, but that's the one I don't under
stand. Do you know what he meant?"

"How should I?"

"You know him better than I."

I stopped and turned to her. "How can you say that? I ca
barely read you through the demon link between us. He's you
species. He's *your* lover. I know nothing."

She just stood there until I resumed walking. "You're wrong
you know," she said quietly.

We did not speak again the rest of the way.

At the beginning of the forest we halted. "We wait here for a moment." Antonia did not question me. This surprised me for a moment, then I knew. She had made her decision and by that had committed us both. It was my turn to carry us the rest of the way.

They were watching us. I knew it the way I knew how to see by night: instinct and nature.

Two Caretakers appeared out of the brush before us. Neither one was Heart.

"Where is she who cried out to Traverse?" I asked.

"That is not your concern, betrayer," said one.

"We come for you and this creature with you," said the other. "Follow us."

"Stand aside, or I will kill you. I will not be led by the lackeys of an insane Ancestor."

"You threaten a Caretaker." The speech was so cold and formal I could not tell who spoke.

"I do. Stand aside." I brought out my claws. "I go to the speakers."

They did not move for many seconds, and I thought I would have to attack them.

"Let her go. The speakers wish her there anyway," said the first, and they moved out of the way.

"What was that about?" asked Antonia.

"Death threats. We bluffed our way through," I said.

"Oh."

All three speakers were waiting for me in front of Traverse's tree. Inside I was trembling. "I demand to speak."

Disapproval cried out: "What *right* do you claim to do this? You who threaten—"

"*Silence!*" I roared through my voice. "Silence!" I said again with speech. "I claim the right taken from me. I claim the right to stand here and be heard without hands laid upon me. I claim the honor given me when I was told to watch these strange creatures. I claim the trust that I earned over these long and bitter months. I claim the right of a cripple to cry out to her accusers. By what right? By all rights. Disapproval is not my speaker, nor is Climber. And Infertility did not speak for me. I claim my own right to speak for myself. Are you going to deny me this? Or have we descended to become beasts?"

They did not answer me. "This," I gestured toward Antonia, "is one of your demons. Has she injured or killed a tree as did Bright?"

"One of them killed me," said Traverse ominously.

"You were killed by your own stupidity! I told you to watch me, but instead you crept close to their device. They did not know you were there. I did not know you were there. The Ancestors said you should watch the watcher, did they not? *Did they not?*"

"They did," said Infertility into the empty silence.

"They killed by accident. They did not murder. We judge them from fear. What have they cost us? What have we lost? Nothing but from accident and clumsiness, our own as well as theirs. They have done nothing." I paused. Still, they did not respond. "The creatures do not lose their lovers. But when they die, they go alone into the dark and are no more."

Traverse cried out. "The demons chose this form to mock us, to trick us! And with cunning they have succeeded. Listen to her. Has she not been changed? Has she been poisoned against us?"

I listened with shock—Traverse crying out against me? Deep inside I never believed it would come to this. "I would have borne your child. Your death hurt me far more than you were ever hurt. I carried your body here! Caretaker and I sealed it ourselves. And I have had to watch what you have become. I will never seek you out again. I will never speak of you.

"Sisters!" I cried to them. "You say these creatures are demons sent to mock and hurt us. You say this because they have no Ancestors. You are correct. They are demons. They mock us because they are better than we. This female is the female who killed Traverse. She presents herself to us for judgment. She has no Ancestors to speak with or hope for. She knows we do and claim her death for that lack. She has come here to be sacrificed in an attempt to become an Ancestor or die. She demands it as repayment for a tragic accident. She demands it for the safety of her clan and her people. She demands it for justice and to stop this stupid, mistaken war."

I had said it all. They watched me, saying nothing. It came to me that I failed—nothing would move them. They were made of stone, of wood, of metal.

Infertility rose. "There has been enough killing."

Slowly, the others murmured agreement. For a moment, I almost had a bit of hope.

"This is not enough," cried Traverse.

"You—" I started.

"You make a great claim of right, Binder—Speaker to Demons! I claim the same right. As an Ancestor. As the male killed by this creature of the dark."

"Speak, then," said Disapproval.

"I still say these are demons who will corrupt us, and we die of it. You know my reasons. You know the evidence. If you will live, you will listen to me. Binder claims this creature will sacrifice herself for the others. I say not. I say you have only Binder's speech—corrupted by the demons—that she will. This thing killed me, and I say it will not pass this test before all others."

"You would have us kill her for you," cried Climber.

"You cannot kill a demon. I say all of them must be destroyed. Let her be the first. It is not only I. All of the Ancestors speak thus."

Infertility turned to the Caretaker speaker. "Is this true?"

She did not respond for a long moment. "It is. The Ancestors demand it. We have already nearly died as a people once. Our lives are too precarious to take any chances. True or false, it must be done. It does not matter how Traverse feels or how we feel, or even whether they are demons. But it does matter if we can trust them, having lost that trust to Bright long ago."

"There are no demons," I said dimly. "There are only evil people. Bright failed to become an Ancestor because she was not properly sealed or because alone as she was she died of loneliness. Demons do not exist."

"Hush, child," said Infertility to me alone. "This is already too dark a day. You undo any good you have done."

Antonia must have understood through the link between us for she touched me and shook her head.

"Then I would do it," I said. "Pick me a tree and let it be done."

"I will also." Caretaker—Heart—came from behind me and stood next to me. "I stand with her. If it must be done, we shall do it."

Disapproval and Climber stirred restlessly. Infertility was still.

The Caretaker speaker held her hands together. "It must be done," she said.

"Very well." I turned from them.

"How do we know they will do it?" asked Traverse.

"Be quiet, male," said Disapproval. "You have shamed us enough."

We led Antonia deep into the forest.

When we were far away from them, Antonia turned to me. "What happened?"

"You know. You must know."

"Only in pieces. I need to know more."

"You know enough. We won, and you will die. What more is there?"

HE AWOKE LISTENING to the forest, the daylight coming into the window. *Shouldn't be open,* Sato thought sleepily, then came awake instantly.

"Jesus!" he said and sat up in air. He closed the window and sealed it again into the side of the ship. "Did you do this?" He turned toward Antonia and saw she wasn't there. The blanket lay on him, and he smiled, thinking of her, of last night. "Thought I was cold, did you?" he said softly and dressed.

The cabin lights were still red, but the corridor was dark. He could see by the light through the other cabin doors—sunlight. "What the hell," he muttered.

No one was in the bridge or the kitchen. He stepped outside and saw no one. "Hello?" he called.

"Here," came Bertini's voice from the other side of the schoolhouse.

Sato turned the corner and saw Bertini stretched out on a tarp in the sun. He sat down next to him. "What's going on?"

Bertini opened one eye at him, looked at him morosely, then closed it again. "Waiting."

"For an attack?"

"No."

Confused, Sato sat next to him. "I feel kind of exposed."

"There won't be any attack."

"Why not?"

No response.

"Damn it!" Sato took a deep breath. Where was the calm he had yesterday? "Okay. Okay. Where's Megan?"

"Taking a walk along the beach."

"Waiting, too, I suppose?"

Bertini groaned and sat up. He stared a long time at Sato. "Don't you understand *anything*? Are you that stupid? When something strikes you in the face, can't you even see it? *There will be no attack.*"

Sato felt a deep chill. "Where's Antonia?"

"The Calibii want us dead because they think we're demons. They think we're demons because when we die we have no Ancestors."

"Damn you! Where's Antonia?" He tried to get up. Bertini held him down.

"If one of us offers to try to become an Ancestor, makes a sacrifice so they might know us as moral, thinking beings, they might just let us go."

Sato tried to break loose, but Bertini's grip was stone. "She can't do it. She'll die!"

Bertini shoved him against the side of the schoolhouse and knocked the wind out of him. "Exactly."

Sato coughed weakly. "Bastard!"

"Maybe." Bertini rose and looked down at him. "She is going to die that you might live. I will not let that sacrifice be in vain."

WHAT HAPPENED to her fear?

Antonia stepped around a tree trunk, over roots. The forest was thick here, shadowy and dark.

"Is it dark here to you?" she asked Thalia.

Thalia did not answer immediately. "This is a holy place. These are the oldest trees. The light from these trees makes our Ancestors and our children." She pointed to Antonia's right. "I bore my first child in that tree there."

"It's not dark to you?"

"No. Not dark at all."

The forest was hushed, appropriate, as a cathedral. She had a sudden image of walking in the light of stained glass. "I wish I could see as you do."

"I, also. If you had, all of this would have been unnecessary."

At last, they came to a grandfather of a tree. The trunk was as big around as the ship. A dozen tall men could have linked arms and not reached around it. "It's beautiful."

Thalia stopped and turned to her. "Caretaker says he has spoken with the Ancestors of this tree. He says they are ready to make you welcome, if it is possible."

She smiled at Thalia. "Tell her thank you."

"I have done so. Stand back, please. We have to dig."

The two of them dug a trench along one great root. How many have been here? How large is the company I am trying to share? She shook her head. Do not be deceived. You have no hope in this.

Then I have nothing to lose in hope.

Thalia stood and dusted herself. "It is ready."

"May I drug myself?"

Thalia stood still for a moment. "What do you mean?"

Antonia looked down. "I do not fear death anymore, but I fear pain. I have with me a drug that will dull the pain and make it easier."

"Take your drug."

For a moment, the curtain parted from between them.

Antonia! Antonia, I never wished this for us. Believe me, I did not want revenge.

Look at me, Thalia. Look inside of me. You know I believe you.

She swallowed the pill. It went down scratchy, dry, and bitter. When it reached her stomach, warmth spread. After a time, she felt drowsy. "All right."

They carried her gently into the trench. Beginning with her legs, they bathed her in some warm substance. Warmth passed all through her. As they were covering her chest and back, she thought of something. "Thalia?"

They stopped. "Yes." Thalia bent next to her.

"I was right, you know. About Sato."

"You were right in a great many things."

They covered her face and she could not see. Breathing seemed difficult, and she stopped. For a long moment, she felt nothing but Thalia holding her. Then something drew her away from the thread between. For a long moment she felt distant and warm.

Then, she heard voices.

BERTINI WAITED OUTSIDE, one part of him watching Sato—or watching where he might be. After he had been told, Sato had gone into the lander and not come out. Occasionally, Bertini heard him cry out.

Damn. He would have liked things to have come to a different conclusion.

He scanned the ridge. They should be coming soon. It was late afternoon. There was the rattling of brush from across the clearing. He turned to it and saw two Calibii come out from under the trees. Where was Megan?

They approached.

"Megan?" he shouted. No answer.

He'd have to do it himself. He waited for them to reach him.

"Hello, Bertini," said Thalia. "Where is Cameron?"

He nodded to her. "In the ship. It is done, then?"

"Yes."

He nodded again. "We are absolved?"

"I have brought the speaker of my band here. This afternoon she was chosen to speak for all of us. Her name is Infertility."

"Hmm." Bertini looked at Thalia. "What is *your* name, Thalia?"

"The name I had once among my people was Binder. I have others now. Thalia is the one I prize the most for what it cost me."

"It has cost us all."

Thalia turned to Infertility and back to Bertini. "Infertility asked, what is your will?"

A cool wind blew up over the water. Bertini crossed his arms out of habit. He wasn't cold. *I feel the cold of death.*

Nonsense.

Rain, you are with me yet.

Always. You will never be without me.

That pleases me.

It is time you took some pleasure out of things.

"We wish absolution for the accidental death of your companion."

Thalia held her hands together. "It is given. What else?"

"That is all. There are several formalities to be dealt with, but they only reflect this one thing."

"May the formalities wait until tomorrow?"

Bertini shrugged. "Of course. Why?"

Thalia did not speak a moment. "It has been a hard day fo[r]
our people. We must grieve over many things."

"Tomorrow will be fine. Then we request a safe leaving."

"That is also given. We will see you tomorrow."

"Until then."

"Bertini . . ."

Something in her voice caught him, and he knelt next to her[.]
"Yes."

"How is Sato?"

Bertini shook his head. "Not well. He also has much t[o]
grieve for. Until tomorrow."

"Yes."

MEGAN FOUND SATO in Antonia's cabin, wrapped in Anton[-]
ia's blanket. The tears fell down his cheeks, but his face was set
like stone. He looked up as she entered, then at the blanket.

"Aren't you warm?" she asked. Dear God, I have *Shenandoah*. Bertini has himself and Cameron. Antonia is dead an[d]
beyond caring. What does *he* have?

"I don't know," he said thoughtfully. "It's hard to tell." He
paused a moment. "It smells like her."

What can I say to that?

"Thalia and a Calibi official of some sort were here a few
minutes ago. I stayed on the beach and waited until they were
gone. Bertini handled them." Never again. I never want to
handle anyone ever again.

"She's dead, then?"

"We don't know. It might work—"

"Don't fucking lie to me! You lied enough!"

Megan looked down. "She's dead. We were hoping the of[-]
fer of the sacrifice would be enough. Apparently, it wasn't. I'm
sorry."

He didn't respond. "All right. All right then."

She looked at him. "What are you talking about?"

He pulled the laser pistol from under the blanket. "Remem[-]
ber this? You gave it to me. The whole thing is your fault. [I]
should kill you."

She stared down the barrel. "I conditioned you. You shoul[d]
remember that. If you're going to shoot somebody, you shoul[d]
shoot me."

"I can't." He grinned morosely at her. "I found that out. I can't shoot me, either. Not that I didn't try. I just couldn't."

"Then give me the gun."

"It's not Bertini's fault at all, so I can't shoot him. Who should I kill, Megan? Who deserves it?"

"Nobody."

"You deserve it, but I can't. A lot of things are owed. You owe a lot to somebody."

"Sato, I'll pay off my debts any way you like, but give me the goddamn gun."

"No. You owe me, but I don't want you to pay me. Thalia and the Calibii owe me a lot more. The pistol's for them." He leaned toward her and stared into her eyes. "No, for you I want something special. I've been thinking about this. I figure you must have a real history."

What does he know? *Shenandoah!* "What do you mean?"

"I'm not sure." He smiled at her. "You have something in your past you did you have to pay for. I don't know what it is, but I'll know it when you take care of it. If you don't, I'll take care of you."

"And how the hell do you think you'll do that?"

He smiled again and nodded. "Hit a nerve. I'll go to the Port Authority and tell them you're hardwired."

She did not speak for a long minute. "I think there's been enough threats."

He stared at her.

How long do I live with this? Another hundred years? Two hundred years? How long do I live with the guilt? Orange! What did I matter so little to you that I suffer so much for it?

Enough.

She stared back. "I owe a lot, and I'll pay. And you'll know what I did before I'm done. *Now*, give me the gun."

He shook his head. "I said the gun's not for you. It's for the Calibii. I'm going to burn down the forest."

INFERTILITY LEFT ME at the ridge. I did not want to return to the village. It was tainted, somehow, of—what? Sin? Death? I did not know. Night fell around me. I had been Binder. I had been Speaker to Demons. Was I now Thalia? The Muse of Rhetoric—never had I been more than a clumsy fool. Why Antonia had laid that name on me I did not know.

I heard movement below me. If it were a beast to finish me I would not stop it.

From under a bush came Cameron.

"You should not be out, small beast." I held him close, and he licked me. It was almost more than I could stand. When I could, I held him away from myself. "You are a beast, but you are not my beast. I must return you." He licked my lips as I spoke. "You are a comforting beast."

I was halfway across the clearing when I heard voices. Bertini shouting at someone, then Megan answering.

"It will ruin what she died for," cried Bertini.

"Then let it! Who are we to say? We are old—too damned old to be making his mind up for him."

"He's crazy."

"They owe me! They owe for Antonia! Them and their fucking trees."

"You're crazy."

"Damn you both! We stand or fall, we leave or boil ourselves in our own damnation, but we are *done* with controlling anyone else."

I saw them now. Sato and Bertini stood facing each other with Megan between them.

"She *died* for this," Bertini shouted at Sato and tried to reach him. Megan took his arm and held it rigid.

"She died for herself." Megan stared at Bertini. "I spent two centuries trying to protect myself by running other people's lives. All it has brought me is pain and loss. It stops here."

"He's going to do us *all* in!"

"He just may. He just may at that. You and I have been around long enough."

They saw me then and stopped.

"I brought Cameron back," I said in a low voice.

I knew what went on here; I did not have to be told. Antonia said I knew Sato better than she did. And I did—I could never have sacrificed myself as she did, nor could Sato. Not so easily, not so well. He and I just hurt and responded to that hurt. It had taken Antonia to teach me there were other, just as painful, ways. "Sato," I said.

He flinched.

I stood beneath him. The metal thing in his hand glowed inside—I could see fire held chained. I took his hand and held it my chest. "I could have stopped this long ago, and I did not. My people are not to blame. I am. Take me instead."

He held the thing against me for a long time. Humans can close their eyes at these times, I thought. Such a gift they have.

Then he dropped it, and I drew him slowly to me and held him. "It just hurts so much. It makes me crazy."

"I know, male child. I am the same."

18

The night before they left, Thalia led them into the village.

"It has been only me watching you for too long," she said.

Calibii had come from all three bands to see them, but it was a strangely formal gathering, compounded of Antonia's sacrifice and the first real meeting between the two species.

Sato smiled twice that night. He remembered both events for the rest of his life.

The first was early in the evening, when Thalia took him deep into Caretaker forest to Antonia's tree.

It was dark. The moon was nearly full above them, but the light could not penetrate here. A second Calibi met them there.

"This is Heart," Thalia said softly. "She and I buried Antonia."

He could not cry. Thalia did not touch him, but he could feel her near him, and the other—Heart—he could feel as well. He strained to feel Antonia in the circle of their bodies, but could not.

She is not here.

"Do you think—"

Thalia cut him short. "Do not think of it now. You must go away for a while, then return. But do not expect ever to speak with her again. She must be dead to you."

He shook his head. "I'd like to hope—"

"You do not. I know how this feels. Go away and come back again sometime hence. Then you will understand."

He nodded. "Have the others come here?"

"The others," Thalia said carefully, "have not been i
vited."

He looked at her, looked away. "Thank you," he said a
smiled sadly.

MEGAN FELT AN OUTSIDER more than she could ever remem
ber being in her long life. The Calibii were gathered togeth
watching them, speaking with each other, and she could n
even tell what they were doing. She could detect radio noise
she wished with her augmented senses, but it was only a ju
bled hash. She sat next to Bertini, in a circle of Calibii, whe
they were presumably doing something, and there was only
lence. She felt lonely. She would get just enough this trip to p
the back installments of the *Shenandoah*'s loan.

And she had to go back to Orange's planet.

She had felt the day she had spoken with Sato as if she h
come awake for the first time. She had debts to pay. How t
hell was she going to pay them?

"Megan?" Bertini nudged her. "You okay?"

She shrugged. "Just worried. I promised Sato something.

"What?"

Confess? Why not start now?

"I used to be on Hanna Pemberton's ship—"

"Who?"

She looked at him. "Hanna Pemberton? Captain of t
Lanford?"

"Had an old rat of a bird?"

"Azul. Right. Why?"

Bertini shrugged. "I met her once. Didn't care much f
her."

She stared toward the trees. "Well, I did . . ." and told hi
the story. It wasn't as bad as she had thought, but the san
thought kept coming to her: *what must he think of me?* Ber
ni's friendship had become more important than she ever wou
have imagined.

He didn't speak for a long time.

Ah, she thought, that's how it is. Did you expect he wou
just ignore it?

"Megan," he said thoughtfully.

"Yes," she said too quickly.

"I've been thinking. I have enough at home in savings to over the *Shenandoah*'s note." He looked at her, and it was as they were the *Shenandoah*'s eyes.

I know you, they said. *And that is enough.*

She took his arm. "I need an engineer for the run to Orange."

"I know of one who needs another job."

She hugged his arm hard, then released it. Her hands were trembling.

IT WAS LATE when the Calibii decided they'd seen enough of the humans and made their way home. Bertini found Sato watching the river where Bertini had guessed he would be.

"Hey there."

Sato turned to him. "Hey yourself."

Bertini stood next to him. Sato seemed different clear through, older. "Thalia, Infertility, and I have been talking."

"Uh-huh," Sato said absently. "I miss her already. Don't they say you feel stunned first, then grieve?"

"Nobody makes rules for these things."

Sato nodded.

"Anyway," Bertini continued, "the Calibii want you to be their liaison. They think you should go home for while, set up relations, and come back."

Sato stared at him. "What do you mean?"

"Don't you understand anything?" Bertini said gently. "They trust you."

Bertini smiled, and like a light dawning, Sato smiled in return.

WE WAITED TOGETHER for the next skiff, Bertini, Sato, Mean, Infertility, and I. Beneath the hot sun I had never seen, amidst the incredible light they never really knew. It was noon before the craft could reach us. Something about orbits, they said.

Once it reached us, they spent a long time with Infertility and me, showing us documents, pointing various devices at us, and always making us say they were absolved of any crime.

Of course they were. We knew that already.

After that, Infertility left us, and we stood around, reluctant to part.

"What will you do now? Map some new place? You will b
gone from me, and I will never know you again."

Megan and Bertini looked at one another. "I have aske
Bertini a favor," she said quietly. "Long ago I did a grea
wrong. He has agreed to help me try to put it right."

"Honorable," I said. "Are you lovers then?"

They laughed. "God no," she said. "Friends, though."

Bertini nodded.

"I will be back," Sato said, looking at me. "I have a pea
to make at home, then I will be back if you will have me."

I took his hands. "Come back soon."

"I have to think for a while. This is the best offer of hom
I've ever had."

They all looked at me, and I wanted to hold them all.

"Oh, yeah." Bertini went back into the skiff and returne
with a large box and a small box. The large box containe
Cameron.

"What is going on?" I put both boxes on the ground.

"I put him in the box so he wouldn't get in the way when w
took off. The little box has his batteries.

"Batteries?"

"Yeah. Here." He opened the box and held Camero
squirming and showed me where they were placed. "He'll sta
getting sluggish and need more of these. Keep them dry. They'
last him about a year each. You've got maybe ten year
worth."

"I'll bring some back with me," said Sato.

"Cameron is yours." I tried to give him back.

"No." Bertini smiled at me. "Cameron is a pet, but he wa
never my pet. Now he is yours."

I held Cameron for a moment and looked at them. Had
been human, I would have wept. "I did not ever expect my li
to be so full." I put Cameron back into the box.

I hugged each of them in turn and watched as they boarde
the ship.

They waited until I carried Cameron and his batteries to th
top of the ridge. In strange, pulsing light the craft rose an
disappeared into the dark sky.

"A sight worth seeing."

I turned. "Heart! I did not expect to see you here."

"I wanted to see the craft before they left. Ugly light. Sic
ening."

"It is that."

I knelt and opened the box. Cameron sniffed cautiously and jumped out. He came over and stood next to me, staring at Ieart.

"What is that?"

"Their small beast. They have left it with me."

"To eat?"

"For pleasure. For entertainment. For friendship."

"I don't understand."

I did not reply.

"I came also to take you back with me to the forest. I am going to wait for the creature to awake."

I turned to her. "She is dead."

"Things are never so simple. Who knows? I am very optimistic."

She turned, and I followed her to the forest.

Cameron followed me.

19

What lives do you lead down there? thought Ruth as she made sure their sleeping forms were strapped in tightly. What dreams have you seen? Did you play them well?

For they were all dreams to her.

Only traveling between the stars was real.

She floated up to the pilot's chamber. There were rituals to be performed. Preparations to make.

Did she think of them then? Did she think of us down here on Caliban? I think not. I who have spent this last year writing this and waiting for Sato to return have written her so.

No, I think she did then what pilots, and the rest of us, do when the interludes of their lives come to an end and they pursue what they think life is for.

The *Shenandoah* blinked once and was gone.

Science Fiction that will take you to the edge of the universe and beyond with...

ISAAC ASIMOV PRESENTS

"...an entertaining novel
with some thought-provoking ideas."
—*Locus*

ISAAC ASIMOV PRESENTS
John Barnes

The planet Randall becomes the focus of human
exploration in the twenty-ninth century when
missionaries arrive to convert the alien races in order
to admit the planet into the Christian commonwealth.
But the human teachings undermine the doctrine that
unite the Randallans creating major hostility among
the races.

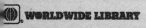